The Wicked Spy

Blackhaven Brides
Book 7

MARY LANCASTER

DRAGONBLADE
PUBLISHING, INC.

Books from Dragonblade Publishing

Dangerous Lords Series by Maggi Andersen
The Baron's Betrothal

Also from Maggi Andersen
The Marquess Meets His Match

Knights of Honor Series by Alexa Aston
Word of Honor
Marked by Honor
Code of Honor
Journey to Honor
Heart of Honor
Bold in Honor
Love and Honor
Gift of Honor

Legends of Love Series by Avril Borthiry
The Wishing Well
Isolated Hearts
Sentinel

The Lost Lords Series by Chasity Bowlin
The Lost Lord of Castle Black
The Vanishing of Lord Vale
The Missing Marquess of Althorn

By Elizabeth Ellen Carter
Captive of the Corsairs, *Heart of the Corsairs Series*
Revenge of the Corsairs, *Heart of the Corsairs Series*
Shadow of the Corsairs, *Heart of the Corsairs Series*
Dark Heart

Knight Everlasting Series by Cassidy Cayman
Endearing
Enchanted
Evermore

Midnight Meetings Series by Gina Conkle
Meet a Rogue at Midnight, book 4

Second Chance Series by Jessica Jefferson
Second Chance Marquess

Imperial Season Series by Mary Lancaster
Vienna Waltz
Vienna Woods
Vienna Dawn

Blackhaven Brides Series by Mary Lancaster
The Wicked Baron
The Wicked Lady
The Wicked Rebel
The Wicked Husband
The Wicked Marquis
The Wicked Governess
The Wicked Spy

Highland Loves Series by Melissa Limoges
My Reckless Love
My Steadfast Love

Clash of the Tartans Series by Anna Markland
Kilty Secrets
Kilted at the Altar
Kilty Pleasures

Queen of Thieves Series by Andy Peloquin
Child of the Night Guild
Thief of the Night Guild
Queen of the Night Guild

Dark Gardens Series by Meara Platt
Garden of Shadows
Garden of Light
Garden of Dragons
Garden of Destiny

Rulers of the Sky Series by Paula Quinn
Scorched
Ember
White Hot

Highlands Forever Series by Violetta Rand
Unbreakable

Viking's Fury Series by Violetta Rand
Love's Fury
Desire's Fury
Passion's Fury

Also from Violetta Rand
Viking Hearts

The Sons of Scotland Series by Victoria Vane
Virtue
Valor

Dry Bayou Brides Series by Lynn Winchester
The Shepherd's Daughter
The Seamstress
The Widow

Table of Contents

Chapter One

B EING AN AMBITIOUS man, Henry Harcourt always entered his neat London house with faint dissatisfaction. He disliked its modest size and unfashionable location. This evening, however, he had more important matters on his mind—matters, which might, in fact, lead to promotion and a larger house before too much longer.

His heart lifted as always at the sight of his wife, Lady Christianne, descending the narrow stairs to greet him. He had married well above his own rank, his wife being the sister of the Marquis of Tamar. Although she was penniless, that had never concerned him, for his was a love match.

Striding to meet her, he realized belatedly that the lady approaching him was *not* his wife but her twin sister. The twins shared the same petite, delicate figures, raven locks, and lustrous, dark brown eyes. Their beauty was almost ethereal. But there, all similarities ended.

Although most people thought them identical, Henry rarely confused them, even at a distance, for Anna lacked Christianne's impulsive warmth and sweet disposition. Anna walked with icy poise, her eyes veiled and watchful, her beautiful face betraying little except bored amusement at life. With her sharp perception and caustic tongue, she was one of the most intimidating women Henry had ever met.

She was not an entirely comfortable house guest either. On the other hand, she had proven surprisingly useful to him in his work, and she was just the person he needed to see this evening.

"Ah, Anna. Come into the study, if you please."

For an instant, her eyes betrayed a spark of interest that was almost relief, but she merely inclined her head, and obligingly followed him into his tiny study.

Henry wasted no time on pleasantries. "Are you on visiting terms with your brother?" He squeezed behind the desk which was really too large for the room.

"God, no," Anna replied with revulsion. "Which brother?" she added as an afterthought.

"Your eldest brother, Lord Tamar."

"Oh, I don't mind him. But I can't imagine his wealthy new wife condescending to our Kensington hovel."

Ignoring her slur upon his home, Henry corrected her. "No, I wish you to visit him up in Cumberland. At Braithwaite Castle."

"Why the devil would I do that?"

Henry frowned. Like Christianne, Anna had grown up wild with little company but her siblings and she clearly saw no reason to mind her tongue with family. "Find your own reasons," he said curtly. "He is newly married, that should be enough. I want you there because it is a mere ten miles from the Black Fort which houses French prisoners of war."

That caught her attention. "Go on."

"In October, an attempt was made to blow up the fort. It was foiled, and the French agents captured or killed. But such a strange act drew the fort to my attention. Why pick on such an obscure prison? Who were they trying to rescue? The men we captured had no idea or weren't telling. So, I've been looking into the inmates and discovered *this* man."

He took a sheaf of papers from the inside of his coat and pushed them across the desk to Anna. "Captain Armand L'Étrange. A man of the same name and the same regiment died at Salamanca. I know because a report was made of his bravery."

"Then who is this?" Anna enquired, flicking through the papers.

"Whoever he is, he surrendered in Spain at the beginning of this year without much struggle and has given no trouble since. I have reason to believe he is Colonel Delon, the commander of all Bonaparte's spies—under Bonaparte himself, of course. An intimate—or at least a past tool—of the likes of Fouché and Talleyrand, the one-time ministers of police and foreign affairs."

Anna cast him a skeptical glance. "What reason could you possibly have for so wild a guess?"

"Well, it *is* a guess," Henry admitted, "for we have no physical description of Delon. He was never a very *visible* commander. But, according to a spy of our own, about a year ago, there was some kind of purge in the ranks of the French police, with several of their spies being killed, or given away to whichever enemy would deal with them. No one has seen or mentioned Delon since, so we think he was pushed out, forced into hiding. He was last heard of in January, in Spain. I imagine his lifespan would have been severely curtailed had he returned to France. He must have a head full of information, dangerous to a lot of powerful people."

"And so, he pretended to be this L'Étrange and gave himself up to us? A rather drastic move, is it not?"

"Perhaps," Henry agreed. "But our man placed this Delon within a few miles of where the supposed L'Étrange was captured. It seems likely Delon surrendered in disguise, and as a result, no one has ever asked him to betray anything. But can you imagine how useful his knowledge would be to us?" He smiled faintly. "And this is where you come in, my dear. I would like you to visit the prison, in charitable spirit, and make friends with the man. Help him escape, find out what you can and bring him to me."

Her face did not change, yet Henry knew that she was pleased. Her very stillness betrayed her excitement.

"To bring such a man to the British side..." she mused. "It would surely help end the war. And it would be quite a feather in your cap, would it not?"

"And in yours," Henry said steadily. "If you succeed. But make no mistake, Anna. This man is dangerous, and not only for what he knows. They say he was once a mere spy himself and rose to control the whole of Bonaparte's secret police system under the likes of

Fouché. He couldn't have done that without being highly intelligent, devious, and utterly ruthless."

Anna smiled and rose to her feet. "Then surely we are well matched. If you procure me a seat, I shall leave on the early mail coach."

TWO DAYS LATER, Lady Anna Gaunt stepped down from her hired chaise. The impressive front door of Braithwaite Castle was already open and a very superior butler regarded her from the top step.

"Be so good as to pay the post boy, if you please," she said carelessly, mounting the steps. "And announce me to Lord and Lady Tamar."

Both instructions appeared to bewilder the butler, though not enough to remove him from her path.

"What name shall I say, madam?" he enquired, making no effort to attend to the impatient postillions who were anxious to return to Carlisle.

Anna gazed at the butler as though astonished. "Lady Anna Gaunt, of course. Lord Tamar is expecting me."

His surprise at least enabled her to sail past him into the house, although he recovered quickly.

"This way, if you please, madam," he said repressively, and led her across the vast hall and oak staircase to an uninspiring reception room. "I'll see if her ladyship is at home."

Anna allowed herself to look slightly offended. "His lordship should have had my letter a week since," she observed. "I cannot be above a few minutes later than I intended."

The butler merely bowed and went on his stately way.

In truth, Anna was not remotely offended since she hadn't written to anyone, and the butler was only doing his duty, preserving his masters from uninvited *hoi polloi*. Her departure from London had been sudden, her journey north urgent and appallingly uncomfortable, though she had no intention of advertising the fact.

The reception room was small and somewhat soulless, though perfectly decorated. It had struck her, on first approaching the castle, that it resembled her own home, Tamar Abbey—another medieval pile. However, the nearer she approached, the fewer were the resemblances. Both the older and newer parts of Braithwaite Castle were clearly in excellent repair, the estate in which it was set well-cared for and prosperous. Here, the best was obviously made of a difficult and wild landscape. And the question uppermost in Anna's mind remained, what on earth had possessed the Earl of Braithwaite to marry his very eligible sister to Anna's entirely *in*eligible brother? The advantages were all clearly Rupert's, and Anna was likely to be merely the first of her siblings to take advantage.

The butler's footsteps returned after several minutes, though rather more hurriedly. "If you'd please to follow me upstairs, my lady," he said with rather more respect, "her ladyship will receive you. And the post boys will be taken care of."

"Thank you," Anna said, and followed him up the grand staircase to an apparently infinite gallery and the first room opening off it. Now the moment was upon her and she would discover what sort of woman had taken on her flat-broke and feckless brother. To say nothing of his awful, grasping family.

But the drawing room—although a much finer apartment—was also empty. The butler bowed again and departed.

Only seconds later, a young woman of around her own age rushed in. Although clearly flustered, she was beautiful, fashionable, and unexpectedly friendly. The kind of woman who had never feared or wanted for anything.

"Lady Anna!" the beauty exclaimed, hurrying toward her with both hands outstretched. "What a delightful surprise!"

Anna almost laughed. She managed to avoid the clearly intended embrace by an adroit sidestep while she briefly shook her sister-in-law's hand. That much contact was unavoidable. "Lady Tamar," she said formally.

Her sister-in-law's hands fell to her sides. Anna might have imagined the flash of hurt in her eyes but the spark of anger was real enough.

"Call me Serena," her brother's wife said at once. A perfect lady, clearly, she would not allow a perceived slight to affect her. "We are sisters, after all. But I hope you will excuse our unpreparedness. Paton said we should be expecting you, but I assure you, we received no word."

"I wrote to Tamar more than a week since," Anna lied. "It would be just like him to ignore it or simply forget! But the matter is easily remedied. I shall be quite happy to put up in Blackhaven. I believe there is a hotel."

"Nonsense, you must stay here, of course. Please, sit close to the fire—you must be chilled through. They're bringing refreshments directly."

Anna took the nearest chair, making up for her old and unfashionable gown by sitting rigidly straight. "Is my brother not here?" she enquired.

"I left him further along the coast, huddled inside a greatcoat and two cloaks painting the sea from a *particular* angle. But I've sent someone to fetch him home."

"You needn't have bothered," Anna said frankly. "He won't be pleased to see me."

Serena blinked. "I'm sure you wrong both of you."

"Oh no," Anna said. She allowed herself to gaze more blatantly at her sister-in-law. The girl lacked neither intelligence nor beauty. Anna was at a loss as to why she had married Rupert. "So, are your brother and mine friends?" Anna asked, wondering if that was how they had met.

"They are now," Serena said cautiously.

"Then Lord Braithwaite did not introduce you?"

"Goodness, no. *I* introduced *them.*" There was a challenge in Serena's direct gaze. "Why?"

Anna opted for honesty. "To be frank, I am wondering what on earth can have possessed you to marry my graceless brother."

"Love," Serena said without apology. She didn't even drop her gaze.

Anna, who had wondered whether Rupert or his bride would be in most need of rescuing, found herself none the wiser. For the first time, she caught a hint of steel in her new sister, a sense that she might just be a worthy opponent. If opponent she turned out to be. Anna reserved judgement, at least until she had seen Rupert.

"How very romantic," Anna said, smiling.

But it seemed Serena was only half-listening for a banging door in the bowels of the castle and a raised, familiar voice heralded urgent footsteps and the precipitous arrival of none other than Rupert himself.

"Serena, guess what? One of the prisoners really *has* escaped the Black Fort and—" He stopped, blinking, brought up short at the sight of Anna. "Good God."

"Good morning, Rupert," Anna said calmly. His blurted news was not uninteresting to her, but at this moment, it took second place to their reunion.

Although she would never admit it, Rupert was one of the very few people she was ever pleased to see. But now, finding him healthy and full of vitality, her sense of relief took her by surprise. If this marriage was the result of some deep game on the Braithwaites' part, she could not yet discern it. Rupert looked happier than she could recall since they were children running wild around the abbey.

Of course, he had luxury and money now, but Rupert had never really been bothered by their lack—at least not on his own account.

"You might have told your wife I was coming," she reproved. "My letter must have reached you at least four or five days ago."

Rupert gave a crooked smile. "Doing it much too brown, Anna. You've never written to me in your life. You're welcome, you know…so long as you haven't brought your brothers."

"Good God, no," Anna said, revolted. "I merely thought it time I unburdened Henry of my presence for a few weeks." She glanced at Serena. "Henry is my sister's husband. We think he makes himself deliberately dull to avoid my brothers descending on him too often."

Rupert let out a snort of laughter. "He's not dull, he just disapproves of us, and who can blame him?"

"Not I," Anna admitted. "So, I was going to return to Tamar Abbey, but the place is in uproar while your renovations begin, with builders and so on all over the place. Henry said I couldn't stay there until you and your wife were there, too. And so, Christianne sent me up here instead to see how you did. And to wish you happy, of course."

"Of course," Rupert said, regarding her a little too keenly. "That must have been uppermost in your mind."

"Well, that and curiosity," Anna admitted. "We're all agog to discover the lady brave enough to marry into *our* family."

"She only married *me*," Rupert retorted, unexpectedly possessive. Normally, he shared his good fortune. "Not the rest of you."

"Don't be inhospitable, Tamar," Serena reproved, and then, as if she could no longer contain herself, blurted out, "But what were you saying about an escaped prisoner?"

"A French officer at the fort. Never gave them any trouble before, apparently, but when the gate was opened yesterday morning to admit a supply cart, he took the opportunity to lay out one of the guards and bolted. Took everyone by surprise."

"Did they catch him again?" Serena asked. Usefully, she was asking the questions Anna needed answers to.

"Not yet. One of the guards shot him, but he just got back up and ran on. They reckon he'll head for the coast, if he isn't dead yet. The soldiers are already watching Blackhaven and the nearby ports."

"Goodness," Anna murmured. "Are we all in danger for our lives from this monster?"

"I imagine he just wants to go home," Serena said with more than a hint of compassion. "And will avoid people rather than seek them out to murder them in their beds—although I'll wager the gossips in Blackhaven are already scaring each other witless with such wild imaginings."

Rupert cast his wife a quick grin, allowing Anna a glimpse of genuine intimacy between them.

"All the same," he added with a frown. "You probably shouldn't go walking or riding alone until the fellow is caught. I expect he must be desperate."

HER BROTHER'S ADVICE was no doubt good for his wife and servants, but Anna had no intention of taking it. Before luncheon, thanks to the tour of the castle provided by her sister-in-law, she knew all the exits. By midafternoon, alone in the castle's fine library, she had poured over all the old and new maps of the Braithwaite estate and the surrounding countryside as far as the Black Fort.

She then drifted up to the well-appointed bedchamber prepared for her and ordered a cold collation to be sent up. She bade the maid who brought it to explain to Lady Tamar that she was overcome with exhaustion and was going to lie down. "Give her my apologies for missing tea and say that I hope to rise for dinner. But if I do not, I am merely sleeping through until the morning and am best left alone. By tomorrow, I shall be quite myself again."

Since they knew she had travelled from London to Carlisle in the fast but exceedingly uncomfortable mail coach, they would not be surprised by her tiredness. Though she might need better excuses in the future.

Left to herself, Anna changed into her old, dark navy riding habit, complete with her favorite stiletto tucked away in its purposely-sewn pocket. She packed the food and a few surgical necessities into a small canvas bag. After all, she was looking for a wounded man. She then slipped out of one of the several side doors and made her way to the stables unseen.

Serena's brother, the Earl of Braithwaite, kept an excellent stable at the castle, even when he was not in residence. Anna, who preferred dogs and horses to people, spent some time there, getting to know the horses and easily charming the stable boy who was the only other person around. Deciding on a spirited but affectionate chestnut mare, unimaginatively named Chessy, she bribed the stable boy to keep her departure a secret and rode out of the castle grounds.

By then, daylight was fading, and she carried a lantern as well as her canvas bag tied to the saddle.

One of the reasons she had chosen the mare, was that the animal knew the terrain, according to the stable boy, and was sure footed over the roughest ground. When darkness fell, she was even more grateful for that, and for the lantern which she held in one hand to light her way, while she controlled the reins in the other.

Beyond the boundary of Braithwaite lands, she made no effort to be silent or to avoid people. However, two hours after she had set out, the only person she had encountered was an elderly man with an injured goat at the edge of the forest. He was carrying the poor creature home and told Anna sternly that she shouldn't be out alone in this country at this time of night. Anna agreed with him and rode on, deeper into the forest. When she emerged at the top of the hill, if she found no trace of the escaped prisoner, she intended to ride the quicker way back to Braithwaite Castle. She might even make it in time for dinner.

However, before she reached that far, the mare suddenly veered to the left, winding through the trees to a more open space. A stream trickled down the hill, forming a pool that gleamed in the cold moonlight. More than that, a man crouched at the water's edge. He appeared to be quite alone.

Anna's heart beat faster. She let the mare walk on, out of the cover of the trees and into the open.

The man had light hair and his coat dangled off one side of his body. He was shaking violently as he used his cupped hand to splash freezing cold water over his shoulder. Perhaps the sounds of the stream and his own washing disguised those of Anna's approach, for he appeared quite oblivious to her presence. Until the mare tossed her head and snorted.

The man sprang up like a startled crow, his worn military overcoat flapping as he swung around, fists raised to defend himself.

Anna allowed herself a small cry of alarm—which was natural enough since his speed of movement had taken her by surprise. She raised her lantern, urging the mare forward with her heels so that the bright light fell full upon him.

His hair was a dark blond, his face lean and far from ill-looking, even with several days' growth on his jaw. He might have been thirty years old, or a little more. His eyes, an intense, piercing blue, darted to all sides before returning to her. Blood stained his coat and his shirt. A lot of blood.

Slowly, his hands fell to his sides. Then, clearly irritated, he waved her away, almost shooing her as though she were a gaggle of geese or an importunate dog. And any young woman alone in the woods in the dark, close to where a dangerous enemy had recently escaped, would have followed his urging and fled. But Anna could barely believe her luck. It could have taken her days to discover him.

"Goodness, you are hurt!" she exclaimed, springing from the saddle. He scowled warningly as she rushed toward him, her lantern in one hand, reins in the other. He even backed away from her, forcing her to seize his arm before he fell into the water. For an instant, he stared down into her face.

Something jolted, deep within her. Surprise, perhaps. She had been prepared to see in his eyes the violence and plain nastiness of his profession. But there was only darkness so deep one could drown in it. He was too weak, surely, to be a threat to anyone. He blinked rapidly and then sagged to the ground, all but dragging her with him as he fell face first.

He was heavy, but Anna sank with him, breaking his fall and turning his face to the side on the rocky ground. She set the lantern down beside him. Beneath the grime and the stubble on his jaw, his features were unexpectedly refined.

He appeared to be out cold, which at least gave her time to tend his wound. He had been shot in the back of the shoulder, no doubt as he ran from his prison, and the ball, presumably, was still lodged inside him. She could only hope it had damaged no vital organs. If it had, she doubted he would still be alive.

At least he had been keeping the wound as clean as he could without being able to reach it properly. He had torn his shirt trying to get at it, so at least she could see it clearly. Peeling off her gloves, she gathered up the bloody rags he had been using in the stream. Then she crouched down at his side once more and set about a more thorough cleansing of his wound.

She found the ball quite easily. Fortunately, it had not penetrated too deeply and did not seem to have damaged any bone, for she could see no splinters. Holding her tweezers in the lantern flame for a moment or two, she hoped he would not come around while she extracted the ball. She had never performed such an operation before. But she had steady hands, and the spy, if such he was, made no movement beyond the involuntary trembling of his body.

She was able to extract the ball quickly and cleanly, after which she took the flask of brandy from her bag and poured some over the wound. She thought he tensed, whether in his sleep or otherwise. She did not pause to check. From common humanity, she needed to get this over with.

She took out the needle and thread, heated the needle in the lantern flame, and sewed up the wound as through it were a torn gown. She had done something similar for Rupert when he had laid his leg open on a scythe blade. And when Sylvester had fallen out of a tree and ripped his arm on a jagged branch. But she had never tended a stranger before.

After she had stitched the wound neatly closed, she applied some of Christianne's healing ointment. She was winding bandages around him when she realized his eyes were open and watching her.

Deliberately, she finished tying his bandage and pulled his ripped shirt and coat back around him. He was shivering more violently from the cold and, no doubt, from the pain.

"Come," she said. "You need warmth and shelter…though I'm not sure there's anything here except an old shepherd's hut." She had passed one just before entering the forest, By the look of it, it had been abandoned for many years.

She rose to her feet, and pulled on her gloves, steeling herself to help him rise, but somehow, he sat up and stumbled to his feet without her aid. The lantern threw deep shadows beneath his high cheekbones, giving him an alarming, cadaverous look. His eyes remained steady on her face, but he made no move toward her.

"Come," she repeated. "Wherever you've been hiding, it's too cold."

The man, who was surely one of her country's most dangerous enemies, perhaps even *the* most dangerous after Bonaparte himself, regarded her without a visible trace of either hope or suspicion. She had never encountered eyes so opaque. It entered her head that, fully fit, he would be her worthiest opponent yet. Even wounded, possibly mortally, he would require all her skill.

Her heart drummed loudly. Her success or failure surely depended on whatever he did now.

Chapter Two

S HE WOULD HAVE liked to turn and walk away. But she had no idea if he would follow her. If he *could* follow her. Bracing herself, she took his arm. "Lean on me. I know where to find shelter."

He appeared to hesitate. Then again, he might merely have been forcing his tired body to work. He had lost too much blood and had already spent two days and a night in the northern winter without care or shelter.

He lurched forward, and she steadied him. He straightened, making a clear effort to walk without leaning on her, but they made slow progress through the wood, Anna leading both horse and man. She had steeled herself to accept his nearness, his weight. But as they walked and stumbled on their way, it wasn't as difficult to bear as she'd expected—perhaps because he was so helpless. Or perhaps because whenever he began to lean on her, he pulled himself away again. And he said nothing to annoy her. In fact, he said nothing at all.

Nevertheless, it was a relief when they finally reached the hut. The door gave easily to reveal one room, bare save for a small, broken bedstead and a mattress. She hadn't held out much hope for a stove, but at least there was a hearth and a chimney.

Leaving him propped against the wall, Anna set down her lantern and hauled the mattress off the broken bed to the floor, close to the hearth. The man watched her without even trying to help. Perhaps he knew he couldn't.

She gestured to the mattress and walked past him, out the door to the tree where she'd tied up the mare. Untying the blanket and her canvas bag, she patted the mare and returned to the hut.

The stranger sat on the mattress, propped up against the wall. Anna shook out the blanket and placed it around his shoulders. A frown tugged at his brow and vanished. Before he could speak, if he truly meant to, she left to gather firewood. This turned out to be easier than she expected, for behind the hut was a lean-to beneath which she found a heap of abandoned logs and kindling. Judging by the wildlife residing amongst it, it had been there for several years.

Having lived for many years without servants, Anna built and lit the fire in the hearth quickly and efficiently. She was pleased to see the smoke drawn up the chimney. When it began to burn merrily, she blew out her lantern to save it for the return journey.

Sitting back on the hard, stone floor, she delved into her canvas bag and brought out the water bottle and the napkin in which she had wrapped her cold meal from Braithwaite Castle. She unfolded it, pushed it across the floor to the wounded man, and set the water bottle beside it.

Throughout it all, he watched her in silence. He hadn't even spoken to her. But, isolated in the warm glow of the fire, the scene was strangely intimate. The firelight flickered across his face, lending it a hard, almost dangerous look. That, she had expected. And yet she wasn't afraid.

He was, after all, weaker than a kitten.

He stirred, and spoke for the first time, his voice quiet and slightly hoarse. "Do you know who I am?" His English was perfect, although his accent was unmistakably French. Which was as well. She'd have hated to have gone to all this trouble if he wasn't the escaped prisoner. Indeed, she could not be sure the man who'd escaped the fort was the same man she'd come to Cumberland for, but it seemed likely.

"Of course not," she said wryly. "We have not been introduced."

His lips quirked with a hint of tired amusement. "Then you really are English."

"Did you imagine I travelled from France on the faint chance that I could save you?"

His eyes remained steady, giving nothing away. "There are many reasons to travel from France."

"And back again. They're looking for you all along the coast."

The news did not appear to surprise him.

Anna smiled. "That was your plan, was it not? To hide here, close to the fort while they scour the ports until they're forced to give up and admit you eluded them?"

"Something like that."

"I imagine you even led them in that direction before you doubled back."

He smiled faintly. "You have a good imagination. Aren't you afraid to be alone with such a devious enemy?"

"Not until you've regained some strength by eating, drinking, and sleeping."

He leaned forward without obvious effort and snagged the water bottle. He took a long drink, then replaced the stopper and reached for the crumbling but still dainty pie. "Why are you helping me?"

She shrugged. "You appear to need it."

"You know I'm French. You know I escaped from the fort."

"The war is nearly over. Besides, I have family and friends in our own army and navy. I hope some French man or woman would be kind to them in similar circumstances."

He swallowed his pie and picked up all the cold meat together in his fingers. "But the circumstances are odd," he pointed out. "You are riding in the woods alone, in the dark. With bandages, blankets, and an al fresco supper."

"Tea, actually," she corrected. "I brought it with me and got lost. I haven't been in the area very long. In fact, I only arrived today."

"Why?" he asked and bit a huge chunk out of the meat. He might have been trying to look savage. Or he might just have been ravenous. She doubted he had eaten in two days.

"Visiting my brother."

"What is your name?" he asked.

"Anna."

He regarded her as he raised the water bottle to his lips once more. "Just Anna?"

"I think so. My family would not approve."

He nodded and drank.

But she would not let him away with silence. "And your name?" she prompted.

"Don't you know?"

She shrugged. "No. No one told me. The excitement is all in your being French and escaping. No one cares about your name."

His lips curved before he pushed a whole handful of nuts and dried fruit into his mouth.

"Louis," he said, when they were gone.

So, he was not admitting to being Captain Armand L'Étrange. Had he plucked the name Louis from the air? No one appeared to know the Christian name of Colonel Delon.

"Just Louis?" she mocked.

"I think so. Will you tell them?"

She blinked at the sudden change of subject. "Who?"

"Your family. The soldiers, guards, magistrates, whoever is looking for me."

She looked away from him into the flames. "The war is ending. I don't want anyone to suffer more."

"What a noble sentiment," he mocked, though he seemed to be deriding himself rather than her. Which was interesting.

"I won't tell," she said. "If you promise to stay hidden and not to hurt any of my countrymen."

"I can't stay hidden forever," he pointed out. "Neither can I promise not to defend myself. However..." He waved a deprecating hand over his person. "I'm not exactly capable of a great deal of violence right now. An average puppy could bring me down without a scratch on him."

She thought that wasn't so far from the truth. But at least he had stopped shaking, and the food had nearly all vanished.

"I'll bring you more tomorrow," she promised. "Can you put more wood on the fire when it burns down?"

"Of course. You brought plenty inside. You are something of a puzzle, Miss Anna."

"I am?"

"You speak like an English lady of quality, but you sew up wounds like a surgeon and build fires like a servant."

So, he had been aware of everything. She smiled wryly. "I had an odd upbringing. Perhaps I shall tell you about it tomorrow."

"Why not tonight?"

She allowed a trace of regret into her voice. "Because I have to go home. And because you have to sleep and heal."

She began to rise, but he moved suddenly, leaning forward and catching her hand. There was no time to steel herself. His bare skin touched hers and she could not prevent her flinch. There was an instant of confusion when the physical revulsion did not strike, when the intense, ugly memories kept their distance. Instead, it was *his* presence which rolled over her, vital and compelling, rooting her to the spot.

And then he dropped her hand. "Forgive me, mademoiselle. I meant only to say thank you."

"There is nothing to forgive," she said hastily. But it was too late. She'd seen the flash of curiosity in his face "I merely want you to take care not to reopen your wounds. Please do not even try to get up." She stood, swinging her cloak back around her and reaching for the lantern. She set a spare candle on the hearth. "Take care. I promise I shall return tomorrow."

He inclined his head, with tired humor. He was no longer hiding the pain that tightened his mouth and tugged down his brow. Perhaps he couldn't. "Goodbye, Miss Anna."

"Au revoir, Monsieur Louis."

As she flitted out of the hut, she was now the one who trembled, and she had no idea why.

THERE WERE MANY reasons Louis Delon did not want her to go. Not least of them was that he could not remember ever having seen anyone or anything more beautiful.

Perhaps it was the moonlight or the firelight, but the soft glow of her creamy skin and the gleam of her raven black hair seemed to accentuate the refined beauty of her face. And even the old-fashioned, loose-fitting riding habit could not hide her delicious figure. Almost delirious with pain, blood loss and hunger, it was no wonder he thought she resembled an angel.

Only he doubted she was. Her appearance had been far too opportune, too unlikely. She had known he was the escaped prisoner from the fort, yet she hadn't been remotely frightened as she had helped him. Or at least, not until he'd touched her.

That was the moment her veil had dropped, revealing, if only for an instant, darkness, horror, and terror. He might have imagined it, only he had seen that look before, in young soldiers after battle, in women and children who had got in the way of a rampaging army. It was more unexpected in a supposedly genteel English lady, which served to increase his curiosity.

He wanted her to stay and tell him the story of her life. He wanted to admire the grace and efficiency of her movements, keep her close for weak reasons of simple human comfort. He wanted to learn who she was and make her spill her secrets. He wanted to watch the expressions flit across her face, to make her laugh while they sharpened their wits on each other. He had no idea who she was, or what danger she presented. But he did recognize a fellow spirit.

And so, he let her go.

And when he heard the soft thud of her horse's hooves as she rode away, he was sorry. She had been kind and whatever she had put on his wounds seemed to have taken the edge off his pain. She gave him something to think about other than vengeance.

Inevitably, the cold fury began to rise, bringing with it, the visions of those men and women, his people, whom Gosselin had sent to their deaths simply to gain favor and power. *His* power. Louis had been unforgivably slow. He had not suspected such massive betrayal from his lieutenant. For when it mattered, it was Colonel Louis Delon who kept France safe, who plugged the leaks created by the Emperor Napoleon's policies and actions.

He had known his power was considered dangerous to others, to the disgraced Fouché and Talleyrand and even the emperor himself. He had known his days were numbered. But he had never expected Gosselin to go after his people. That was unforgivably stupid, short-sighted, and dangerous. To say nothing of cruel and inhuman.

For a moment, the agony swamped him again. The faces of Marguerite and her son, and all those others arrested, executed, or betrayed deliberately to the enemy, swam through his mind, accusing, shaming. Brave men and women of various ages and places in life, who had risked far more than Gosselin ever would, to save France from its ever-growing number of enemies. Marguerite and Jean most of all. They had trusted him, and he had failed to save them from his own over-ambitious underling, Gosselin.

Gosselin, you will die, he promised as he had every night for ten months. His visions of the betrayed slid away into the back of his mind, until he was left only with the dark beauty of the English girl who had undoubtedly saved his life. *Anna.*

Warm at last, fed and almost comfortable, he knew he would drift quickly into sleep.

And he knew that he would see her again.

"I'M GLAD ANNA is here," Serena said to her husband the next morning as he brushed out her hair. It was a duty he had taken over from her maid, although he was not so good at dressing or styling it. He seemed, mostly, to enjoy winding it through his fingers. "Only I don't think she likes me."

Tamar shrugged. "Anna doesn't like anyone very much. Except Christianne."

"Then why did she come here?"

"Curiosity, probably. And perhaps Christianne's husband made it difficult for her to stay there. It's probably quite unsettling to have someone in his house who looks so much like his wife and yet is so unlike her in character. Besides, he's probably jealous. The twins have always been close." He laid down the brush and gave her hair a gentle tug until she turned up her face and he could kiss her. "She'll grow less prickly in time. Just leave her be and you'll find she's actually quite fun company when she chooses. Come on, let's go to breakfast and see if she's up yet."

Lady Anna proved to be not only up but eating breakfast while being entertained by Serena's young sisters. Serena had expected her to be bored or even irritated in such company. But in fact, she was laughing at something Alice had said, and didn't seem to mind when Helen commanded her attention by simply calling her name.

"Why didn't you tell us you had such a *good* sister?" Alice demanded when Tamar and Serena entered the breakfast room.

"I never said she was a bad sister," Tamar objected. "In fact, I have no objections at all to my sisters. It's my brothers who are awful."

"Thank you for such fulsome praise," Anna said wryly.

Serena, finding a letter from her mother by her place at the table, sighed and sat down to break the seal.

"What is Mama saying?" Maria asked. "Is she still outraged by Miss Grey having the temerity to marry Mr. Benedict?"

"Oh, no, she isn't outraged, exactly," Serena said. "Merely inconvenienced. It must be infuriating to have one's forgiveness proved *unnecessary*. My mother dismissed the girls' governess," she explained briefly to Anna, "over something that was quite unfair and untrue. And by the time she'd come to realize this and wrote our Miss Grey a very handsome letter of apology, appealing to her to come back to us, Miss Grey had married our neighbor!"

"Most galling for her," Anna said, faintly amused.

"Well, I think it was. Plus, she does not like people stepping out of their station. The girls now go up to Haven Hall three days a week to be taught by the new Mrs. Benedict..." She broke off, frowning. "Actually, they probably shouldn't go until this prisoner is recaptured."

"I doubt they'd be in any danger," Tamar said, heaping his plate with ham and eggs. "Haven Hall is inland, and I can't imagine this fellow would draw attention to himself by attacking a carriage full of schoolroom misses. But, if you're worried, I'll go with them. Better still, send Jem or one of the footmen, armed to the teeth."

"We could," Serena said doubtfully, spreading open her letter. "Perhaps he was even recaptured last night. Do we know who he is? What kind of a man he is?"

"Infantry captain," Tamar said, taking his place opposite the girls. "L'Étrange. Armand L'Étrange. A gentleman, apparently, who had accepted his captivity with grace. So why he didn't just stick it out for another few weeks until the war finally ends..."

"Perhaps he had bad news from home," Serena speculated. "Or he'd just had enough and snapped. After all, does anyone *really* accept captivity?"

Anna cast her a curious glance, as though reassessing her, though Serena doubted it would be in her favor. Hastily, she turned her attention to the letter and read her mother's latest instructions. "Oh, for the love of—Just when we were comfortable again!"

"What?" Maria demanded.

"Mama has engaged a new governess for you and she is arriving tomorrow. Mrs. Elphinstone."

"But we like Miss Grey!" Maria objected. "I mean, Mrs. Benedict."

"I know," Serena said ruefully. "But you must admit it isn't convenient when she is at Haven Hall. And you may like Mrs. Elphinstone excessively."

"We won't," Helen said flatly.

"It's also possible that Mrs. Benedict no longer wishes to teach, now she is mistress of Haven Hall. I suspect she is merely being kind to us. Anyhow, Mama has spoken and we must make the best of it." Turning to Anna with something close to relief, she asked, "What would you like to do today? We have some charming countryside and

Blackhaven is a pleasant town, although quiet at this season…"

"Please don't feel the need to look after me," Anna replied at once. "I arrived uninvited and am quite happy to look after myself. In fact, I prefer not to disturb you."

"Well, if you enjoy parties, there is a musical evening at the vicarage tonight and on Friday, there is a masquerade at the town assembly rooms."

"A masquerade?" Anna repeated, apparently amused. "How very decadent!"

"Well, it won't be, since it is sponsored by the vicar's wife and Mrs. Winslow," Serena said frankly. "But it did seem a harmless form of fun leading up to Christmas. We can easily find you a mask and domino cloak. Also, if you can sing or play at all, please come to the musical evening or it is likely to be torture."

"That isn't encouraging," Anna pointed out.

"It raises funds for the vicar's charities," Serena said apologetically. "His wife holds them every so often and besides, it lets the young ladies practice their accomplishments somewhere unthreatening."

"I could threaten them if it would help," Anna offered.

ANNA WAS OPEN about her expedition that morning. She even asked for a luncheon to be packed so that she could go further.

"You don't want to go far with that Frenchie about," the cook said darkly.

"Oh, I shall be very careful, and take someone with me," Anna lied. She had no intention of taking anyone. While she set off in the direction of Blackhaven, she quickly doubled back once she was out of sight of the main part of the castle and galloped across country toward the Black Fort.

Her heart was beating fast with excitement as she drew nearer the wood and the hut where she'd left "Louis". Captain Armand L'Étrange was the escapee, and that was the name Henry had given her, while convinced it was an alias. If he was right, then this prisoner, Louis, was in reality, Colonel Delon, Bonaparte's spymaster.

And Anna, had come to learn his secrets.

He was certainly a more interesting man than most, which had to be the source of her excitement. She wanted him to be well and she needed to convince him to change sides. She didn't underestimate the difficulties, nor the advantages if she could succeed. And she *would* succeed. There had been something between them last night, even in his poor state, even in the short time she'd been with him. And today, she intended to build on it, win his trust, his liking, and the beginnings of his loyalty.

She all but flung herself off the mare, tying her loosely to the same tree branch as last night. From her continued, keen observation, she knew there was no one else around. They would be isolated here, undisturbed, and she had several hours.

Her heart drumming, she walked up to the door and pushed it open.

The hut was empty. There was nothing to show he had ever been there. Even the mattress was back on the tilting bed.

Slowly, she crossed the room to the hearth. He'd even taken the ashes away. Only the warmth still in the stone betrayed last night's fire.

"Damn," she whispered.

He was good. Far more perceptive than she'd given him credit for, he hadn't trusted her at all.

Chapter Three

HAD HE BEEN fit, Louis would undoubtedly have stayed and met her on her own terms—while taking sensible precautions, of course. As it was, isolated and wounded, his only safe choice was to leave, which he did at first light.

As he walked into the woods, brushing over his footprints as he went, he acknowledged that without her, he would have been in a much worse state. But with his wounds dressed, food in his stomach, and a night's sleep behind him, his strength had begun to return. Although, perhaps he was more delirious than he thought because the ridiculous plan that came to him first and made him grin, seemed to be the one with the best likelihood of success.

In easy stages, resting frequently, he walked back up to the vicinity of his prison and the village beyond. There appeared to be no extra soldiers around it any more. They were, no doubt, watching the coast as Anna had told him. And the guards from the fort had obviously returned to watching their remaining prisoners.

The village inn was a coaching establishment. While imprisoned, Louis had made it his business to learn when the stagecoaches arrived and departed. He chose the busiest time for the inn staff when they were all rushing around, changing horses and drivers, and fetching ale and breakfast for hungry stagecoach passengers.

Wandering into the inn yard as though quite familiar with it, Louis went straight to the kitchen and helped himself to a loaf and some cheese while the cook was screeching at someone to get out of her hair. In the tap room, he found a disreputable leather coat abandoned on a stool. And outside again, on the coach box, he found what he really wanted—a pistol and some powder. And as a bonus, a tatty, floppy-brimmed hat. Stuffing those all into his pockets, he clambered awkwardly down again and growled at the man who seemed about to ask what he was about. Apparently satisfied, the man returned to harnessing the horses and Louis went to the stables, where the boys were busy brushing down and feeding the tired horses who had just arrived. They ignored him, so he led out a large nag and saddled her in front of them before mounting and riding off.

He had often found that if you did the outrageous with enough conviction, no one questioned you. He was glad he had not lost his touch during his months in prison.

SOME HOURS LATER, dressed in the stolen coat and hat, riding his stolen horse, he lurked on the main road between Blackhaven and Carlisle. He was so bored waiting for the perfect carriage to hold up that he would have welcomed any traffic at all. He wanted a wealthy young man of about his own height and build, alone. Someone who could be robbed and relied on to exaggerate the story of the hold-up beyond recognition of the actual facts. Instead, beyond a couple of farmers' carts and a few cattle, he saw barely anyone at all. It was not a busy stretch of road. A couple of private carriages had passed earlier, but since their occupants were elderly and female, he rode straight past them without stopping.

Time was running out and he did not wish to spend another night in the open. So, when he heard the sounds of another approaching carriage, he sprang out of his hiding place to see a hired chaise and accompanying postilions. Without troubling to observe who was inside it, he rode recklessly into the road to force it to halt.

The driver and outriders slowed from instinct. Even before he raised his pistols, he must have looked a disreputable sight in his tatty and torn leather coat, his fair hair hidden under his stolen floppy hat, which he had pulled low over his muddied face.

"Stand and deliver!" he shouted in a rough London accent, brandishing his pistol as he grabbed at the lead horse's head and all but dragged it to a complete standstill. His wound protested, sending sharp pangs of agony through him. Ignoring the pain, he levelled the pistol at the driver.

"Come down. Everyone, dismount and stand over there."

"I say," an irate male voice sounded in the chaise doorway as a young man stepped out. "What the devil is the hold up?"

"Exactly that, young sir," Louis said amiably, noting with some pleasure that his victim was well-dressed and close enough to the same build as he. "This is indeed the devil of a hold up. Got anyone else in there with you?"

A scream went up.

"Oh God, she's having hysterics," the young man cried in despair, clutching at his already disordered locks.

Louis changed position until he could see the young lady prostrate upon the seat inside, drumming her heels as she wailed like a banshee.

"Looks more like a tantrum to me," he said judiciously. "But either way, I don't envy you. Tell you what, young sir, just hand over the blunt and your baggage. I'll spare the lady's."

"That's damned good of you," the young man said nervously. "Only how can we elope with no money?"

"Live on true love," Louis advised, accepting the young man's fat pocket book and his portmanteau. "Here, we'll share it," he added, seeing just how much money was inside the wallet. He kindly handed a wadge of it to his victim and pocketed the rest. "Best be off! And take my advice and don't stop on the way. You'll never get married once you start involving the law, whichever side of the border."

"Good point," the young man said, climbing back into the coach with a wary glance at his rigid beloved.

Louis waved everyone back to their proper places and let the chaise go. Only when one of the postilions paused to level a pistol at him did he raise his own. The man turned back and rode on, presumably deciding that discretion was the better part of valor.

Louis dragged himself and his horse off the road to investigate his plunder.

IT WAS GROWING dark by the time Louis disturbed the peace of Henrit, the snug country estate of Mr. Winslow. In truth, by then, he was so tired and his shoulder ached so abominably, that he all but fell off his horse without acting and called imperiously for the help of a magistrate.

"I've been robbed! Highway robbery!" he told anyone who would listen, until Mrs. Winslow gave him a cup of tea in her drawing room. This at least told him he appeared to her to be a gentleman is his second set of stolen clothes. A few moments later, the lady's husband came bustling in with some concern to hear his tale.

As though pulling himself together, Louis uttered an apology for bursting in on them. "My name is Lewis. Sir Lytton Lewis, at your service," he said more calmly. "I was told you were the local magistrate, and in truth, I don't quite know what to do. I've never been robbed before. I was travelling to Scotland for my health—I'm told the air is more bracing—and now I'm stuck here with neither vehicle nor baggage! I was lucky just to find that nag wandering around, for it happened in the middle of nowhere."

"It is quite outrageous how lawless the local roads have become," Mrs. Winslow agreed. "Why, only a few weeks ago, a lady was *shot* on the Carlisle road! And now this! What can be done, Mr. Winslow?"

"Well, we'll make a search for your belongings and the fellow who took them, but between us, sir, he is likely to be long gone, probably into Scotland! There is a hotel in Blackhaven, if you have the wherewithal to put up there for a couple of nights while we investigate."

Louis allowed himself a small smile. "I confess I hid some funds against just such an event as this."

"The hotel is very good," Mrs. Winslow assured him. "Also, there is a bank close by which can help if you find yourself short. And if you are travelling for your health, sir, many people swear by the Blackhaven spring waters."

"I'm overwhelmed by your kindness," he said, allowing a faint look of shame to cross his face. "I apologize for the rude manner of my entry. I'm afraid I am not at my best…"

"Have some tea with us," Mr. Winslow invited, "and then I'll drive you into Blackhaven. I'm going anyhow. Now, how would you describe this ruffian?"

"He was a big, dirty brute, wearing a long, tatty leather coat. I couldn't see his face. I think he'd deliberately smeared mud on it."

"Didn't have a French accent, did he?"

Louis raised his eyebrows. "French? Lord no. London gutter, I'd say. Why would he be French?"

"Oh, it was just a thought. We had a prisoner of war escape from the fort a few miles away, and we can't find a trace of him. But it seems we have a highwayman, too!"

THE AMIABLE MAGISTRATE was kind enough to enter the Blackhaven Hotel with Louis and explain his lack of baggage. As a result, he was given a decent, front-facing room and the best of service.

By the time his dinner had been brought to him in his bedchamber, his whole body ached and he wanted to fall into bed and sleep for a week. Worse, as he eased himself out of his stolen coat, he saw a little dried blood on his bandage. But at least the stitches appeared to be holding. If he could just avoid infection and fever over the next few days, he might just survive. By the time Gosselin came, he should be recovered enough to kill him. That he would come, Louis did not doubt.

He would have to, for he could not trust such work to anyone else. The news of his escape would reach France via the maze of spies and dupes Louis himself had set up from excisemen and other officials to smugglers. And Gosselin, who must have been furious at his escape into British custody, would come to finish his self-appointed task. And that would be his final mistake.

The trouble was, Louis needed to do more than wallow in his bedchamber for a fortnight. To hide was to invite investigation. He needed to be seen again, to establish himself more firmly as Sir Lytton Lewis.

At the last moment, he asked the maid to buy him some laudanum.

As she scampered off to do his bidding, he eased himself onto a chair by the window, tore off his badly tied neckcloth, and began to eat his dinner while he watched the world of Blackhaven pass by in the well-lit street below.

Blackhaven was a growing spa town, newly fashionable with the wealthy who attributed all sorts of cures to the spring water that flowed there from the nearby hills. And although the chills of a northern English December must have driven off many health-seekers, enough remained to give the town an air of bustle.

A few carriages trundled up the street, while on either side of the road, respectable working folk hurried home, avoiding the gentry who strolled along the swept part of the street in their furs and finery, no doubt on their way to dinner parties or the theatre.

The maid returned with his laudanum so quickly that he gathered the hotel kept a supply. He took the bottle, setting it down on the table by his dinner, and thanked the girl with a coin. She curtsied, and he turned back to the window in time to see a familiar figure below.

He leaned forward, fatigue falling away from him like a discarded coat. She wore an elegant evening cloak trimmed with fur over a pure white gown that hung like silk over her graceful person. Her gleaming, raven hair had been piled high on her head and held with a wisp of some glittering net that may have been sewn with jewels. She took his breath away all over again, even before she laughed at something uttered by the handsome if carelessly dressed gentleman beside her.

"Wait." Louis managed to stay the maid just as she reached his bedchamber door. "Do you know who that lady is?"

The maid, perhaps scenting romance, bounded back to the window.

"The black-haired young lady across the street, walking with the hatless gentleman and the fair lady," he said, keeping the urgency from his voice with some difficulty.

"No idea who *she* is," the maid said regretfully. Somehow, he hadn't really expected a different answer, although he'd hoped. "But the other is Lady Serena—well, Lady Tamar as she is now. She's the Earl of Braithwaite's sister. From the castle. And Lord Tamar is the gentleman with them."

"Ah. Thank you," Louis said vaguely, and nodded dismissal.

He watched the raven-haired lady as she walked the length of the street with her companions, until they vanished around the corner. His whole body hummed with excitement, with the fresh plans forming in his mind.

He could justify those plans, of course. His meeting with her in the wood was unlikely to have been an accident, and so he needed to know how she fitted into the web of his enemies. And if he could make her an ally instead, this woman who walked with such careless, aristocratic grace, as though no street dirt would dare cling to her pristine white gown. Who appeared to face enemies, gory wounds and solitary rides in the dark with quiet efficiency, and yet flinched at his lightest, most unthreatening touch. Not so fearless, perhaps, as she pretended. If so, he could not but admire the calm manner behind which she hid the fact.

And it could have been that admiration which really lay behind his new plans. He wanted to see her again.

ANNA, WHILE FURIOUS to find her Frenchman gone, and annoyed to discover no trace of him around the shepherd's hut, had not quite given up hope of discovering him again. If she truly had lost him, this would be her first failure. Unfortunately, it was also the most important task she had yet been given.

She'd been foolishly overconfident. But he should not have been capable of leaving the hut as he had. Her one hope was that he would still need help and look for it somewhere she could find him.

And so, she swallowed her ill-nature and returned to her other, self-appointed task of investigating Rupert's marriage, which meant accompanying him and his wife to the dire musical evening at the vicarage. Of course, the idea of Rupert and herself in a vicarage at all, was amusing. Until she met the vicar's wife, the stunningly beautiful Mrs. Grant.

Anna recognized Mrs. Grant as the one-time Lady Crowmore, the "Wicked Kate" who'd scandalized London for years, hovering on the verge of social ruin. Not that Anna had ever moved in such exalted circles—until now—but Kate Crowmore had been pointed out to her in the park and in the street. The idea of this dashing lady as the vicar of Blackhaven's wife should have been funny, or even tragic, but neither Mrs. Grant nor her guests appeared to find it so.

Rupert certainly seemed to be on friendly terms with her, but then, so was Serena. And when Mr. Grant finally walked into the room, the way his wife's whole face lit up left Anna in no doubt that Wicked Kate had eyes only for her dull vicar.

Who turned out not to be so dull. He made a point of welcoming Anna to Blackhaven and to his home.

"I hope you will sing or play for us, Lady Anna," he invited. "Our evenings, as you see, are quite informal, a fun way to raise donations. You merely put your donations in the bowl at the back to show your appreciation of each performer."

"Of course," said Anna, smiling. She had no money with her and none at all to her name except the small sum Henry had given her—and that she might well need to pursue her Frenchman into Scotland.

"Tamar, you have all the money," Serena said unexpectedly. "Divide it up and let us choose our own favorites!"

The idea of Rupert with any money at all was an alien one to Anna. But he had married an heiress. Exchanging banter with his wife, he duly emptied his pockets into Serena's lap and let her divide the coins evenly between the three of them. Anna, watching their faces rather than listening to their nonsense, was surprised to find not only contentment but fun there. They *liked* each other.

Well, Rupert deserved that. Although she didn't understand it, she was glad he had married for more than the money, and glad, too, that Serena seemed happy with the outcome.

I have nothing to do here. I can chase my Frenchman into Scotland, or I can go home... Neither prospect explained her restlessness, her unspecific discontent.

When invited, Lady Serena sang first, without any show of reluctance or embarrassment, and yet with a pleasing modesty that proved flattery had never gone to her head. There was a lot to like about Serena. That, too, was unexpected.

When Serena's song was finished, Anna duly dropped some coins into the bowl. They collided with those thrown at exactly the same time by a quietly dressed man who gave her a conspiratorial and rather charming smile.

Almost immediately, her attention was distracted by Mrs. Grant, who introduced her to Mr. and Mrs. Winslow and their daughter Catherine.

"And so, you have come from London to visit your brother?" Mrs. Winslow said as they strolled toward a sofa. "How charming! My daughter is going to London for the season next year. Perhaps you will look out for her."

"Oh, I don't go much into society," Anna said. "I live quietly with my sister and her husband."

"Oh, well, but you might at least meet in the park," Mrs. Winslow said, disappointed but making the best of it.

"I shall bow to you," Anna assured Catherine. "And I won't be the least offended if you give me the cut direct."

Catherine laughed nervously, betraying that she knew exactly how Anna's family stood in the world. At least before Tamar's extraordinary marriage.

"I would hope my daughter incapable of such rudeness," Mrs. Winslow said, bridling.

"Lady Anna was joking," Catherine said hastily. "Will you sing tonight, my lady?"

"If anyone's brave enough to listen. But I believe it is your turn, Miss Winslow. Mrs. Grant is beckoning you."

Catherine turned out to have a pleasant voice, well enough trained to reach all the right notes so at least there was no difficulty in complimenting the proud parents.

"And are you coming to our masquerade on Friday?" Mrs. Winslow asked. "I shall be sure to send a card to the castle for you. It's the first time I remember such an event in Blackhaven!"

"You do seem to have an exciting town," Anna observed, "what with masquerades and escaping prisoners-of-war!"

"And highwaymen," Mrs. Winslow added.

"Highwaymen?"

"Why yes, only today some poor man was robbed on the Carlisle road."

"Goodness!" Anna had no need to pretend her avid interest. "And who is this villain?"

"Well, we don't know! He doesn't appear to be a local ruffian, but my husband, who is the magistrate, thinks it likely that wherever he came from, he has vanished into Scotland."

"I was thinking of travelling north myself to visit other friends," Anna said. "You must give me the description of this villain before I do!" She hesitated, then, "I don't suppose *he* is your escaped prisoner?"

"We thought if that," Mrs. Winslow admitted. "And I suppose he could be, although he did not speak with a French accent but with a low London one. Do you think he could have *copied* such a thing?"

"Perhaps," Anna said. Her Frenchman had certainly spoken with a distinctly foreign accent, but knowing who he was, she didn't put anything past him.

"Lady Anna," Mrs. Grant said. "Might we call on you for a fresh voice? This is Mr. Banion, by the by. He refuses to perform for us but has kindly agreed to turn your music."

Mr. Banion turned out be the man who had smiled at her over the coin bowl.

"I have no music," Anna said. "But he is welcome to play along, if he wishes!"

It was the sort of tactic Anna often used to repel male encroachers, but in this case, it did not result in her victim's embarrassed retreat, Instead, he sat down at the piano.

"What are you singing?" he asked. "Or shall I just improvise?"

"Oh, improvise," she replied, "by all means."

But if she'd hoped to humiliate him for his boldness, she was disappointed, for although she chose an obscure Cornish song she doubted had ever been written down, he quickly followed her lead. In fact, they ended by playing a musical game, piano and voice chasing each other with echoes and harmonies that appeared to charm their audience. And since it was unexpectedly good fun, Anna laughed and forgave him.

She even allowed him to take a turn with her about the room while the next performer was decided upon. Until he broke off in mid-sentence to say, "Do you have any idea how beautiful you are when you smile?"

Disappointed in him, she said, "No, for I never smile in the looking glass."

"You should."

She sighed, and perhaps he recognized that he was losing her, for he added with a hint of desperation, "No wonder Tamar has kept you hidden from the world."

It was meant to be amusing, but she wouldn't allow it. "Actually," she said in bored tones, "Tamar is the only man I've encountered who *doesn't* try to keep me tied to his wishes."

At that, seeing no doubt that he'd caused unintentional offence, he tried to catch her hand. She had only time for the beginnings of her most freezing glare before Serena suddenly stood between them.

"Anna, lend me a sovereign? I put all of mine in for Catherine and now have run out."

Anna accepted the rescue for what it was, though it struck her Serena might know more of her history than she was comfortable with. But, fortunately, Serena didn't try to discuss the past. Instead, she said abruptly, "I heard what you said to Mr. Banion. Tamar doesn't need it, but you defend him like a lioness."

Because he had once defended her, to the death. They never spoke of it, but it was always there.

"I will always defend him," she said shortly.

Serena's lips quirked. "I'm not his enemy."

"I know," Anna muttered.

Serena cast a quick glance around her to be sure no one could overhear. "Is that why you came? To be sure?"

"To be sure I didn't need to rescue either of you," Anna said deprecatingly.

Serena blinked. "How would you have rescued me while defending him?"

"If it came to it, I'd find a way." Her lips twisted. "I always do."

Serena frowned, not skeptical or even frightened, but as though trying to understand. In spite of herself, Anna rather liked her new sister. It was time to do her a kindness.

"You needn't worry," Anna assured her. "I thought I'd go to Scotland for a few days."

"Oh, not yet," Serena insisted. "You must come to the masquerade ball first! Besides, you know, the border roads will be terrible so late in the year."

"Well, I can find out," Anna said lightly. There was a lot she had to find out.

Chapter Four

ANNA ROSE EARLY the following morning. A night's sleep had convinced her that she should indeed stay at the castle, at least until after the masquerade.

Judging by the romps she had witnessed at Vauxhall Garden masquerades in London, people dropped their guard at such events, safe behind the anonymity of a costume and mask. And if her Frenchman wasn't dead—there was a whole tangle of reasons why she didn't want him to be dead—then someone in the neighborhood must surely have been helping him. If he was indeed the highwayman the Winslows had told her about, then someone must have given him a change of clothes, whether or not they were aware of his identity. Before she chased after him into Scotland, she needed a clue, a direction to begin her search.

Or the highway robbery could be a distraction while he returned to his old hiding place...or hid on a fishing boat or a smuggling vessel and sailed back to France. Which would be the worst possible outcome for her and for Great Britain.

So, she rode up toward the fort once more, just to see if he'd crept back to the hut, or if she could find any trace of him nearby. Finding none, she made her way to the road and rode past the fort, where she paused to make conversation with the bored guard by the front entrance.

"Good morning!" she greeted him.

"Morning, Miss," the soldier returned.

"It's a beautiful day, is it not? Though cold, I imagine, for guard duty!"

"That it is, Miss."

"This will be the Black Fort?" she asked innocently.

The soldier nodded.

"I hope your charges are not all monsters," she said with a shudder.

"Good as gold, most of 'em. Just like you or me. Well, not you, Miss, obviously! And they don't all speak a godly language, but I suppose that's just their way."

"I suppose it must be," Anna said gravely. "Tell me, is there a respectable inn in the village where I might get some water and a bite to eat?"

"Yes, ma'am, The Duck and Apple does decent breakfast. You can't miss it from the road. Don't get much quality there, but Mrs. Wiggs don't stand for anything untoward."

"Thank you! It sounds just what I need before I ride back to Blackhaven. Thank you for your help."

"Welcome, Miss, I'm sure," the soldier said, preening slightly as Anna urged her horse forward.

Anna looked back over her shoulder, as though she'd just remembered something. "Oh! Didn't you lose one of your prisoners the other day? Have you caught him again yet?"

"No, Miss, can't find him. I reckon he crawled into some cave or a hollow tree and just died."

For some reason, the soldier's words chilled her as she rode on in the winter sunshine. It might have been better than him carrying whatever dangerous secrets he harbored back to France, but still...

Mrs. Wiggs, who was preparing to receive the Manchester stagecoach, did indeed give her breakfast, and allow Chessy the mare to rest in her stable, though she made it plain she didn't hold with ladies of quality riding around the countryside alone in such a ramshackle manner.

"I suppose it was foolish," Anna agreed, hanging her head. "To be honest, I had forgotten all about the escaped prisoner, too. I shall get a tremendous scold."

As she had hoped, this did distract Mrs. Wiggs into talking about the escape, though she inclined to the belief that smugglers had already conveyed the miscreant to France.

"Good riddance, I say," she finished comfortably. "Got enough of our own riff-raff coming and going. Why, only the other day, poor old Harry had his coat stolen from the taproom! And a pistol was taken from one of the coaches right under our noses."

Anna's heartbeat quickened. "Goodness. Not the weather for losing a coat! Did he get it back?"

"Not yet," Mrs. Wiggs admitted. "And to be honest, it was a horrible old thing, leather all ripped and flapping. His wife will be glad to see the back of it, but that's not the point."

"No, it isn't," Anna agreed, finishing her coffee. Surely the Frenchman would not have walked in here openly to steal his highwayman's costume. Someone must have done it for him, someone above suspicion. She rose to her feet. "Well, I must get back before they all worry."

"Back where would that be?" Mrs. Wiggs enquired with blatant curiosity.

"Braithwaite Castle. I'm visiting my brother, there."

Mrs. Wiggs manner changed alarmingly at that. Anna was bowed out of the inn most obsequiously and only just managed to refuse an escort back to the castle. In the end, the arrival of the stagecoach saved her by distracting everyone, and she bolted.

She rode next down to the town of Blackhaven itself. After the musical evening at the vicarage, she had walked with Rupert and Serena for a little, admiring the pretty harbor and the High Street and the gallery which sold some of Rupert's paintings. She was glad of his growing success with his art and pleasantly surprised by how proud Serena was of this not terribly aristocratic career.

Yet, for all that, Anna had imagined hidden eyes boring into her as she walked. Not that she had seen any signs of anyone following them or observing her with more than the sort of curiosity the locals appeared to reserve for strangers associated with the castle. In the light of day, she felt no more than her usual wariness.

Now, in winter sunshine, the sea was a glorious shade of blue. Anna brought the mare to a halt while she admired it and took stock of the fishwives and fishermen repairing boats and nets. She bade one or two a cheerful good morning but received only slightly sullen responses. No one here was likely to talk to her about smugglers. The tavern was probably a better place to overhear that kind of conversation, though it sounded precisely the sort of establishment she didn't want to enter. Indeed, she couldn't without a heavy disguise.

So, for now, she turned the horse around and rode back up to the castle. There, she discovered Rupert and Serena in the drawing room, introducing Serena's sisters to their new governess.

Although the girls were too well-mannered to voice their displeasure, Anna could tell at once that they were not happy. Mrs. Elphinstone was large but appeared far from jolly. As Anna entered, she was explaining to Serena that she had been with Lady Watters for the last seventeen years but had been obliged to seek a new position when her ladyship finally ran out of children.

Anna regarded her with unexpected interest, not so much because of her words or her perfect English, but because of her accent, which was unmistakably French.

"I am acquainted with Lady Watters, of course," Serena said. "She is a great friend of my mother's. Oh, let me present you to my sister-in-law. This is Mrs. Elphinstone, Anna, our new governess. Mrs. Elphinstone, Lady Anna Gaunt, Lord Tamar's sister, who is staying with us for a while. A bedchamber is prepared for you close to the girls and the schoolroom.

"Girls, show Mrs. Elphinstone the way and get to know her a little. I'm sure there is no need of lessons before tomorrow."

The girls swept their new governess from the room in friendly spirit, although Alice did make a face over her shoulder at Serena.

Tamar sighed. "Miss Grey she is not," he murmured with regret. "In fact, Serena, she's got a face like a kicked bottom."

"She can't help that," Serena said reasonably.

"Yes, she can. It's ill-nature, if you ask me."

"It's more likely to be fright," Serena retorted. "The poor woman has only ever had one position before and she probably feels quite isolated up here among strangers."

"I suppose she is an émigrée," Anna added.

"I suppose she must be," Serena said. "I must admit, I didn't expect her to be French."

BY FRIDAY, THE day of the masquerade, Anna knew little more for certain. From casual conversation with Serena and Rupert, she gathered smuggling was endemic in Blackhaven, despite its distance from the continent. She even met a retired "gentleman" known unimaginatively as Smuggler Jack, who claimed not to have heard of any person smuggling in either direction. He might have been telling the truth. With no more highwayman attacks, Anna was fairly sure her quarry had headed north by land with his ill-gotten gains and a little sympathetic help.

Her lowering suspicion was that she had lost everything when she had left him alone in the hut. She would be forced to acknowledge her failure in the most important task she'd been given, which was humiliating. She would go to Scotland, but it would be like searching for a needle in a haystack.

In the meantime, she admitted to being sucked into the excitement surrounding the masquerade. Not least because it was, probably, her last hope of learning anything useful before she pursued her quarry north. However, the day before the ball, she took time between her morning ride and luncheon to try on her second evening gown.

It was of palest silver-grey with an overdress of silver gauze. She had always thought it lent her dignity, but it was not a ballgown. Perhaps no one would notice since the domino cloak would cover it for most of the evening.

A knock sounded on the door.

"Come in," Anna said reluctantly, and Serena stuck her head around the door.

"Oh, is that your gown for tomorrow? I would never have thought of that color for you, but it suits you very well."

Anna wrinkled her nose. "It's very well for dinner parties and the odd visit to the theatre, but it isn't a ballgown. I don't possess such a thing, since I never go to balls."

Serena came in and closed the door, regarding her critically. "Hmm, its charm is its simplicity," she allowed, "But for a ball...do you know, Madam Monique in High Street has rather beautiful lace of almost precisely that shade? If we trimmed the gown in that, and I lent you my garnet set, I think it would do very well. Oh, and I know the perfect domino for you!"

And so, Anna found herself in the sort of frivolous shopping expedition she had always vaguely despised. The lace was indeed beautiful, and Serena also insisted on buying lengths of silver and red ribbon to dress her hair. She added a chemise and a few wispy handkerchiefs for herself to the pile, which Anna suspected was simply so that she could pay for everything together without fuss. It was an unexpected delicacy that Anna found herself appreciating.

"How are you with a needle?" Serena asked as they left. "I confess to being indifferent, but my maid will sew on the trim in no time if you like?"

Anna regarded her. "You're very kind to me."

"You're Rupert's sister. Besides, for some reason, I like you. He told me you had grown a hard shell, but I prefer to think of you as prickly."

Anna laughed. "Like a hedgehog? I assure you, I am not so amiable."

A sudden shiver passed through her and she glanced over her shoulder. Mr. Banion, whom she'd met at the vicarage the other night, emerged from the coffee house and raised his hat, bowing to her. She inclined her head and walked on with Serena, but still she felt as though other eyes watched her.

THE FOLLOWING MORNING, shortly after Anna returned from her ride—during which she had learned nothing new—guests arrived at the castle. These were the Benedicts from Haven Hall, who were staying the night to avoid the long drive back home after the ball. There were four of them, Colonel and Mrs. Benedict, an older Miss Benedict, and a shy child of around ten years old. Mrs. Benedict was the former Miss Grey so beloved by Serena's sisters, and her presence precipitated the first major mutiny in Mrs. Elphinstone's schoolroom. The young ladies bolted as one to greet their old governess, erupting downstairs while the guests were still being shown into the drawing room.

Colonel Benedict stood back, observing with tolerant humor as his wife was enthusiastically embraced.

Serena called her sisters to order as Helen hugged young Rosa Benedict. "What hoydens! Stand aside and let the rest of us in!" Serena duly greeted their adult visitors and then turned to the child.

She was shy, Anna saw. But more than that, there was old pain in her young eyes. A protective wave swept over Anna, ready to drown whoever had hurt the child. But even as her hackles rose, the girl's eyes sought those of her stepmother, who nodded, smiling.

The child swallowed and parted her lips. "How do you do, Lady Tamar?" she whispered.

And tears sprang to Serena's eyes. "Oh, my dear girl, so much better now! How clever of you to have found your voice again!"

There was shy pleasure in the child's eyes as everyone hugged her again.

"She didn't speak for two years," Rupert murmured beside Anna. "Someone frightened her."

"Who?" Anna demanded. The father was looking proud of his daughter, but there was a harshness about his scarred face, especially in his eyes and around his mouth.

"A man now in prison and awaiting trial for other crimes. Thanks in part to Rosa. And now, finally, she's begun to talk again."

Young Rosa, clearly had enough people to protect her, and she would grow stronger. Perhaps not in the same way Anna had, but at least like Christianne, who could enjoy a normal life.

Anna, who was only just growing used to her sister-in-law, found herself almost enjoying the company of the Benedicts, too. They were intelligent, amusing, knowledgeable, and, in Colonel Benedict's case, pleasingly sardonic. Interestingly, he had been a prisoner of the French until he had escaped more than a year ago. There seemed to be too many French connections in Blackhaven.

THE EYES ANNA had felt on her the previous afternoon had belonged to Louis. From his favorite place by his bedchamber window, he had glimpsed her with a ripple of excitement. It seemed almost bizarre that she should do anything as mundane as shopping. But she was again in the company of the young woman who was Lord Braithwaite's sister. He guessed she would be at the assembly masquerade everyone was talking of.

And it was time they met again.

He'd seen her glancing over her shoulder, as though she felt herself under observation, but could not quite detect the observer. Unless it was the man who emerged from the coffee house across the street from the hotel and bowed to her. An admirer whose head was turned the wrong way for Louis to see his face. But such a woman would have a whole host of suitors.

Louis had spent the last few days largely resting and recruiting his strength. He had even managed to change his own dressings in a haphazard and not terribly neat way, but he could smell no hint of corruption in the wound and he had managed to sleep the previous night without laudanum.

When the town was quiet, he had taken gentle strolls to the hotel dining room, to the harbor—where a soldier always lurked among the fishermen—and to the pump room where he drank the curative waters. Perhaps they helped.

And he had received a morning call from Mr. and Mrs. Winslow. The former came to tell him there had been no further sightings of his highwayman, who probably had indeed fled into Scotland. Mr. Winslow was in touch with the authorities over the border, but so far, he had heard nothing. Louis pretended to be surprised that his robber should disappear into thin air.

Mrs. Winslow came to leave him a card for the masquerade ball she and the vicar's wife were sponsoring at the assembly rooms. Louis almost laughed, because it was such a perfect vehicle for him, and he had every hope that Anna would be there.

So, with the money robbed from the eloping young man, he bought a theatrical black domino cloak and mask, and then hired a horse from the livery stable for the morning and rode gently out to the hollow tree near the Carlisle road, where he had hidden the same gentleman's bags. It saved him the cost of black satin knee breeches and an evening coat.

On Friday evening, he donned his "borrowed" evening clothes—which really fitted rather well—and managed to knot his cravat respectably. Then he swung the black domino around his shoulders and tied the black mask over his upper face. His lips twitched, for he certainly looked mysterious and slightly villainous, in a ridiculous kind of way. In his profession, he had perfected the art of blending in and was rarely noticed unless he chose to be. He only hoped every other man present would look similarly absurd.

Leaving his chamber, he walked downstairs, crossed the foyer, and went out into the street where he strolled among several other masked figures in the direction of the nearby assembly rooms.

He had made sure to arrive in the earlier part of the evening so that he could familiarize himself with the building and discover all the alcoves and doors in the ballroom. At the same time, he could observe everyone as they entered. Men and women of all ages trickled constantly into the ballroom, which was exotically decorated for the occasion in hothouse flowers. Their heavy scents filled the air and their bright petals added to the dazzling colors of the dominoes and the glittering jewels on display.

Masked young bucks strutted around the ballroom, emboldened by anonymity to ogle young ladies until they blushed or flirted behind their fans, according to temperament. But it was a small town, and many people merely pretended not to recognize neighbors they must have known most of their lives.

The Winslows were there from the beginning, of course, and instantly recognizable. Mrs. Winslow wore a distinctive puce silk domino and her daughter one of ivory. Mr. Winslow retreated early to the card room. When the dancing began, some proprieties were still observed, with the masked gentlemen asking permission of the masked chaperones for the honor of dancing with their daughters. And Mrs. Winslow and the vicar's wife—a ravishingly beautiful woman, even masked—were kept busy presenting potential partners.

Louis moved among them all, picking up snippets of gossip and information as he went. He was not the only avid observer either. A youngish man in a burgundy domino also scanned the guests and the new arrivals, as though seeking someone in particular. Was he awaiting an anxious lover? Or did he fear some threat to his own secrecy? The answer, finally, walked into the ballroom in a scarlet domino and matching mask sewn with glittering silver thread. Garnets dangled at her ears and around her creamy white throat. Red and silver ribbons intertwined in her artfully styled black hair, braided at the back of her head and allowed to fall in a smooth wave over one shoulder. She walked with a grace and confidence that caught at his breath, and the cloak parted in the middle to reveal a gown of ethereal silver.

She was breathtaking. Louis and the other observer were not the only men to notice either.

She entered with the handsome couple he had no difficulty in recognizing as Lord and Lady Tamar.

"My," a woman whispered behind him. "Who is the lady with Serena Tamar?"

"I think it must be Tamar's sister. I heard she had come on a visit."

Louis smiled at this piece of news. At least now he knew who she was. Although what a marquis's sister was doing riding alone in the dark and tending the wounds of escaped French prisoners was even more of a mystery.

While strolling in the direction of the card room door, Louis surreptitiously watched the vicar's wife greet the newcomers, clearly pretending not to know them.

Meanwhile, the man in the burgundy domino had managed to secure the attention of Mrs. Winslow and was nodding toward the lady in the scarlet domino. Mrs. Winslow smiled, tapped him on the wrist with her fan, and led him across the room to where the Tamars were sitting down together with some friends.

Louis leaned his shoulder against the wall next to the card room door and watched.

Mrs. Winslow introduced the burgundy domino to Anna, then walked away with an indulgent smile. Anna did not give her hand to her admirer, merely inclined her head. The man talked, inviting her to dance. Louis watched Anna's shapely lips, reading them as clearly as if he had heard the words.

"Oh, no, I do not care to dance. But if you wish, you could fetch me a glass of champagne."

The burgundy domino, obviously cast down at the beginning of her speech, sprang back to life and trotted off to do her bidding. She didn't appear to watch him, but as he began his return journey, she rose and flitted away. Louis would have assumed he was not a favored suitor, except that within the space of ten minutes, he saw her perform the same trick three times with three different men. Lady Anna, it seemed, simply did not care for admirers at all.

And yet, she did not give the impression of hiding or wishing to be elsewhere. With the vicar's wife, she joined in an apparently lively conversation that included several other people, and a little later, he saw her strolling about with a young man in a green domino.

She's listening. She's doing exactly the same as I am...

Eventually, he chose to intercept her as she made her way back to her sister-in-law's place. He could not allow himself to be side-stepped, ignored, or sent for drinks, and so he simply strode out from behind a pillar into her path, and she was forced to stop.

It did not upset her poise in the slightest. She was not startled. She had been waiting for him. Because she knew him? Or because she didn't?

Behind the red and gold-threaded mask, her eyes glittered, alluring and mysterious. She was dazzling, the most desirable woman he had ever encountered. She took his breath away.

Almost of their own accord, his lips began to smile. *"Madam, will you walk?"*

Chapter Five

S HE HAD KNOWN he was there, watching her. A large man in a black domino who didn't dance or converse, merely strolled around the ballroom, observing. And she became increasingly sure he was observing *her*. So were several other men, of course. It was a masquerade, and guests were constantly trying to identify those they couldn't at once recognize. But there seemed something different about this man, something poised and confident about the way he held himself, the way he moved, lithe, economical, subtly predatory.

Intrigued, she had deliberately wandered closer to him, and found she was actually piqued when he neither spoke to her nor asked for an introduction. And so, she veered toward Mrs. Winslow.

"Satisfy my curiosity, ma'am, if you will. Who is the gentleman in the black domino? *Please* don't tell me to wait until the unmasking!"

"Would you like me to introduce you?" Mrs. Winslow asked, apparently amused.

"I could not be so forward," Anna said at once. "But was he not at the musical evening?" There *was* something familiar about him.

"Oh, no," Mrs. Winslow said with certainty. "But I believe I met him for the first time on the same day."

Possibly, she thought the clue would mean nothing to Anna. She could not have known that Anna always remembered everything, that she guessed at once her observer was very probably the highwayman's victim. She hadn't realized he was still in Blackhaven. For some reason, she had assumed he'd continued his journey north.

And so, to learn more about the highwayman himself, she had

commenced the dance, shadowing him, moving closer, drawing him in until he waited for her behind the pillar. It was almost a relief when he stepped out into her path at last.

Something jolted hard inside her, something she neither recognized nor understood. It was all she could do to preserve her expression of tolerant contempt. And then he spoke.

"*Madam, will you walk?*" He quoted from a familiar country song, his voice deep and pleasing, reaching far inside her, perhaps with warning. But his accent was unmistakably that of a gentleman.

"No," she replied lightly, and quoted from the next line of the song. "And *neither will I talk with you.*"

"But you are already talking to me," he pointed out. "And we both know you could have avoided me if you chose."

She curled her lip. "I never choose to let a man divert me from my course."

Apparently undeterred, he offered his arm. "Then perhaps you would allow me to accompany you upon that course."

Anna hesitated only a moment. She preferred not to touch him at all, but neither did she wish to send him away. Feeling as if she took a huge step, a huge risk of some kind, she laid her fingertips on his arm and allowed him to guide the direction of their promenade.

"You do not dance," he observed.

"Neither do you."

"I would," he said at once, "if you would dance with me."

"Well I won't, so you must make do with walking and talking."

"Oh, I am not *making do*," he assured her.

"What do you want, Sir Black Domino?" she asked bluntly.

"A few moments of your time. What do *you* want?"

She laughed. "To win my wager. My sister-in-law and I are in disagreement over whether or not you are the gentleman who was held up on the road to Carlisle."

His face gave nothing away. The faint smile continued to play around his lips. "Why should either of you imagine that I am?"

"Something Mrs. Winslow said. Don't be imagining she gave you away, for she didn't. I merely guessed. Am I right?"

"What do you win if you are?"

"My sister-in-law's garnets," Anna lied with aplomb, touching the necklace at her throat.

He blinked. "That is a large wager."

"My sister has a large fortune."

"And, alas, she will keep the garnets."

A frown tugged down her brow before she could help it.

"I am not the highwayman's victim," he explained.

She searched the eyes behind the mask. "Then who are you?"

He smiled. "I am the highwayman."

Abruptly, his arm straightened and her hand fell to her side. He bowed and walked away into the throng.

Anna couldn't help it. She laughed. It was too good an exit, even when the implications swamped her, depriving her of breath.

She had already been more than half-convinced that the highwayman had been Louis. And yet, here she had been fooled by his mask—not just the black one over his upper face, but by his easy grace, his pain-free eyes and English accent. Yet the clues had always been there, that dark blond hair, those deep blue eyes, the sheer *presence*.

Dear God, she was not half as good at this as she had imagined. And she was letting him elude her again.

The man in the burgundy domino—whom she suspected of being Mr. Banion—was bearing down on her from the dance floor. Rupert was bringing some friend of his toward her from the opposite direction, and nowhere could she see the man in the black cloak.

Instinctively, she hurried toward the ballroom entrance, slipping between her brother and her admirer and swerving around several couples as she went. As she reached the foyer, the doorman was bowing in a group of late arrivals, but she was sure she glimpsed a swathe of black vanishing into the night.

She almost followed him, so keen was her desire not to lose him again. Fortunately, after a brief struggle, sense and self-preservation won. She could not draw attention to herself by haring off down the street after him in her dancing slippers and bright red domino. And she had to remember he was the enemy. He must have been suspicious that she was more than she seemed, and he could have been luring her to harm, even to her death.

In any case, whatever his reason, he had come to her. Excitement soared as she whisked herself back into the ballroom. He would come again.

So lost was she in plans for their next encounter, that she failed to avoid Rupert and his friend who reached her at almost exactly the same time as the man in the burgundy domino.

"This insolent fellow wants me to introduce him to you," Tamar said carelessly. "Though I can't see the point when I'm not supposed to tell you who he is. Or who you are."

"You came in together and sat together," his friend argued. "You must be acquainted. Fair Lady Red Domino, will you do me the honor of waltzing with me?"

"I thank you for the invitation, Sir Blue Domino," Anna replied, "but alas, I do not waltz."

"Not with strangers, of course," the burgundy domino said from her other side. "But you and I have already been introduced." He even held out his hand to her.

She regarded it with distaste. "I do not waltz," she repeated.

"And that," Rupert said with a hint of steel in his voice, "is the end of the matter, gentlemen."

As both men, who obviously knew him, by reputation at least, turned to him in surprise, Anna stepped smartly back out of their circle and spun away straight into the arms of another man who, instead of merely steadying her, as had seemed to be his intention, suddenly swept her onto the dance floor.

"I do not waltz," she uttered once more, this time with cold fury as she attempted literally, to dig her heels in.

"Why ever not?" enquired a voice that paralyzed her. Her partner took unfair advantage of her astonishment, whisking her among the couples on the dance floor, just as the music struck up.

"It bores me," Anna said. However, she didn't quite achieve the cold contempt she had intended, for her partner wore a black domino, and despite his educated English accent, sounded remarkably like the Frenchman. Between the slits of his mask, his eyes were a deep, intense blue. He moved to the light yet relentless rhythm of the waltz, and somehow, she was following him, blindly, trying only to keep her feet until she could escape with dignity.

He said, "I don't believe you and I need to bore each other. Like this we can have a long and uninterrupted conversation."

"You left," Anna blurted. She strove to squash the panic, to relax the rigidity of her body.

He smiled. "I wanted to see if you would follow."

"Why?"

"You intrigue me. I hear you are the sister of a marquis, and yet..." He trailed off, leaving her in no doubt he was referring to their first meeting.

"He is not just any marquis." Anna lowered her voice further. "As any Englishman would know. We Tamars grew up like wild animals, fending for ourselves. I go where I please, whenever I please."

"Then I am all the more thrilled to be holding you in my arms."

Anna never blushed. And yet she felt the blood seep into her face and neck. It distracted her from the discomfort of his nearness, his touch. And yet, curiously, the discomfort was not revulsion. This was new. And strange.

"Against my will," she pointed out.

"I took you by surprise. I apologize. I thought I was saving you from your other admirers."

She searched his eyes, so much more mysterious, so much less revealing surrounded by the black mask. "No, you didn't. You hoped to catch me off guard."

"That also," he admitted.

"You are insane to come here. Mr. Winslow, the magistrate, is present. So is Major Doverton, the commanding officer of the 44th who are stationed here. For all I know, there are officers from the fort present, too."

"There aren't."

She ignored that. "Why did you come?"

"Mostly to see you."

He was lying. She knew that and yet she couldn't help her pleasure in his word. She, who loathed flattery.

"Why?" she asked.

"I refer you to my previous answers concerning your beauty and fascination—"

"I've forgotten those."

"—and my own curiosity," he finished, apparently undeterred.

She considered him. He danced with grace and elegance, guiding her with so much easy skill that she followed him without thinking. No one watching, surely, would guess that she had never waltzed with a man before. Or that this man had been shot barely a week ago.

"And so, you are the highwayman," she said thoughtfully. "Did you hold yourself up?"

"No, I'm afraid I held up a young couple in a hired chaise and may have spoiled their elopement. The young lady had hysterics, but *he* took it very well. We parted on amiable terms."

"You probably seemed preferable to the hysterics," Anna said flippantly.

"I was. In fact, I felt so sorry for him I didn't take everything."

"I don't understand why you took *anything*," Anna admitted.

"I needed clothes and money to live."

A frown tugged at her brow. "Just to come to Blackhaven? As your own victim?"

"It seemed a good place to wait."

"For what?"

He smiled beneath the mask. "For you."

In spite of herself, her heart fluttered. Not that she believed him.

She tilted her head, allowing amusement to fill her eyes and curve her lips. She heard his intake of breath and knew he was not immune to her. Men rarely were.

"I would imagine you wanted my help," she said. "Only, on your own, you have already committed theft and highway robbery and disguised yourself among Blackhaven society. I doubt there's anything I could do for you if I wanted to. Except keep my silence."

"Do you really have family and friends fighting in the war?" he asked unexpectedly.

"No," she admitted. "I don't have friends. And none of my family could afford a commission if they wanted one. Or at least they couldn't before my brother married a Braithwaite heiress."

"Then why did you help me?"

"I really don't know," she said. "But trust me, it's an impulse I'm regretting."

His thumb moved over her gloved fingers, sending a jolt through her body. It should have been unpleasant, and yet it wasn't. "I don't think you are, though I don't understand why not. Have you ever been to France, my lady?"

She blinked. "How the devil could I have got to France? We've been at war for as long as I can remember. Are you *stuck*, sir? Do you *actually* need my help getting home to France?"

"I might," he said. "If I had any intention of going there."

She stumbled, and he tightened his grip, steadying her while she stared into his eyes. "You don't want to go home?" she asked. "If that is true, sir, why did you bother to escape in the first place?"

His lips quirked. "That is a very good question and the answer is likely to exhaust me. I'm afraid my desires, yet again, outweigh my strength. I need to sit down and I know the very alcove."

She allowed it. Now that he had begun to talk, she would have gone anywhere with him. But she wasn't prepared for the excitement of the escape, of dancing toward the edge of the dance floor and all but spinning into the corner alcove. The concealing curtain fell behind them before she could even draw breath.

For an instant, she stared up into his face. The earth seemed to tilt. She didn't want to move.

It was he who did so first, releasing her to sink onto the sofa provided for those wishing a rest away from the bustle of the ballroom.

She swallowed and sat beside him, recalling reality with an effort. "Why do you not wish to go home?"

He shrugged. "I have enemies in France."

Her heartbeat quickened once more. This was a better beginning than she'd hoped for, than even Henry had hoped for. "What kind of enemies?"

"Powerful ones."

She met his gaze. "It can only be a month or two more until the war ends at last. You should have stayed safely in prison."

"I wasn't safe. I was meant to die in October, on the day the prison was attacked."

So, Henry had been partly right. The attack was what had drawn Henry's eyes to the prison inmates and to the discovery of M. L'Étrange. He had assumed the attack had been to rescue the valuable spy. Could it have been to kill him? Why would the French go to such trouble to kill their own man? Unless he had a good deal of information that would benefit the British if he chose to divulge it.

"Why?" she asked bluntly.

"Because they think my…knowledge is dangerous. Because they are afraid I will take revenge. And change sides."

Her heart leapt into her throat. It was proving to be simple, after all, this task that had given her so much trouble. "Will you?" she asked.

"Change sides?" He smiled. "No."

He did not even think about it. He meant it. Which was a blow after her surge of hope, but at least he was still here and still talking.

"Then what do you want of me?"

"Your silence," he said softly.

She dropped her gaze. "I already told you, you have that. On the conditions I made."

"Why?" he asked.

The lie was easy. She'd told similar ones before. And yet for some reason it stuck in her throat. Not *because* it was a lie, but because she was suddenly afraid it was the truth.

She stood, swinging away from him. "Because I like you," she said carelessly. "I was sorry for you, and then I liked you."

She had thought him too tired to move. But without a sound, he stood suddenly in front of her. Neither of them had removed their masks. She jumped when his fingers tilted up her chin.

"Then why," he asked softly, "do you flinch when I touch you?"

The intrusion was too much. Fury surged and she swung up her fist. Just as he caught it in his free hand, the curtain swished. The Frenchman's face swooped down and his mouth covered hers.

Shocked beyond belief, she could not move. A woman's voice, surely Serena's, seemed to be talking, mercifully on the other side of the curtain. Relief flooded Anna. He was not assaulting her, but providing a romantic excuse for their assignation, whose true purpose was much more dangerous for him. With the rush of knowledge, her instinctive fear disintegrated and she realized the light pressure of his lips, softly caressing hers, was not unpleasant at all.

Butterflies stirred in her stomach. Without meaning to, she actually reached up and touched the silk of his mask. And then the curtain swished again with more purpose, and this time, someone definitely came in and halted in their tracks.

"Sir, unhand the lady and deal with *me*," Tamar's voice said ominously.

A hiss of quite inappropriate laughter escaped Louis's lips as they left hers. He straightened and turned to face her outraged brother and Serena.

"Sir," Louis protested. "I have absolutely no desire to kiss *you*."

Rupert was still protecting her, because what had happened all those years ago still tore him up. It warmed her, and yet she couldn't let him ruin everything.

"Go away, Rupert," she managed. "I thought such things were *meant* to happen at masquerades."

"Not if you don't want them to," Tamar growled.

She regarded her brother until a smile flickered over his face.

"Really?" he said, sounding more pleased than angry. He was an unusual brother in many ways.

Anna, unsure yet exactly how she felt about the kiss, began to walk to Serena. Escape seemed to be necessary after all. However, she cast a flickering smile back over her shoulder at the Frenchman before she said carelessly, "I presume this gentleman may call on us?"

"Not until we know who he is," Serena said at once.

"Lewis, my lady," the Frenchman said. "Sir Lytton Lewis, at your service." Though he didn't remove the mask, he bowed elaborately.

Lewis. Louis. "You should be clapped up," Anna said unsteadily. "In Bedlam."

"Anna!" Serena objected. Anna gave in and walked out of the alcove with her sister-in-law before she was dragged out.

LOUIS REGARDED THE marquis with interest. He had been involved in thwarting the autumn attack on the fort. In fact, so had the lady who now appeared to be his wife. Lord Tamar, distractedly turning a pack of cards in his hand, stared back at him, with more suspicion than aggression.

"How do you know my sister?" he asked abruptly.

"We met by accident in the woods last week," Louis said readily. "I was much struck by her as you might imagine and managed to secure myself an invitation to tonight's event."

Tamar scowled a little and scratched his head as though wondering what the devil he was supposed to do now. Then his hand fell back to his side.

"She seems to like you, so I won't come the heavy-handed brother," he said at last. "But you'll treat my sister like a lady, or you'll answer to me." His lips twisted. "And to her." He seemed to become aware of the packet in his hands and cocked one eyebrow at Louis. "Game of cards?"

"Why not?" Amused by the sudden change in the marquis's manner, Louis sat down in the chair Anna had vacated and stretched out his legs.

However, after a couple of games with Anna's amiable brother, exhaustion drove Louis from the ballroom and he returned somewhat wearily to his hotel. His mind wanted to stay for the unmasking, to seek her out and spar with her, not just for information but for the pleasure of her company. Alternately sweet and sharp, funny and prickly, brave and timid, her contradictory character drew him like the proverbial moth. And he could still taste her lips, stunned, virginal lips, which he had taken to conceal the true purpose of their meeting. And yet there had been a moment...

He curled his lip at himself. A moment when he'd imagined a true awakening passion? *Keep dreaming, coxcomb. The woman eats men like me for breakfast.*

Only they didn't usually get to kiss her. He understood that much. They ate out of her hands, probably, in the vain *hope* of those kisses.

Easing off his coat, he all but fell into the chair by the window and splashed some brandy into the waiting glass. There was a lot of French brandy in Blackhaven, which meant smugglers. They could bring people in, too, and take them away. Gosselin would have to come himself now. No one else would be able to recognize him in person.

And when Gosselin was dead...then he could think beyond vengeance. He could never go home, of course. France was surely denied to him now, whoever ended up in power when Bonaparte finally fell. There was a certain charm in losing himself in England, in becoming Sir Lytton Lewis for good. A man like him could always hide.

But Anna knew the truth. She had kept silent already, and so he'd told her a little more to engage her help as well as to watch her reaction. She could be exactly what she said, the wayward sister of an eccentric and poverty-stricken nobleman. In fact, he didn't doubt that part. But there was more to Anna, much more.

He raised the glass to his lips, drinking while he remembered how she had felt in his arms, how her rigid shock had slowly relaxed. He wasn't sure she needed protection, and yet he wanted to shelter her, hold her... Her beauty, the scent of her hair, every movement of her graceful body, stirred his blood. The way her eyes laughed, the curve of her lips, the humorous twitch of her eyebrow... It all captivated him, coiled his body into a ball of lust he was too tired to do anything about.

A knock sounded at the door.

Or was he?

The chamber maid had been fluttering her eyelashes and flirting. Perhaps she was here now. And perhaps he should take up her offer and assuage the hunger.

It wouldn't work, of course, but just for tonight it might make things better.

He swallowed the remains of the brandy in the glass and reached for the bottle. "Enter."

A quick glance showed him not the chamber maid but a lady in a black domino cloak and mask, leaning against the door she had just closed. Just for an instant, the black fooled him, because it wasn't red, but a moment later he stumbled to his feet. "Anna."

Chapter Six

H<small>E WAS THE</small> epitome of the carelessly attractive male. Anna regarded him from his rumpled blond hair to his shirt sleeves, and even the casual way he reached for the bottle while poised, she suspected, to use it as a weapon if necessary. He reminded her of a large, dangerous cat who hadn't yet decided whether to sleep or to hunt. Though he shot to his feet quickly enough when he recognized her.

"Anna."

"Louis."

"Every instinct tells me you have not come to while away the night in carnal pleasure. And yet, I can't shake off my natural optimism."

Anna, who was well aware of the one-sided nature of such pleasures, laughed at him. "Abandon hope," she mocked. "I've merely come to look at your wounds and change your dressings. I assume you haven't been near a doctor."

"How did you find me?" Louis asked.

"There is only one hotel suitable for Sir Lytton. I bribed one of the maids to tell me which room you were in. She still gave me the evil eye."

"I think she likes me. Does your brother know you are here?"

"Of course not. He is aware I have no interest in dalliance."

There was a faint pause. Across the room, his eyes seemed to glitter. "Have you not?" he said with deliberation.

Her body flamed. Without meaning to in the slightest, she recalled the feel of his sensual lips on hers, the rough warmth of his jaw beneath the mask, the heat, the scent of his body so close to hers.

She lifted her chin. "You think that because I like you, I am prepared to be your lover?"

"As I say. I am optimistic by nature. Please, sit down. I only have brandy, I'm afraid, or I can send for tea."

"No, thank you." She untied the domino and threw it over the back of the sofa. It was only black because she had reversed it. "A simple disguise," she observed. "More for Tamar and Serena's sake than mine."

"Where are Lord and Lady Tamar?"

"Enjoying supper, so I don't have long," She untied the mask, which had also been reversed, and threw it on top of the cloak before indicating he should sit on the sofa.

He didn't obey at once. Disconcertingly, his gaze remained steady on her face for several seconds before it dropped unhurriedly to her throat and lower over the rest of her body.

"Louis," she said impatiently, peeling off her long, silver-grey gloves.

A choke of laughter escaped him. "You have not come for dalliance," he said, as though making an agreement, or perhaps just remembering. He advanced to the sofa, pulling his shirt over his head and dropping it on the floor before he sat on the sofa. He clearly felt no modesty at thus revealing his broad, naked chest and his thickly muscled arms and shoulders.

For some reason, Anna's throat felt dry. Somehow, it had been easier in the cold forest, by the lantern light, when he was simply a task, and not this very physical human being. She had never thought before that men could be beautiful.

He is still a task, she reminded herself. *Nothing more and nothing less. He is merely, a harder task to accomplish than most.*

Forcing herself, she went to him, her heart beating an annoying tattoo as she unwound his bandage. He'd changed it for himself, clearly, and hadn't made a bad job of it. The wound itself looked clean and was clearly healing. She only hoped he was healing inside, too.

She nodded. "Do you think we should leave the stitches in for a little longer?"

"Yes," he said, without further explanation.

She took the little jar from her reticule and, with a very odd feeling in the pit of her stomach, smeared the ointment over his wound.

"Do you always carry such things to a ball?" he asked.

"Everywhere," she said. "Just in case."

"How many wounded people do you encounter in a day?"

"You'd be surprised. But there is no room in my reticule for dressings. Do you have something clean I might use?"

"In the drawer by the bed."

She knew his eyes followed her as she walked across the room and bent over the drawer in the bedside cabinet. "You have done this before," she observed, taking the pads of soft cloth and closing the drawer.

"Like you, I am always prepared."

"Then how did you come to be captured?" she retorted.

He smiled faintly, and she thought that Henry had been right. He *had* been prepared for capture, perhaps even intended it. Which presented another mystery.

"You are an enigma, Sir Lytton," she said lightly.

"I try, in the hope it makes me more appealing," He tilted his head, watching her as she bound his wound. His skin was warm and velvet-smooth whenever her fingers brushed against it. And she, who never touched anyone if she could avoid it, knew a sudden desire to lay her palms flat against his chest and his back. Which made her uncomfortable in a completely different way.

She drew in a breath. "Louis, if your own people are trying to kill you, you must come to some agreement with ours."

His lips twisted. "Who would not, of course, ever consider killing me."

"They wouldn't," she insisted. "Not if they knew you had severed ties with Bonaparte's France."

"France is still France, whoever claims to lead it."

"Then you are prepared to take your knowledge to the grave?"

"That depends," he said, cynically. "Is blind loyalty more appealing than mystery?"

"It is not me you have to appeal to."

"Who, then?"

"I don't know," she said, carefully reserving Henry's name for now. "But I can find out. My brother has a new-found ambition to go into politics, and Serena's brother, the Earl of Brathwaite, will know exactly who you should talk to. Between us, we know many people who could help you."

Having neatly tied his bandage, she swept his dropped shirt from the carpet and handed it to him. "It's your only hope, Louis. Please think about it, because you will be discovered here eventually, by people who have no idea that you possess such knowledge. *They* might kill you from ignorance. I must go."

She took a step away from him, but his hand closed around her wrist and her gaze flew back to his face. It bothered her that she had no urge to hit him.

"Will you tell them, Anna?" he asked steadily.

"I have kept silent this long."

"Will you tell them?" he repeated.

She stared into his face, listening to the rapid beats of her own heart. "Even I have loyalty to my country."

"The war is almost over. It will not matter soon."

"It must matter or you would not have done what you have. Louis, you have my silence for the moment, but you *need* the protection of my government." She meant it. Her urgency and sincerity must have stood out in her voice and face, for after a moment, he released her wrist.

"I almost believe you care," he said flippantly.

"I care," she muttered, hurrying around the sofa to grasp her domino, which she swung around her shoulders, black side outward.

The mask had fallen to the floor, but before she could retrieve it, he had already picked it up. "Turn around," he said.

She almost snatched it. But he was her task. She obeyed, every nerve alert and sensitive as he slipped the mask over her eyes and tied it at the back of her head. The faint brush of his knuckles against her cheek, of his fingertips in her hair, set her skin tingling. Then he walked around and gazed down at her before making a minor adjustment to the mask's position.

"Perfect," he observed. When his gaze dropped to her lips, she couldn't breathe for wondering how his kiss would feel if he did it from no motive but his own desire, with no one watching. She shivered, and it wasn't all fear.

"Good night, Louis," she said walked swiftly out the room, closing the door softly behind her.

Leaving the hotel, she walked back along the road to the assembly rooms, where the doorman merely bowed her discreetly back inside. She made her way to the ladies' cloakroom where she changed her shoes once more, lingering a few moments until the ladies beside her left. Then she quickly reversed her mask and her cloak and returned to the ballroom, where it was almost time for the unmasking.

It came to Anna that with or without their outward disguises, she and Louis were always masked. She couldn't understand why the thought made her sad.

THE FOLLOWING DAY, Anna stayed in bed late, forgoing her usual ride since there was now no need to discover Louis's whereabouts. At least, she hoped there was no need. She hoped he hadn't done exactly as before and vanished as soon as she found him. But she could hardly go to the hotel undisguised and inquire without causing a great deal of talk.

She had made progress last night. Not only had he shown himself to her, but he had admitted to valuable knowledge. She might not yet have convinced him to tell all to her or to other servants of His

Majesty, but she had sown the first seeds. And, providing she had "hooked" him—and she thought she had, to some degree at least—she would have more time to persuade him.

Her hope now was that he would pay a morning visit to the castle. After all, she had blatantly invited him in the hearing of both Tamar and Serena.

She lay for some time, listening to the fading patter of rain on her window, and then to the song of the birds as the wintry sun broke through, shining in her open curtains and onto her face. She liked the feeling of hope and comfort that filled her. It felt almost like...happiness.

Eventually, she rose and, with the aid of Nora, the housemaid who had been assigned to serve her during her stay, she washed and dressed in her more becoming day gown of delicate turquoise cambric. Having a high neck and graceful folds, she knew she looked well in it without it appearing deliberately seductive.

The breakfast room was full, since Serena and Tamar had risen to join their guests from Haven Hall, and the children were all demanding details of last night's masquerade. Mrs. Elphinstone, the governess, looked somewhat tight-lipped at the apparent lack of discipline of the children in adult company, but neither Serena nor Mrs. Benedict appeared to find it unusual. Anna found it quite endearing, a charming balance between the untamed wildness of her own and Tamar's upbringing, and the strictness of most noble households.

She could understand why Rupert was comfortable here, with Serena's easy-going family. Although rumor had it the dowager countess was more of a high stickler. Without her, this all reminded her just a little of herself and the other Tamar children before.

She veered away from the memory, refusing to spoil the unusual gladness of the day. She stood on the front step with her brother and sister-in-law to wave off the Benedicts, and then prowled the castle until luncheon was served. She could settle to nothing, even reading from Braithwaite's impressive library. Having spurned company since she had arrived, she felt she could not now request Rupert and Serena to join her in conversation, games or walks, just to pass the time. They had their own apartments in the old part of the castle.

During luncheon, she received a letter from Christianne, who regaled her with a couple of amusing domestic stories and passed on the news that Henry had, apparently, asked when Anna was coming home. In this, Anna recognized a summons. Henry was assuming her failure, on the basis of her past message, also sent via Christianne, that after initial fun, things at Blackhaven were not quite as expected.

At least the letter gave her something to do after lunch. Retreating to her own bedchamber, she wrote her reply, telling Christianne all about the masquerade, adding, after a moment's hesitation that she had waltzed with a man whom she'd found quite entertaining. No doubt Henry would read that, too, and know to whom she referred. But she didn't write it for Henry. She wrote it for her sister, because for some reason, she wanted her to know. For Henry himself, she wrote. *Please tell Henry that I am amazed he looks for me so soon. I shall give him a longer reprieve since I am quite settled at Braithwaite Castle and enjoying myself immensely.*

By the time she took her letter downstairs to add it to the others for posting, there were, finally, visitors in the drawing room. Her heart beating faster, Anna walked in. But there was no tall, fair man among the callers.

Mr. Banion had come, however, as had Rupert's friend who had wished to dance with her. For lack of other amusements, she let them quarrel discreetly over her while her eyes strayed to the window in the hope of seeing a distant yet instantly recognizable figure riding up the winding drive.

Of course, she didn't know if his stolen money would stretch to hiring a horse.

But eventually, the callers all left, and Anna began to feel uneasy. Had he truly vanished again? Gone for good, this time? If so, why had he sought her out?

Perhaps he has been recognized and recaptured... Which wouldn't be so very bad, for she could arrange the escape she had intended for him when she first left London. On the other hand, if the French had got to him…

She shivered.

"Who is that, I wonder?" Serena said from the window. "Another of your admirers, Anna?"

Without much interest, Anna sauntered up to the window in time to see a figure just striding out of her view. "I can't tell from the top of his hat," she said. "Do you know, I might walk into Blackhaven. Would you care to come?"

"I think I would rather go in the carriage. It's sure to rain. But we could go and beard Rupert in his studio, if you like. I suspect that's where he's gone, and you haven't seen it yet. We could be *not at home* to whoever this is."

"What an excellent idea," Anna approved, just as the footman entered with a card on a tray, which he presented to Serena.

"Thank you, James…" Her eyes lifted to Anna's face. "Sir Lytton Lewis. *Are* we at home?"

The news, which she had given up hoping for, made Anna smile, though at the same time, Serena's arch look brought embarrassed color to her cheeks.

"What can another half hour matter?" Anna said carelessly. "*I* shall be at home."

"Then I shall play chaperone." Serena said, nodding to the footman who trotted off again. "What a pity Tamar has sloped off. He could have done a little more glaring."

"Oh, I think he gave that up. They were playing cards together before supper."

Serena gave an unladylike snort of laughter, just as Sir Lytton was announced, and Louis strolled into the drawing room.

He was perfectly dressed in skin-tight pantaloons and a dark blue coat over a tastefully embroidered waistcoat. His snowy white cravat was simply tied but would not have disgraced the most fashionable in London society. As he bowed over the ladies' hands and enquired politely after their health, Anna wanted to laugh, because he understood the banal rituals of English society so well.

Serena ordered fresh tea and invited her guest to sit, which he did, though not on the sofa beside Anna. Instead, he sat closer to Serena, directing most of his conversation at her. Perhaps Anna would have been piqued had he not caught her gaze as she brought his cup of tea, and discreetly but definitely winked.

After that, she sat back and watched. Was he playing a part, or was this simply Louis as he would be in his real life? Once he had gauged Serena's character, he relaxed more, answering her humorous quips with his own, and drawing Anna so subtly into the conversation that she barely noticed he had done it. If their roles had been reversed, if he had been seeking information from her, she suspected she would have succumbed in minutes without realizing what she'd said until too late.

"Did you ride up from town?" Serena inquired.

"No, I walked."

"Well, Anna and I mean to drive into Blackhaven, so you are welcome to a seat in the carriage."

It must have taken some effort to walk up to the castle and it seemed to Anna that he was genuinely grateful for the offer. There was a moment, when, during the confusion of fetching cloaks and bonnets, Anna found him alone in the entrance hall, waiting for her and Serena.

"Are you well?" she asked as she approached him. "Is something wrong? Something else!" she corrected herself with a rueful smile.

"No, I am merely obeying your command to call."

She lowered her voice as she came to a halt beside him. "Have you thought more about how to solve your problem?"

"What problem?" he countered, provokingly. "I am exactly where I wish to be."

"Why?" she demanded.

"I'm waiting for someone."

She curled her lips. "And that someone is clearly *not* me as you claimed at the ball. Behold my devastation."

He gazed upward and turned, taking in his surroundings. "Ah, if only I thought that was true. I had many plans that did not include you. I chose this one. The castle must be a magnificent place to grow up in." He glanced at her, perhaps hoping his sudden change of subject had confused her. "Is your home like this, too?"

She laughed. "Lord, no. Well, it probably was once. Tamar Abbey is a great medieval pile in Cornwall, acquired by no doubt nefarious means, by our ancestor from Henry the Eighth. When we were growing up, it was already falling around our ears from neglect and lack of funds to repair it. We had fun there, for a little, but it was more like playing in a huge ruin than living in a grand house."

A faint smile played around his lips. "I can see you in such a place. Was there just you and Tamar?"

"God, no. We have two other brothers, and my twin sister, Christianne."

"Twin?" he repeated. "You mean there are *two* of you?"

She laughed. "Oh, no. Christianne is nothing like me. Well, we may look alike, but there it ends. Christianne is the best of us."

"But she is not here with you?"

"No. She is in London with her husband."

"Another great nobleman?"

"No, a lowly gentleman who actually works for his living. A civil servant." She stepped closer. "But he may know someone who could help you."

His eyes locked to hers, searching, yet giving nothing away. Even so, she somehow had the impression of thoughts flitting furiously through his mind. Not all good thoughts. Had she blundered?

Since Serena came hurrying downstairs at this point, Anna merely turned and walked toward the door.

A quarter of an hour later, they alighted from the carriage in Blackhaven's High Street in front of a milliner's shop. Louis handed the ladies down and Serena said carelessly. "Come with us, if you like. We're going to interrupt Tamar in his studio, where he may be hard at work or holding an impromptu party."

Serena, it seemed, had few illusions about her husband.

"In either case," Louis pointed out, "I can't imagine he would be pleased to see us."

"On the contrary, he's always pleased to see people. People he likes, at any rate."

Rupert was indeed discovered in his studio, entertaining a couple of disreputable looking friends and painting at the same time. The friends looked somewhat alarmed at their arrival, though Rupert himself appeared delighted.

He worked amongst the same kind of clutter Anna remembered, but amiably shoved and kicked things aside to make way for them and offered "Lewis" a glass of brandy.

Anna took in the huge number of paintings leaning in piles against the walls as well as hanging on every available space. "I never dreamed you were quite so industrious."

"Oh, a lot of them are mere dross, pieces that didn't work or were too dull to finish," Rupert said modestly.

"But you may still find a few hidden gems," Serena told her.

"What are you working on now?" Louis asked, approaching him to look.

With his paintbrush, Tamar pointed commandingly away from his easel. "I'll show you if it works."

Louis bowed ironically and examined the paintings on the wall instead.

Anna wandered the one-room cottage which was her brother's studio, examining paintings at random. Crouching down in the far corner, she flicked through the unframed canvasses stacked there, until, near the back, she came upon a caricature of a stout, self-important little man, his eyes all but popping out of his head as he grasped greedily at money falling from various different hands scattered around the edges. His expression was avaricious and unpleasant, but that wasn't what drove Anna backward so quickly that she clattered into the paintings piled under a little window. She recognized him.

"Anna?" came Serena's concerned voice.

But Louis was already there, crouched in front of her. "What is it?" he asked urgently. Only then could Anna wrench her gaze away from the caricature. Louis was looking from her to the picture and back.

Anna tried to laugh. "Nothing. It is just an ugly picture."

Rupert strode over and swept it up, breaking it over his knee and throwing the bits into the corner. "Christ, I'm sorry, Anna, I forgot it was there. I thought I'd burned it with the other rubbish."

Anna swallowed. "Where is he?"

"Gone. Defeated. Powerless."

She looked up at her brother over Louis's head. "Your doing? Again?"

"Partly. Mostly Serena's."

Anna's gaze flickered to her sister-in-law. How much did Serena know? God, how much was she giving away at this moment? She drew in a breath, trying to gather her wits, her hard shell, her knowledge that no one would hurt her ever again.

To her surprise, she found that Louis was holding both her hands, helping her to rise to her feet. And she was clinging to his fingers as if they were her only salvation.

Appalled by her weakness, she pulled her hands free. She couldn't look at him. Instead, she hurried across to Tamar's drinking friends, to make some witty observation on the picture above their heads, as if it had just caught her attention. They laughed and she sat beside them, strangers she could wrap around her finger and enslave for practice, just until the trembling had stopped.

"Serena, what about this hat shop of yours?" she called, jumping to her feet. "Are we too late, or may we go now?"

Chapter Seven

S HE WAS A chameleon, ever-changing. Her sudden collapse had been shocking, the way in which she'd clung to Louis both alarming and gratifying.

Until that moment, Louis had doubted she needed anyone's protection, that she ever lost her formidable self-control. For an instant, all he wanted was to shield her from harm. And then, before he'd properly grasped what was happening, she'd pulled free, ignoring him to become the society beauty, deigning to charm the less respectable fringes of her brother's acquaintance. And then she was gone. To look at hats.

Tamar clapped him on the shoulder. "Cheer up, my friend. She affects most people like that."

"What just happened?" Louis asked, lowering his voice so their arguing companions could not hear.

Tamar shrugged. "Bad memory."

"Who was in the picture?" Louis asked, holding his gaze.

Tamar grinned. "Just a bailiff. He used to frighten us as children. Here, have another brandy. And then I'm going to throw you all out and go home for dinner."

Tamar didn't fool him. The young marquis was far more easily read than his sister, and he was covering something up. Something he would not tell a stranger. Or perhaps anyone.

Everyone had a past. He'd suspected Anna's of being more interesting than most, considering the fascinating woman she had become. But somehow, he had never expected it to terrify her. He wasn't remotely offended by her rejection. He understood it was necessary to her recovery. But he found, as he walked thoughtfully back to the hotel in the gathering dusk, that he had a new ambition—to be the one she leaned on, to be the one to whom she revealed her secret. He wasn't even thinking now of secrets he could use.

Louis, you poor fool, she is defeating you...

It was fortunate that he had trained himself so well. Otherwise, his distraction might have caused him to miss the man who crossed his path just as he emerged into High Street. But even when deep in thoughts and plans, Louis automatically observed who came any-where near him. Passers-by, watchers at windows, or at coffee houses. And the man hurrying up the high street in the growing dark almost brushed against him.

His heart leaping against his ribs, Louis merely swerved and walked in the other direction. Stopping at the jeweler's window, he pretended to examine the wares on display while he gazed after the man who hadn't even noticed him. Gosselin. The man he had drawn here by his escape. The man he meant to kill before he left Black-haven.

ANNA RARELY ATTENDED church. In fact, she had deliberately avoided clerics ever since one of the local vicars in the vicinity of Tamar Abbey had sought to improve his social standing by marrying one of the marquis's sisters. He hadn't seemed fussy as to whether Anna or Christianne should have the honor of becoming his wife. In fact, it was doubtful he could tell them apart. In the end, Anna had got rid of him with a few graphic threats and a glimpse of the stiletto she carried everywhere with her. He'd given them both a very wide berth after that. A week later, they had accompanied Rupert on a trip to London where he wished to consult a solicitor. There, at a rare visit to the theatre, they had met Henry Harcourt, who had married Christianne two months later.

Vicars had remained low on Anna's list of people to tolerate. Tristram Grant, vicar of St. Andrew's Church in Blackhaven, had quickly become the exception to her rule. Neither sanctimonious nor self-righteous nor venal, so far as Anna could gather, he appeared to combine fun and wit with good works. Prepared to give him the benefit of the doubt, Anna accompanied Rupert, Serena, her sisters, and their governess to church. Since it was a dry day, if cold and blustery, they all walked down to the town together.

The picturesque church was packed. Many servants, towns people, and country folk had to stand at the back. Serena and Tamar, however, led the way to the front of the church, nodding and murmuring greetings to people as they went. The young ladies did the same, waving enthusiastically to Rosa and the Benedict ladies seated toward the front.

Inevitably, the Braithwaites had a family pew, separating them from the riffraff. This enabled Anna to observe the rest of the congregation. She recognized the Winslows and several other people including Mr. Banion. But of Louis, there was no sign.

I expect he's a Roman Catholic, she thought morosely. *If he has any religion at all.* But it was annoying not to have a chance to meet. Partly, of course, she wished to recover her loss of position when she'd fallen apart on seeing Rupert's drawing of John Rivers. And partly, she found she just wanted to see him. To assure herself of his wellbeing. To talk to him further about changing sides, or at least into giving her the information she needed.

Mr. Grant preached a wonderful sermon, simple, articulate, humorous, and curiously uplifting. Even for Anna, who had believed herself immune to such "nonsense".

Outside, while Serena spoke to Mr. and Mrs. Grant, Anna explored the little churchyard, with the girls following her to show her their favorite gravestones, some of which were hundreds of years old. Eventually, they spilled out of the side gate and walked all round the outside of the yard, past the vicarage, and round toward the front gate once more.

Anna's heart jolted because there in front of her stood Louis, wearing much the same dress as yesterday, in conversation with Mr. and Mrs. Winslow, their daughter and a group of town worthies.

Somehow, she was sure Louis had already seen her, but he remained attentive to the thin, middle-aged lady who was chattering away to him. Instead, Anna caught Mr. Winslow's eye and smiled.

"Good morning, Mr. Winslow," she said, and of course, his eyes lit up on seeing her and he moved at once to intercept her.

"Lady Anna!" exclaimed his wife. "Do allow me to introduce everyone to you. They have been so looking forward to meeting Lord Tamar's sister! First, will you let me present Sir Lytton Lewis?"

Anna smiled. "But there is no need, ma'am. Sir Lytton is a friend of my brother's. How do you do, sir?" In a moment of recklessness, she offered her hand. Which gave him a false respectability in Blackhaven, but also served to remind Anna that not all touches were disgusting.

"Ah, then you know all about his adventures with a dangerous highwayman?" Mrs. Winslow was clearly disappointed.

"I do," Anna admitted.

"Alas, I am seen in a most unheroic light," Louis sighed, releasing her hand and leaving it cold while Anna acknowledged the other introductions.

"You were held up by a highwayman?" Lady Alice said in awe to Louis. "How wonderful!"

"Did he command you to *stand and deliver?*" Lady Helen demanded.

"I believe he did," Louis replied.

"He clearly had no imagination," Anna interjected.

"I am sure he was just a traditionalist," Louis said firmly.

"These are my youngest sisters-in-law," Anna said, swallowing down the surge of laughter. "If you have not yet been formally introduced. Lady Maria, Lady Alice, and Lady Helen Conway."

The children curtseyed in a faultless manner that must at least have mollified their governess, advancing from the churchyard to gather up her charges. Not far behind Mrs. Elphinstone came Serena and Rupert.

"I suppose you also know Lewis's history?" Mr. Winslow greeted them before Anna could hustle everyone away.

"What history?" Tamar asked without much interest.

"Why that he was the highwayman's victim!"

Serena frowned. Tamar blinked, then let out a bark of laughter. "Kept that quiet, didn't you?" he threw at Louis.

Louis sighed and hung his head. "Ladies are so much more under-standing of such humiliation."

Tamar slapped him on the wounded shoulder. "Come up and tell us all this afternoon. Have dinner, if you like. Ladies, Mr. Winslow, your servant!"

To his credit, Louis never flinched at the friendly blow, though it must have hurt. He merely smiled and raised his hat to everyone before walking on and leaving the Braithwaite party to climb into their carriages.

LOUIS WAS AN alarmingly good liar. The tale he told that afternoon to Tamar, Serena, and the girls, was highly entertaining and did not spare his dignity. Anna was prepared to believe it did not even contradict the story he had already given Mr. Winslow.

"How can I ever believe a word you say?" she murmured under cover of the general laughter. She sat beside him on one of the drawing room sofas.

"By using your skill and judgement," he replied at once. "Would you care to take a walk while the sun is out?"

It was exactly what she needed to do, spend time with him, make him comfortable, make him tell his secrets. And she would not refuse. But for an instant, the hint of danger that had always surrounded him, even when he could barely stand, showed in his eyes. He didn't trust her.

It was a blow at this stage. Still, she was sure she could recover from it. She just couldn't understand why it should *hurt*.

She stood. "I'm going to show Sir Lytton your gardens," she told Serena.

"Take my sisters as chaperones," Serena said at once, her eyes gleaming. "As once they were mine."

Tamar laughed, and Anna was briefly distracted by this window into their courtship. She had grown used to the idea that Rupert and Serena liked each other, but courtship and marriage she had always found distasteful.

The girls were delighted to accompany them, having formed a liking for "Sir Lytton". Maria even blushed when he spoke to her.

"Where shall we go?" Helen asked as they emerged from the front door and descended the steps.

"Wherever you like. You know your own home better than either Sir Lytton or I."

"I doubt that," Alice observed. "You have been out and about so much since you arrived, I suspect you know the land better than any of us now!"

As the girls moved ahead, leading them toward a walled orchard, Anna felt his sardonic gaze on her face.

"I was looking for you," she said with dignity. "I was afraid you would die after you vanished from the shepherd's hut."

"I probably would have if you hadn't sewn me up."

"And still you don't trust me," she said bluntly.

His lips twisted. "I am an escaped enemy of your country with secrets I am unwilling to share. Why would I trust anyone in such circumstances?"

"Because they *did* sew you up *and* kept all your damned secrets," Anna retorted.

His lips stretched. "Why Anna, I believe I have hurt your feelings."

"You would have if I had any."

"It's a good role you play, but you needn't bother for me. I see beneath it."

She pushed down the panic, for she didn't put such perception past him. "To what?" she asked mockingly. "Some poor, delicate, helpless lady?"

"Not helpless. And we both know there is a lot more to you than that. Besides, you may have noticed I am already trusting you. You could expose me at any time, and yet here I am."

"Then you need my help after all? In what? Escaping England?"

"Oh, no, I have an arrangement with a free-trading captain, introduced to me by an individual known somewhat indiscreetly as Smuggler Jack. He claims to have retired."

"And where did you encounter such upstanding members of Blackhaven society?"

"In the town tavern. Which is quite a den of vice."

"And when do you sail?"

"In a day or so, maybe," he said vaguely.

"I thought you were afraid to go home."

"I shan't go home. I'll go to the Isles de la Manche. Or to Ireland, perhaps, and from there to the Americas. Who knows?"

She searched his eyes, genuinely afraid he was slipping away from her in every way. And made a discovery. "You're lying. Again. You're not going anywhere. You know the soldiers are still watching the smugglers."

"I'm not sure they watch them very well—not those coming in at any rate. There is another Frenchman in Blackhaven."

"In the tavern?"

"He is too well dressed for the tavern. Nor does he stay at the hotel."

She frowned. "Why are you telling me this? Is he a friend?"

"Not to me. He has come to kill me."

A week ago, neither the news nor the word kill would have disturbed her. She looked away. "Let me take you to safety," she pleaded, and God help her, she meant it.

"To your friends who are so interested in my secrets? No, I thank you."

"Then what will you do?" she demanded.

He raised one eyebrow. "I shall kill him."

She shivered, chilled by the casual certainty in his voice. "Does there have to be killing?"

"Apparently so. But if not at the hotel, where else would such a man stay? Where would he go?"

"He could have hired rooms, or a whole house anywhere in the town," Anna said. "Many people do. As to where he would go, there are a limited number of entertainments in Blackhaven. Gentlemen do slum it at the tavern on occasion, I'm told. The coffee house opposite the hotel is popular. Otherwise, there is really only the hotel itself, the theatre, the pump room, the art gallery, and the assembly rooms..."

She broke off, her eyes widening. "Do you think he could have been at the masquerade ball?"

"It is possible, though I would not have expected him to be in the country so soon. I wasn't looking for him. I could have missed him."

She frowned. "Then you *know* him?"

"Oh, I know him."

She shivered. "You are quite...frightening, you know."

He met her gaze. "But I don't frighten you, do I, Anna?"

You do. God help me, you do. Before she could answer, they were interrupted by the girls, dragging them out of the orchard again. They wished to walk around the other side of the castle to show "Sir Lytton" the best sea views.

A COUPLE OF hours later, once changed for dinner, Anna was walking along the gallery to the drawing room when, through the open door of the library, she glimpsed Louis.

His back to her, he was gazing along the shelves nearest the fireplace. Soundlessly, she walked in.

"Your brother-in-law appears to be interested in politics," Louis observed, without turning.

"I believe he is," Anna replied, moving further into the room.

"How did you know I was here?"

Louis glanced over his shoulder. "I heard the faint rustle of your skirts. And your scent is unmistakable."

"I hope that is a compliment."

"I thought you didn't care for such."

"As a rule, I don't. In this case, the alternative is unthinkable. I shall assume the compliment and move on. Are you not interested in politics, too? Isn't everyone in these times?"

"I don't see the point. People corrupt even the best of political ideals."

"People," she repeated. "Do you mean Bonaparte?"

"The Emperor Napoleon," he mocked. "Who came to power believing in liberty, equality, and fraternity. And what did we achieve? Military dictatorship, constant war, the death of thousands, and an emperor instead of a king."

"Then you are not a Bonapartist?" she said carefully.

"I was once." Just for an instant, there was sadness in his voice that tugged at her heart. And then his lips twisted in self-mockery. "Ardently so. But I want the best for my country and my countrymen. I don't believe that is the emperor any longer. A purist might say he betrayed the revolution that allowed him to rise to power. Certainly, he is now leading France into disaster and defeat."

"Everyone says the war is almost over."

"I expect it is. We have been kicked out of Russia and Spain. The whole of Europe is allied against us. Even he cannot win against such odds."

"*Even he*," she repeated. "Did you fight in his army?"

He shrugged. "I have done."

"But you are not Captain L'Étrange."

"My rank is higher, but it is largely honorary."

"Because you are noble?" she asked, doubtfully.

A breath of laughter escaped him. "There is nothing noble about me, in rank or nature. I am an orphan brat recruited from the streets of Paris." He paused, as though searching her face for signs of disgust or scorn. He shrugged. "I thrived in the new France, on liberty and equality if not so much on fraternity. And now we shall lose and no doubt be forced to take back the king we deposed more than twenty years ago. There will be an unseemly grab for land and wealth and power all over again."

"Do you have land in France?" she asked curiously.

"Yes. I am considered a wealthy man. Does it help you warm to me?"

"No, since you're about to lose it."

He laughed and inclined his head. "Well said." He advanced until he stood facing her, close enough to touch. "Why *do* you help me, Anna?"

"Why do you think?" she countered.

"Perhaps compassion, as you said. And perhaps you seek danger for the thrill, just to feel *something*."

She couldn't help the twitch of her frown, but she refused to let him see how close he came to truth. "Is such a reason compatible with compassion?" she wondered.

"People do things for all sorts of contradictory reasons. Whatever yours are, I thank you."

Warmth seeped into her face. She could think of nothing to say. She liked the way his hard eyes softened as he gazed down at her. He raised his hand slowly, brushing his fingertips against her cheek, her hair. She didn't flinch. On the contrary, her skin seemed to sing under his tender touch. She almost leaned into his hand to prolong the caress.

"We could have been friends, you and I," he murmured.

"If we were not enemies?" she managed. "Does that matter?"

A smile flickered across his lips. "Not to me."

For an instant, she could not breathe. And then the arguing voices of the young ladies could be heard coming along the gallery.

Louis turned aside, offering his arm, and she laid her fingers on his sleeve before walking out the door with him and across the gallery to the drawing room. It was only later, as she relaxed into the general laughter and banter, and met Louis's humorous gaze across the room, that her stomach jolted with fright.

What is happening to me? After everything, is he *seducing* me?

Chapter Eight

FOREWARNED WAS FOREARMED, and Anna resolved to use the genuine closeness forming between them to win him over. Such had always been her plan, after all. She just hadn't expected any actual *feeling* to be involved on her side. What the feeling was, she had no clear idea. It was new and oddly delightful and seemed to provide something of the same excitement she found in risk. Well, he presented just a little more danger than the previous tasks she had undertaken for Henry, so perhaps that explained it.

At any rate, when Serena mentioned they might attend the theatre the following evening, his gaze immediately fell on Anna.

"My mother took a box there when it first opened," Serena explained. "Just to support it, you understand. I don't believe she has been there once! It doesn't have the best-known players, of course, but we have spent a few enjoyable evenings there."

"I shall do my best to look in," Louis murmured.

It gave Anna something to look forward to the following day, but before the evening trip to the theatre, there came a curious incident involving Mrs. Elphinstone.

Lady Braithwaite had granted the governess leave every second Saturday, and every Monday afternoon. And this Monday, she had chosen to take herself to the nearest port town of Whalen. The larger ships all put in there, and in fact, even five years ago, before Blackhaven's expansion, it had been the most notable town along this part of the coast. So, for a lady used to the hustle and bustle of London, it was not an unexpected choice of visit.

However, she returned early, much to the clear annoyance of the Braithwaite under coachman, who had no doubt looked forward to an entire afternoon in Whalen. Anna saw her agitated arrival from the library window, all but leaping from the carriage without waiting for the steps to be let down and vanishing up the front steps.

A moment later, Mrs. Elphinstone's voice could be heard demanding to know Lord Tamar's whereabouts. Intrigued, Anna went to track him down, and found him with Serena in the drawing room, only a few moments before the governess's precipitous arrival.

"My lord!" she exclaimed, panting and barely pausing to curtsey. "My lady. I have important news and I am at a loss as to whom I should tell!"

"Begin with us," Serena encouraged. "We love news." Her flippant manner was lost on Mrs. Elphinstone, who was clearly too disturbed to notice such nuances.

"I have seen him!" the governess announced dramatically.

Anna exchanged glances with her brother and Serena. "Seen whom?" she asked, when no one else did.

"Him! The one they all seek, the French prisoner who escaped the Black Fort."

That certainly drew everyone's attention. Anna's stomach twisted as she stared at the governess. But her outward reaction was no doubt similar to Serena's and Rupert's.

"Where?" Rupert demanded. "How do you know it was him?"

"Well, I didn't, at first. It was only later it came to me...I was walking around the harbor area, admiring the ships, and stopped to look at the wares in the nearby street market. I struck up a conversation with a woman there. And almost as soon as I moved on, a man came to me and asked me in French if I would buy him passage on a ship sailing to America."

"Did he, by God?" Rupert said, interestedly.

"He did. And when I suggested he buy it himself, he told me his English was not good enough. Of course, I was immediately suspicious it was some trick or other to part me from the few coins in my purse, so I merely held it tighter and hurried away. And only then did it strike me."

She paused, as though for dramatic effect. "He could be a fugitive. He could be the prisoner everyone is looking for!"

"He could at that," Tamar agreed, far too interested to please Anna. "I think we should probably send to the fort and Major Doverton. And to Winslow, too. What did he look like, your French-man?"

"Tall." Mrs. Elphinstone shuddered. "Dirty fair hair poking out from under a floppy, wide-brimmed hat. He was not ill-looking, just very furtive. Oh, and he wore a torn leather coat."

Anna's eyes fixed on the governess's face. Was she lying? Why would she? This made no sense to Anna, for while it was perfectly possible that Louis had gone to Whalen, it was highly doubtful he would have done so in his highwayman's disguise. Was this the other Frenchman Louis had mentioned? Coincidentally resembling Louis's highwayman? Dubious.

"Come, Mrs. E.," Tamar said cheerfully, striding to the door. "We had better call on Major Doverton at the barracks. Have tea without me, my dear," he threw over his shoulder at Serena. "I'll be back in time to escort you to the theatre."

ANNA AGAIN DONNED the silver-grey gown and joined her brother and sister-in-law to go to the play in Blackhaven. As they took their seats in the Braithwaite box, she was already searching for Louis in the rows of boxes and the seats in the pit. She kept her anxiety hidden but she could not banish the fear that Mrs. Elphinstone's information might have led to Louis's capture. Even though she could not quite believe the information.

The governess's motives eluded her, but the woman was French by birth and she bore watching.

Rupert said Doverton and Winslow were taking the information seriously and had moved their patrols from Blackhaven to Whalen. It made sense in many ways, since from Whalen, Louis could easily take ship directly to Ireland, America, or anywhere else he chose.

Only, Anna was sure he had no intention of going. Not yet. And never if she won him over.

The theatre was like a miniature of those Anna had attended in London, and because of its size, it created an atmosphere of coziness that made her slightly uncomfortable. Acquaintances from the other boxes bowed and smiled to her, a civility she returned, just as if there was not only one face she wished to see.

In the pit, sat men and women of the lower orders, cheek-by-jowl with several young gentlemen, including Mr. Banion, who, quizzing glass raised to his eye was searching the boxes with more open fervor. He dropped the glass to smile and bow when he came to Anna and Serena.

"He does pay you particular attention," Serena murmured.

"I cannot imagine why."

"You are new here, and beautiful, and no doubt you pique his desires by appearing to be unaware of his existence."

Anna cast her a cynical glance. "But I am the worst of all possible worlds. I combine the highest birth with the lowest income—none at all—and a scandalous upbringing. Trust me, he is not considering marriage!"

"Oh, I don't know," Serena murmured. "I more than considered marriage with Tamar, after all."

"Tamar is a man," Anna pointed out.

"I am," Rupert agreed, catching the tail-end of their conversation. "Everyone agrees on that."

The curtain went up on stage and most of the theatre quieted as the farce began. A few minutes later, the curtain dividing their box from the passage outside, swished. The hairs on the back of Anna's neck prickled. She knew before she turned that Louis had entered the box, and sheer relief swamped her. Her smile of welcome was spontaneous and the answering glimmer lit his eyes before he moved to formally greet Serena.

Anna's excitement had little to do with the play as he pulled a chair up and sat behind her, in the relative gloom by the right-hand curtain.

"You are a creature of the shadows," she mocked.

"I am. And I don't want to give those officers down there any help to recognize me."

"Are they from the fort?" Anna asked quickly.

"One of them is."

She lowered her voice further. "Were you in Whalen today?"

"No, why?"

"What did you do with the highwayman's coat?" she breathed.

"I buried it," he said unexpectedly.

Could someone else have found it? Or was Mrs. Elphinstone leading the authorities on a wild goose chase? Improbable. Instead, it was far more likely that Anna had just grown too suspicious. Mrs. Elphinstone had been accosted by a suspicious Frenchman and possibly endowed him unconsciously with the escaped prisoner's description. The important thing was that he was here and free. And in spite of everything, Anna's spirits soared.

She turned her slightly breathless attention back to the stage and soon even found herself laughing. Everything, from the play to the danger still presented by the officers in the audience, seemed to be heightened by his presence.

Then, he leaned forward abruptly, his breath stirring her ear. "Who is the man in the natty puce waistcoat? In the pit, just behind the girl with orange hair."

Anna looked down. "That is Mr. Banion. Serena thinks he admires me."

His gaze burned into her face, thrilling and yet unyielding. The man even Bonaparte found too dangerous to live.

"Then you have known him some time?" he murmured.

She shrugged. "No, just since I came to Blackhaven. But I believe he has *been* here for some time. Why?"

"No reason."

Anna looked into his eyes, colder and harder than she had ever seen them. Fear coiled in her stomach, squeezing. Dear God, had she really imagined she could get the better of *him*?

Yet it was not in her nature to back down. She would fear nothing and no one ever again.

"I don't believe you," she said flatly.

FOR LOUIS, ANNA'S answers changed everything. Well, not that he would kill Gosselin, but everything else. Catching sight of his enemy the other day had been a shock. He had not expected him so soon, but even so, Louis had immediately imagined his plan was working, that his escape had lured Gosselin to Blackhaven so speedily. Fierce elation had filled him, because after six months, his moment was finally at hand.

Until Anna had spoken. Gosselin, as Banion, had insinuated himself into local society *before* Louis's escape from the Black Fort. Which meant Gosselin's English had improved drastically. And that either he had come here for reasons that had nothing to do with Louis, or that he had come to kill Louis personally when his attempt by proxy had failed.

The latter was not in character if he had believed Louis to be safely out of the way in prison. But it was not impossible either…

As the curtain came down for the first interval, Gosselin—Mr. Banion—rose from his seat at once, making his way to the stairs that led to the upper boxes. For an instant, mindless emotion almost seized control of Louis. He would turn and face his enemy, kill him where he stood with his bare hands…

But, of course, that was insanity. For one thing, he would be overpowered and imprisoned, probably even before the killing was done. For another, a lifetime of training convinced him there was more to learn here.

Visitors were already streaming into the Tamars' box, so Louis was able to slip out unnoticed by anyone. Except possibly Anna. Though she did not so much as glance at him, keeping her gaze fixed instead on the gentlemen Serena was presenting to her. And yet, he was sure she knew he left.

He did not go far, merely milled among the people in the corridor, waiting for his quarry to appear from the staircase. "Banion" sauntered by without even looking. Of course, Gosselin had never been used to getting his hands dirty and putting himself in this kind of danger. He did not know how to look out for enemies in a crowd. And he did not try, which meant he didn't expect to see Louis here at the center of Blackhaven society. And yet everyone knew of the escaped prisoner. Did Gosselin, too, believe that he was the highwayman who'd ridden north into Scotland? And if so, why was he still here?

No, Gosselin had come for some other reason entirely. The question now, was whether or not Anna knew that reason. Was she simply a slightly damaged aristocrat playing with fire in the shape of an escaped enemy prisoner? Or did she have deeper motives?

He didn't return to the box but left the theatre to avoid being seen by Gosselin, aiming to pick up any information he could about "Mr. Banion".

In the street, by chance, he came upon the two gentlemen he'd encountered at Tamar's studio. Sauntering along in the direction of the theatre, they greeted him like an old friend.

"Not going to the theater, old man?" one asked cheerfully. He was a young officer of the 44th, whose name, Louis thought, was Gordon.

"I've just left," Louis said, deliberately morose. It was time to play the jealous lover.

"Acting that bad?" the other asked sympathetically. His name was Fenner.

"I barely noticed it to be truthful," Louis replied. "Just couldn't bear the sight of some fellow fawning all over Tamar's sister."

Lieutenant Gordon cocked an intelligent eyebrow. "Banion?"

"That's the fellow."

"I wouldn't worry," Fenner said. "The clever money's on you."

Louis allowed himself to frown. "You're betting on this?"

"Only discreetly," Gordon said hastily. "Ignore Fenner, he's half-cut."

"Who is this Banion anyhow?" Louis asked.

"Decent enough fellow. Came here to get over a bad bout of measles. His father has land in east Yorkshire, apparently, and his mother was a French émigré."

Which would cleverly explain any slip-ups of accent or words, Louis thought, impressed in spite of himself. Gosselin had never been lacking in intelligence.

"Where does he lodge?" Louis asked.

"Got a neat little house on Cliff View," Fenner told him. "But, I say, Lewis, you ain't going to call him out?"

"Lord, no."

"Good," said Gordon. "Because it was you she danced with at the masquerade. We all know that. And he don't have anything like your address."

"What do you mean?" Louis asked, temporarily thrown.

"I mean you're a much more appealing cove. Ladies all like you, give you my word. Come on, Fenner, let's get to the play before it finishes! Sure you won't come with us, Lewis?"

"No, I won't, but I thank you and wish you a pleasant evening."

Louis watched them go, then waited in the shadows until the patrons began to spill out of the theatre. Gosselin came out alone and walked straight down the road as if he were going home. Ever wary, he would be careful not to expose himself too much and risk making mistakes.

Louis walked casually into the light, meaning to follow him. Only, the Tamars emerged from the front door just in front of him, and he paused. Serena had stopped to talk to someone while Anna held back, as she often did. Few people appeared to interest her. She found normal social civilities constricting and unnecessary. Louis rather liked that in her. The child who'd grown up wild with little or no supervision, was only partially tamed. For the rest, she went her own way.

"Anna," he murmured.

Her body seemed to still. She didn't spin around in fright at his suddenness. In some way, she trusted him.

She turned with grace. "Sir Lytton. I thought you had abandoned us."

"Of course not."

"Tamar has bespoken supper at the hotel. I'm sure he meant you to join us."

"Alas, I cannot."

She merely inclined her head, as if she did not care, and yet for some reason, he was sure she did.

"I would rather see you alone," he murmured before she could walk away. "Tomorrow morning, in the Braithwaite woods."

She regarded him for an instant. "Is this an assignation or a conspiracy?"

He smiled. "Both. Neither. Whatever you like."

"Nine of the clock," she said abruptly. "Or I shan't be there."

She walked away without a second glance.

His dying smile slightly twisted, Louis strode off in the other direction after Gosselin, who was no longer in sight. However, by the time he reached Cliff View, he had caught up enough to see his enemy walk up the path of a neat little house and let himself in with a key.

Since a watchman with a lantern was approaching, Louis merely sauntered past and said a polite good evening to the Watchman. There would be better opportunities to search the house, when Gosselin was not in it. Instead, he kept going until he came to the beach.

A path wound down the rocky cliffside to the sand. Before taking it, Louis stood at the top like a slightly morose drunk taking in the view while feeling sorry for himself. There were no soldiers watching the cove below. Had they given up on him escaping that way?

Louis strolled only a little way down until he found a comfortable rock to sit on with his back against the cliff. From habit, he chose the place because it hid him from the road and some scrubby bushes concealed him from the sea side. Though, in fact, he was mostly there just to rest and to watch any smuggling activity that might take place. It would be too lucky to catch Gosselin making plans with the smugglers, although he could hope. As it stood, he had no idea what was going on.

His wound still pained him, often in sharp, nagging ways. But he believed it was healing inside as well as out, and he had no intention of pushing himself into any unnecessary fights and risking his recovery. It was a cold night, too, with frost forming and glistening, so he meant only to stay and think for a little. But the fine view of the moonlit sea and the ship anchored in the distance was curiously soothing, and he stayed until he was too cold.

As he began to rise, his gaze focused on a darker blur in the sea surrounded by rhythmic ripples. It was a boat rowing ashore from the ship.

Louis dropped back down again, no longer noticing the cold. He more than half-expected to see Gosselin slip down to the beach to wait for the arrival, but no one did. As the boat drew nearer, he made out the shapes of several men and a woman. Two of the men jumped out in the shallows and heaved the boat onto the beach for the others to jump out on to dry sand. One man lifted the woman out, carrying her ashore so that her feet didn't get wet.

Leaving the others on the beach, three men and the woman began to walk up the path. The men were all armed to the teeth. One carried a lantern and one carried a bulging carpet bag. If they were smugglers, they clearly weren't doing much business. Unless...the woman was a spy returning from France? Or a French spy sent to Britain? Or she could simply be a refugee.

And then, as they silently climbed the path, so close he could hear them breathing, the lantern light fell across several faces. And with a jolt, Louis recognized the saturnine features of the man who walked beside the young woman.

Captain Alban.

As a prisoner of war, Louis had been transferred from a naval vessel to this man's ship. The captain, an abrupt Englishman, had a somewhat piratical past and not much reputation for loyalty until recent years when he had shown both willingness and an annoying ability to engage and defeat unsuspecting French ships. These days, he had every right to come ashore in his own country.

So what was this silent, moonlit landing all about?

From the road, came the unmistakable sound of horses' hooves approaching at a slow pace. As though someone had been waiting with the animals not far from there.

At the top of the cliff, Alban gave the carpet bag to one of the other men and took the woman into his arms. She was young and pretty enough, and well-dressed, too, but she looked far too respectable to be one of Alban's women. She even wore spectacles that glinted in the lantern light. Nevertheless, Alban kissed her thoroughly and she appeared to cooperate fully.

"Take care," her voice whispered on the breeze.

"Always," came Alban's deeper murmur. "Go." He released her and she walked off with the other two men while Alban strode and slid his way down the path back to his boat. His men were already waiting to push off.

His curiosity thoroughly roused, Louis crawled on his stomach to the top of the cliff, where he was in time to see the young woman and her escort mount on waiting horses and ride away out of Blackhaven.

Well, it was interesting. But did it have anything to do with either himself or Gosselin? Louis waited a little longer, but his enemy never emerged from his house.

ANNA RETURNED FROM her early morning ride, reaching the woods with only about five minutes until nine o'clock. Although not sure exactly what she had been looking for, she liked to know the lie of the land and anything odd that might be happening in the extended neighborhood of Blackhaven. Especially after Mrs. Elphinstone's curious sighting. But she had seen nothing odd, unless it was the absence of soldiers watching the coves and the harbor.

A figure stepped out of the trees right in front of her.

Her free hand—for she held the reins only in her left—flew to her wrist, where the stiletto fitted snugly into a pocket in the seam of her gloves.

"Good morning," said Louis mildly. "I thought you might keep me waiting."

"Well, there is no need to *sneak*," she retorted.

"I felt it was *de rigeur* for a clandestine assignation."

From habit, she was about to deny pithily that their meeting was any such thing. But she had already acknowledged that Louis was not a man she could lead by the nose, not without giving something in return. That "something" made her heart race, but it did not seem to be with revulsion. More, with…excitement.

"I suppose it would ruin my reputation if I were seen alone with you at this time of the morning," she agreed. "So, by all mean, let us be clandestine. I had better come down and let poor Chessy rest."

He raised his hands to her waist to lift her down, and she did not stop him. His grip was strong and sure without being rough. She would have thought him a gentle man, had she not been aware of his profession.

Her feet landed lightly on the ground between him and the mare, who snuffled and shifted restlessly at her back. His hands remained lightly on her waist as he gazed down at her.

"There is something about you, Anna Gaunt. You make me forget why I'm here. Why you are. You do not even seem to care that I am a gutter rat who got rich on Bonaparte's back. *Why* do you not care?"

She shrugged. "I have learned to take people as they are, not how they are regarded by the world because of who their father and grandfather were."

"That is a very revolutionary sentiment for a daughter of one of the oldest noble families in Europe."

She shrugged. "Their noble birth didn't stop most of them from being total swine."

"Like Tamar?"

She laughed. "Tamar is different. He and Christianne. The rest of us are vile."

His brow contracted and she pulled away, looping the reins over Chessy's head to lead her.

"Have you killed your enemy yet?" she asked lightly.

"No. I want to know why he's here first."

"I thought he was looking for you."

"Then he was looking for me before I escaped. Which is not impossible, only why has he done nothing about finding me?"

"Perhaps he has legions of servants to do it for him."

"Perhaps," he allowed. "Or perhaps something else is happening in Blackhaven."

"I gather something is *always* happening in Blackhaven," Anna replied, "though usually nothing more important than smuggling and illegal gambling."

"Do you know Captain Alban?"

She blinked. "No, I've never met him. But Tamar and Serena know him. Tamar calls him a friend."

"Then he has some connection to Blackhaven?"

"Well, yes. Alban isn't his surname. Lamont is. His family own the Roseley estate near…" She paused, remembering the bustle and the overheard conversation on her ride. "Is Alban back?"

"No, but he left someone here last night."

"*Another* Frenchman?" she asked wryly.

"No, a woman, who sounds as English as you do."

"*You* sound as English as I do," Anna retorted.

"Setting that aside, she is perhaps a few years older than you, small and pretty in an unusual kind of way, wearing spectacles."

"Oh, that will be his wife, who was Lady Arabella Niven. I am sure *she* is not connected to your French spies!"

"Then why did she come in secret?"

"To avoid Blackhaven society?" Anna suggested. "I hear she is reclusive by nature."

"Hmm."

"I could take Serena and go and call on her."

"But would you tell me what you discovered?"

"That would depend on what it was. But if it helps, Serena and Tamar both like her."

"They also appear to like me," he said wryly.

She took a breath for courage. "Louis." She took his gloved hand, gazing up at him seriously. A flicker of surprise showed in his veiled eyes and vanished. "You are involving yourself with events and people that should not concern you. You are an enemy French...officer on British soil. You have to seek protection."

"How would I do that?" he asked steadily.

"Negotiate for your freedom. With information. Give up this other Frenchman to them to show your good will."

"And let myself be taken along with him?"

"No." She had thought this all through already. Letting her grip on his hand tighten, she said, "I will go to Major Doverton for you. Or I'll go through my brother-in-law, Henry Harcourt, if you prefer. Give me something, any little piece of information to impress them, and then we'll negotiate your freedom for the spy."

His steady eyes never blinked. "You would be admitting to helping me."

"I would have to say you had told me from the outset that you wished to seek asylum with us."

He raised his hand and hers to his cheek. "Oh, Anna, you are undoubtedly a temptation few men could resist."

Her lips twisted. "Except you."

"Oh no, I would succumb in an instant. Except..."

"Except what?" she asked impatiently.

"Except I don't want to seek asylum with you. I am French."

She threw his hand from her. "Then go home to those who will kill you."

She strode away, forcing the surprised mare to trot behind her.

"Perhaps I would rather die with you," he said, keeping pace easily beside her.

"Damn you, do you have to die at all?"

"Not today."

"At least think about what I have said," she pleaded. She swallowed. "I don't want you to die." The truth was terrifying in her own ears. She should not care if he lived or died. She never had before, about anyone, except Christianne. And Rupert. Maybe Serena now. But the point was, Louis was her enemy, her task that she had to complete. And she would, whatever it cost her.

His gloved fingers touched her cheek in a caress that brought both sweetness and pain. "I'll find a way," he promised. "I always do. But I will think about what you said."

She smiled, leaning her cheek into his hand. "Tell me about your home, Louis."

Chapter Nine

I T WAS AFTER eleven o'clock before Anna returned to the castle, happy and triumphant over the victory she could sense was very close now. At least, she assumed that was the reason for her elation. He might have some strange effect upon her, but she was not foolish enough to let that cloud her judgement or interfere with her task.

And she saw no sense in not using the information she was given. Encountering Serena "by accident" as she finished conferring with the housekeeper, Anna threw herself into a chair and enthused about her delightful ride in the direction of Roseley, and casually mentioned that some member of the family had apparently arrived there to stay while the lady of the house was absent.

"Oh, it will be Alban, probably," Serena said carelessly. "Lady Roseley, his sister-in-law, is in London with her children. He looks after the place for her, I believe."

Anna allowed herself to look impressed. "The famous Captain Alban?"

After that, it was quite easy to manipulate Serena into riding over there to call. "Or we could wait until tomorrow," Serena said doubt-fully, "when Rupert might come with us. He is poring over books and plans sent up from Tamar Abbey and deciding what next to set in motion. I don't like to disturb him."

For the first time, it struck Anna that her brother might actually manage to restore their old home into something habitable, and the land into something profitable, something decent for their people to live on. Which would be a great thing, something she never imagined could happen.

But it would be Serena's home, not Anna's. Anna was not destined to be the lady of any manor. Or any home.

"Oh, no," Anna agreed. "He has taken on a massive task, and of course we must not try to drag him away. But we don't need him to go out riding, do we?"

Serena, whom she already knew to be surprisingly good company, was a fun and interesting companion on their ride. She pointed out the best views and landmarks and told amusing tales of the trouble she had got into in various places with her older sister and brother. But more than that, she took uninhibited joy in her surroundings. She was one of those rare people who loved life and somehow spread her enthusiasm to everyone she touched. Even the cynical Anna.

"I can see why Rupert married you," Anna said once.

Serena glanced at her. "Do you mind that he did?"

Anna could have turned that one off easily enough, but she chose to tell the truth. "I thought I might. But I don't. I'm glad. And not just because you make it possible for him to restore the estate. It's good to see him happy. And full of purpose."

Serena held her gaze. "And what of you, Anna? Tamar could give you a dowry now. It might not be anything great considering your rank, but it makes a good marriage likelier."

Anna curled her lip. "Why would I wish to marry?"

"For a home and children. And happiness, such as I have found with your brother."

Anna looked away. "I'm not like you. These things don't interest me."

"And Sir Lytton?" Serena prodded. "Does he not interest you?"

Anna smiled. "Yes," she admitted. "But not in the way you are imagining. He could be a friend." For a moment, she thought Serena might probe further, and in a direction, Anna had no intention of going. She had a feeling Serena knew more of her history than she was comfortable with. For, of course, Rupert would have told her his own part in it. He could only recently have shaken off the "other" Rivers, the extortioner he had caricatured.

But Serena said only, "This is Roseley land, now. The house is just ahead."

There was a lot of activity around the house and grounds. Everything was being cleaned and repaired, which was only natural if a member of the family had turned up unexpectedly. Everyone bowed and tugged their forelock to Lady Serena, whom they obviously recognized. A boy ran up to take both their horses while a rather villainous looking man sloped inside the house through the front door.

"Don't be alarmed," Serena said with a hint of amusement. "That will be one of Alban's seamen."

Anna, who had already presumed this, and wasn't remotely alarmed, merely nodded and smiled.

They were met at the door by a much more respectable footman, who bowed them into a sunny front parlor. Here, a slightly vague, bespectacled young lady came toward them with her hand held out.

"Lady Tamar, how unexpected," she murmured. "And how pleasant to see you again."

"I hope we haven't come at a bad time," Serena said, her easy manner contrasting with the slightly awkward shyness of her hostess. "We heard a rumor you were here and just had to call in during our ride. Forgive me, I haven't yet introduced you! This is Lady Anna Gaunt, Tamar's sister. Anna, Mrs. Lamont, whom we all still call Lady Arabella because her husband has too many other names!"

Lady Arabella shook hands most civilly, rang for tea, and invited her unexpected guests to sit.

"How did you know I was here?" Lady Arabella asked with surprising directness.

"We didn't," Serena admitted. "It was a mere rumor, but I am very glad to find you here."

"And I'm very glad you did," Lady Arabella said. "Only...you will not tell anyone else, will you?"

"Not if you don't wish us to," Serena said at once. "Forgive me, but is everything well?"

Their hostess smiled in a way that raised her pretty face to beauty. "Oh, very well indeed. And I am delighted to see *you*. It's just that I came alone because that is how I particularly wish to be." She blushed. "I am *enceinte* and have been feeling a trifle too sick for seafaring. Alban landed me here, where I can be both useful and quiet!"

"Oh, how wonderful," Serena said warmly. "I am so glad for you. We shall say nothing to anyone, and leave you be unless you send for me—which I hope you will if you need anything at all."

Anna, on the other hand, felt somewhat deflated by this news. There appeared to be no mystery here. The woman had landed at night merely to avoid visitors because she was suffering in the early stages of pregnancy. Of course, she might have been more comfortable in her own home which Anna knew to be in Scotland, or with her own family.

In the room above, the sounds of moving furniture and cleaning could be heard. The inside of the house was clearly getting the same treatment as the outside. A clean and tidy house, would, no doubt, make Lady Arabella more comfortable in the end. Only, it did not seem very *restful*.

And Lady Arabella herself, while certainly shy and a little vague, was far from being a stupid woman. Or the kind who turned households upside down unnecessarily. Was she mixed up with foreign spies? Anna doubted it, though the husband was, perhaps, a different matter. Was she up to something? Possibly, though Anna could not imagine what.

They did not stay long, since the lady had already told them of her desire for solitude. And in any case, it was a long ride home.

AT DINNER THAT night, Tamar was full of enthusiasm, regaling them with his plans for the abbey lands. "It will take years of course. But we can make a start immediately and do more every year. If we keep out of the way, they'll get the work on the house done faster, too, so I was thinking we could just stay here after all, perhaps until early spring? And then we can go down and be comfortable while you order the inside of the house to your liking."

"I admit I am dying to see it," Serena admitted warmly.

Tamar cocked one eyebrow at Anna. "What about you? Will you stay here for Christmas? Or go back to Christianne? Go to the abbey if you'd rather."

"I'll probably go back to Christianne's," she said easily, "if the weather permits."

It was fortunate and somewhat touching that Serena tried to persuade her to stay at the castle over Christmas at least. For she wasn't quite sure how long her current task and its aftermath would take. She found she was in no desire to leave. Or to break off all ties with Louis, whatever she persuaded him to say and do. But she would not think of the future, only the present.

"Oh, do you care to have dinner at the hotel tomorrow evening?" Tamar said suddenly, fishing a crumpled note from his pocket. "Lewis invited us to dine with him."

IN THE END, Anna didn't have to wait for the next evening before she met Louis again. She encountered him in the woods that morning while walking alone, as she had more or less trained the household to expect of her. She was sure Mrs. Gaskell threw up her hands in frustration at such unladylike behavior, but by this time, they were all used to Tamar's eccentricities, so her own, she hoped, were all the more forgivable.

It was no part of her plan to fall out with her hosts, their servants, or their neighbors. In fact, considering why she was there, she felt remarkably...comfortable.

The weather had turned much colder in the last couple of days, though the trees shielded her from the worst of the icy wind. As she walked, she was aware she would be disappointed if Louis did not come.

This time, he did not surprise her. She knew, as soon as she heard the snap of a twig close by, that it was he, and she was already smiling by the time he fell into step beside her.

"I cannot make up my mind," he said, without any greeting, "whether you look lovelier in sedate morning dress, silken evening gowns, or this delightfully mysterious ensemble from another age."

"What a kind way to describe my comfortable old riding habit," she said dryly. "And I suspect I looked best of all when masked!"

"That, too, had a definite charm."

"Why are we discussing my appearance?"

"Perhaps I hope to flatter you into doing me a service."

"What?" she asked suspiciously.

"Remove the stitches from my back."

She frowned. "If you would just do as I ask, we could safely ask a physician to perform the task. He would hurt you less, for one thing."

"That is by no means certain. Will you do it?"

She sighed. "Of course, I will. But I have no scissors with me, no—" She broke off as he produced a pair. "Sit," she said resignedly, and he took off his greatcoat and coat before sitting down on the large trunk of a fallen tree and removing his shirt. Even knowing what she had to do, a secret thrill ran through her at the sight of his broad, naked back.

She knelt behind him and began to talk nonsense to distract him while she worked. Although he must have been freezing cold, he was very stoical, letting out no more than the odd hiss of pain when it took him by surprise. Taking the ointment from her pocket, she smeared some more along the red-ridged seam of his wound, then placed a clean dressing over it and began to wrap the bandage around him.

He caught her wrist. "I can do that."

"So can I," she said steadily, and after a moment, he released her. She was getting too used to the delicious tingles caused by his touch. She found herself looking forward to them, wallowing in them, remembering them at night before she went to sleep. She wished she could speak to Christianne about it, about what it meant.

It may have been the cold or simple pain that caused his shivering as she helped him back into his shirt.

"The sun has gone," she murmured, casting a quick glance at the sky as she rose to her feet. "I think that is the end of the fine weather. I hear predictions of rain and wind, and snow to come before long."

"So do I." He struggled into his coat, then stood. He was a little white, but otherwise seemed no worse for her ministrations. "So," he continued, picking up the great coat, "what do you think is going on at Roseley?"

She frowned, pausing as she pulled on her gloves. "How do you know I was there?"

"I knew you would go. What did you find?"

"Lady Arabella, Captain Alban's wife. She is *enceinte* and spending some time there to be quiet and peaceful, instead of voyaging with her husband."

"Do you believe her?"

"Yes." Anna hesitated. "Although she is conducting a major house cleaning. There may be more than she says going on, but it needn't be anything to do with you."

"I know."

"And your Frenchman?"

"I found a letter," Louis admitted. "It's in code, unsigned. But I know who it is from."

"Who?"

"Fouché."

Her eyes widened. Fouché had been the French minister of police before Bonaparte had dismissed him. But rumor said the emperor still sought his advice. "Can you prove that?" she asked eagerly.

"Not without the code, and even then, it could as easily have been written to me or anyone else. I have copied it to see if I can make sense of it. But it shows he is here at Fouché's command, not because he's gone into hiding before he falls with Napoleon."

"And this Fouché... Do you trust him?"

"The butcher of Lyon?" Louis said with contempt. "God, no."

MARY LANCASTER

And yet, Fouché must once have been his superior. He had been deserted by those who had commanded his service. Worse than that, they were now trying to kill him for his knowledge before he took it to the British, or perhaps hurt them with it at home. She felt the pain of his betrayal almost as if it were her own. She should have been pleased. He had no one in France to turn to. Only Anna and the shadowy friends she had mentioned could help him. It was all working out, slowly but surely.

He said, "My one hope was that Talleyrand would come back, but he seems to have deserted the sinking ship, too."

It had never seemed to Anna that the Prince de Talleyrand, lapsed priest, one-time bishop and foreign minister of France, was trustworthy either.

Louis's smile was twisted, as if he guessed her opinion. "He hates Fouché," he explained.

"You have no choice, Louis. You must trust me."

His gaze dropped from her face to her gloved hand, which he took in his. Unexpectedly, he peeled back the edge of her glove and pressed his lips to the inside of her wrist.

She gasped. And yet she didn't pull free. She would need to give something to win him. A few kisses was little enough to grant. To him, at least.

"If I cannot trust the woman who saved my life and kept my secrets," he said softly, "whom can I trust?"

Suspicion twisted inside her, for she wasn't sure he meant the words honestly. Did he know? No, he couldn't, but he *always* suspected betrayal. There was more to do before he was won. But he was close, so close…

What would he do when he was won? Kiss her? Make love to her? The question, surely, was what *she* would do. And she didn't know. All her energy had to be focused on winning this strange, secretive man whose eyes could laugh, beguile, and threaten at the same time. After that…*could* she tame him?

"I should go," she said breathlessly, withdrawing her hand at last.

"I am only thankful we were not discovered while I cut your stitches."

"I believe you are joining me for dinner this evening. That is a much more respectable assignation."

It was, of course, as long as it never came out in Blackhaven that Sir Lytton was the escaped French prisoner, and worse, Bonaparte's commander of spies. At best, Tamar would look a foolish dupe, and the town would no doubt be annoyed because they had taken their lead from him. And from Winslow, of course, the magistrate Louis had also duped.

BY EARLY EVENING, when the Tamars were driven into Blackhaven, the weather had taken a turn for the worse. The fierce, freezing wind hurled rain at the carriage windows, and the damp made everyone feel chilled to the bone. It reminded Anna of long winters at Tamar Abbey, huddled around the kitchen stove, even to sleep, because the bed-chambers were so cold and damp.

The Blackhaven Hotel, however, was deliciously warm, with fires burning merrily in the large foyer and the dining room.

At the reception desk, a young couple with two small bags, appeared to be arguing with the staff.

"No, I want the largest suite of rooms on the first floor," the young man said belligerently, just as Louis emerged from the dining room to greet his guests.

"Good evening," Louis said, bowing to Serena and Anna before offering his hand to Tamar. "I feel I should apologize for dragging you out on such a night."

"Oh, it's perfectly cozy for us," Tamar observed. "And the horses don't care. It's the poor coachman I feel sorry for."

Louis cast an irate glance at the young man who was growing increasingly loud and angry, and then he looked again. A breath of laughter escaped him.

"Sir, you clearly have no need of such large rooms," the goaded clerk was saying, indicating the couple's sparse baggage with a contemptuous wave of one hand.

"Well, the reason there is now so little is that we were held up when we last left here, not an hour away from your wretched little town!" the young man retorted.

And suddenly, his identity was clear to Anna. No wonder Louis had looked twice and laughed. These must be the people he had held up, the eloping couple.

"Goodness," Serena murmured, awed. "Another hold up."

"I don't feel nearly so paltry now," Louis said. "Excuse me one moment." He walked immediately to the reception desk, but nothing could have kept Anna or her companions from following him.

What would he do, Anna wondered, if—indeed, when!—the couple recognized him? Look blank and rely on the social standing of his companions? And the apparent history he had already built in Blackhaven?

Anna's heart beat with excitement as well as concern. If she had to, she would run with him. It would, after all, be a good opportunity to win the rest of his trust. But, on the whole, she would have advised discretion in this situation. The newlyweds were so incensed and concerned for their dignity, they would never have noticed him. Now, he risked everything...for what?

The furious young man was exclaiming to the clerk, "If you are concerned by our lack of servants, they are on their way. Now, hand over the key to the rooms I was promised—"

"Sir, you were *not* promised," the clerk insisted. "You were told they *might* be available, depending on which day you returned. And these rooms are no longer available."

"Then *make* them available," the young man blustered.

"I wonder if I might be of assistance?" Louis said politely, bowing to the blushing young lady.

Distracted, the young man stared at him suspiciously, then jerked out a bow in return. "Why, have you taken our rooms?" he demanded.

"Alas, no, or I should, of course, have given them up to the lady. I have a room you would regard as barely large enough for one let alone for two."

"Then you'll forgive my shortness, sir, but I fail to see how you might help," the man exclaimed crossly. "Unless it be by beating *this* fellow until—."

Louis laughed, a curiously calming sound. Anna felt as if she were at the theatre enjoying a particularly fine performance. "Well, *this* fellow's hands are clearly tied. But I know for a fact, they have more than one set of excellent rooms which would be quite suitable for you and your lady."

This appeared to be a possibility that had not struck the tightly wound young gentleman before. He opened and closed his mouth without saying anything.

"I hope you will forgive my informal manners," Louis added winningly as the clerk hopefully produced the key for what he said were an equally good set of rooms. "But I could not help hearing that you had been held up and robbed."

The young man scowled as though suspecting derision of some kind. And in truth, it must have been galling to be robbed while one was trying to elope.

"You see," Louis mourned, with just the right degree of shame and fellow-feeling, "the same misfortune befell me not two weeks ago, so I have every sympathy with your plight."

The young man brightened. "Truly? I suppose it was not on the Carlisle road?"

"It *was* on the Carlisle road."

"But this must have been close to when we were robbed! Did the villain take much?"

"Everything, more or less," Louis said with a sigh. "You?"

"Oh, yes, the same," the young man agreed hurriedly, presumably not wishing to be outdone by someone who had lost more. "Rough, insolent fellow he was, too–utterly terrified my wife. I should like to meet him again and punch him on the nose!"

"I should like to see you succeed," Anna murmured below her breath.

"I hear he is long gone, sadly," Louis said, ignoring her. "But you should most definitely report the incident to the local magistrate...if you have not already done so."

So that was it, Anna realized with awe. He wanted them to report the robbery to reinforce his own story, his own character. And the couple suspected nothing. Even though Louis stood before them in the young gentleman's own coat, shirt, and necktie. In fact, the victim blushed a fiery red. So did his lady. He began muttering about the urgency of his business in the north preventing him speaking to the authorities until now. But first thing tomorrow, he would indeed seek out the magistrate.

Eventually, Louis took pity on him and interrupted the painful tangle of promises and self-justification by introducing himself and his friends. Of course, there were so many titles that the couple, Mr. and Mrs. Bradley, were quite overwhelmed and grateful for the notice.

They parted cordially, Mr. Bradley now quite reconciled to the alternative accommodation offered by the hotel.

"I wish them happy," Tamar murmured as they walked toward the dining room. "But, frankly, it's unlikely. He's far too concerned with his dignity to have grown up enough to marry anyone. Let alone face the scandal of elopement."

"Don't preach propriety, Tamar," Serena advised. "Some of our best friends eloped."

"They weren't seventeen years old," Tamar pointed out, "but I take your point."

As they were shown to their table, they drew both curious glances and bows of recognition from several patrons. Anna waited until Tamar and Serena were involved in one of their own bantering arguments, before she spoke quietly to Louis.

"How did you know they would not recognize you?"

He smiled faintly. "Experience."

"It still might come to them," she warned.

"But they will never believe it. They are already...*invested* in my being Sir Lytton, the friend of marquises and beautiful ladies."

She frowned. "You understand people quite horribly well."

"Don't you?"

Anna opened her mouth and closed it again. "No. I thought I did, but I don't. I only understand the viler impulses."

His gaze was too perceptive and she hurried back into speech. "Did you really cause that scene simply to add to your credibility?"

"Only partly." He lifted his brandy glass, swirling it gently. "I wondered why the hotel was so determined not to give him that particular set of rooms. They're empty."

Her eyes widened. "You saw the hotel's book."

"I glimpsed it."

"They must be expecting someone more valuable than Mr. and Mrs. Bradley."

"Even so, why not give the Bradleys those rooms and save the other vacant set for the future guest? Why make such a fuss?"

"I suppose you will tell me why."

"Perhaps because the room is set up in some way for that particular, important guest. And they are not sure exactly when he—or she—will arrive."

She regarded him. "Nothing is ever straightforward for you, is it?"

"Not when I know something is happening. Will you meet me again tomorrow?"

The change of subject threw her for an instant. As if he didn't already know what she was going to say.

Chapter Ten

DINNER WITH THE Tamars was undoubtedly a fun way to spend an evening. Louis would have found it so, even without the thrill of Anna's presence by his side. As it was, he rejoiced in her nearness while making the most of the company. Outside, the windows of the cozy dining room, snow began to fall and blow against the panes, adding a touch of magic to his contentment.

His plans, always, fluid, began to alter once more. Whoever Anna was, *whatever* she was, he could very easily make her part of those plans. If she would play. If he could convince her. If he could see this through to the end.

But he was making too many assumptions, running ahead of himself.

As he waited with his guests in the foyer for their carriage to be brought round, he placed Anna's cloak about her shoulders. She glanced up with a smile to thank him. He wondered yet again what it was about her that fascinated him. It was more than beauty, though undeniably that helped.

For a little, they stood together by the window, watching the snow in silence.

"What are you thinking about?" he asked, at last.

"You," she said, disconcertingly. Her gaze strayed to his face. "But then, you know that already, don't you?"

"I wish I did."

"You are still clutching Serena's cloak."

He accepted his dismissal with a twisted smile and walked over to the sofa where Serena and Tamar sat in quiet conversation. He came from behind them, and they obviously did not discern his approach, for he heard Serena murmur, "You know you should not encourage them, Rupert. It could so easily end in scandal."

"I'm not encouraging anything," Tamar protested. "Though I'll not deny he's good for her. He makes her..."

"What?" Serena asked.

"I don't know. Softer, happier. Normal."

It wasn't a conversation for his ears, so he swerved around the sofa at a wider angle to pretend he hadn't overheard them. "Your cloak, my lady," he said with a civil bow. "And your carriage, I believe."

But in the flurry of departures and farewells, he was only too aware of his triumph and the rapid beat of his heart. Almost like a boy approaching his first love with naive hopes and dreams. *Almost.* If Louis had ever been naive, it had been so long ago he couldn't remember it. With Anna, he had no illusions, only a drive to know more.

She gave him her hand as they parted, and her fingers clung to his just a little too long.

"Tomorrow," he murmured, and her face flushed adorably as she turned and hurried after Serena to the carriage. The snow had gone off for now but lay in wet white splodges on the road.

As the carriage pulled away, he found himself gazing across the road at the coffee house opposite. A few old soldiers and a couple of drunk youths sprawled in the window. And one man whom he knew very well indeed.

Gosselin.

And he was staring straight at Louis, his eyes wide, his jaw slack with shock.

Louis laughed aloud and gave him a mocking bow, before he turned and walked back into the hotel.

Discovery had always been inevitable. In fact, Louis welcomed the coming encounter. Gosselin needed to die. After he had given up what Louis needed to know.

He strode upstairs to his room and lit a few candles before he shrugged off his coat and threw it on the bed. The slim dagger was already in position in his stocking. He loaded the old pistol he had used playing the highwayman and sank into his favorite chair by the window.

Across the road, Gosselin still sat at the same seat in the coffee house. Louis settled in to wait.

It was well after midnight by the time Gosselin left. Louis's waning excitement surged back, but his enemy didn't even glance at the hotel, merely trudged through the freshly falling snow all the way up the high street until he turned off to the right, as if he were going home.

Louis would have thought Gosselin was avoiding him, if he hadn't taken so long to leave. As it was, perhaps he meant to double back.

After another hour, Louis grew tired of waiting. Rising, he shrugged into his greatcoat, put the pistol and a spare dagger in his pocket, and pulled on his boots.

The snow was still falling as he left the hotel and walked to Cliff View, every nerve alert for attack. There was none.

Even as he approached Gosselin's house, he knew his bird had flown. The house was in darkness. Of course, it could have been to lure him into a trap. Just in case it was, Louis walked around the back of the house and broke in through the kitchen window, as he had the last time. But the house felt empty, Louis only went through the motions of searching for his enemy. He knew he was wasting his time.

Eventually, he sat back on his heels by the dying kitchen stove and thought. Gosselin wanted him dead, for fear of what he might tell the British, or whoever ended with the power in France once Napoleon fell. That was a given. But it seemed he would not risk himself over the endeavor. Why? What was he about in Blackhaven that was so precious?

Gosselin had been watching the hotel from the coffee house, but he hadn't been watching Louis. It wasn't outside the realms of possibility that he was watching for whoever the Bradleys' rooms were being kept for. Someone secret, someone important. Surely someone

British.

So how was Gosselin even aware of him? No one knew better than Louis that the French had no spies close to the British government any more. Even the one they used to have had never been much help. But Gosselin must have found someone in the last few months, someone who was working with him, perhaps, providing him with moment-by-moment information. Someone, who could have arrived in Blackhaven recently and unexpectedly.

Anna had a bother-in-law who was a civil servant. She had arrived unannounced to visit her brother less than two weeks ago. It had crossed Louis's mind that she had come for him, but what if she had another task?

It didn't ring true to him. She didn't strike him as someone who would betray her country. But people did things for all sorts of reasons that made no sense to anyone else. She had secrets, motives she had never explained. He could not be sure of her, and he needed to be. He had no more time to woo her. He had to win her.

WITH THE HEALING of his wound, Louis seemed to be returning to his old habit of sleeping only a few hours in a night. Despite his busy evening, he woke early, Anna and the deliberately vacant hotel rooms jostling for attention in his mind.

He rose and dressed by the light of one candle, which he carried with him as he left the room, for the hotel was still in darkness. The only servants stirring at this hour would be in the kitchen. Louis walked quietly downstairs to the floor below, and along the passage to the corner rooms which Mr. Bradley had so coveted.

Skills learned from a Paris burglar before he was ten years old had been honed by years of collecting information people did not want to be discovered. Unlocking the door, with the aid of instruments adapted from scissors, tweezers, and a comb, was the work of moments.

He closed the door softly behind him and looked around. Several doors led off the main sitting room, to bedchambers. And in the sitting room, pride of place had been given to a large table in the middle of the floor. Six chairs surrounded it, and at each place had been set a neat sheaf of blank paper, an ink stand and several pens.

A room for work, not relaxation.

Louis swiftly checked the furniture in each room, but the desks, chests of drawers, wardrobes, and night stands were all empty, with no obvious space for any secret compartments.

He stood by the central table, frowning. The setting up of this room was a minor matter for a squad of well-trained servants, the work of minutes. There was nothing here to cause the kind of resistance offered to the Bradleys yesterday evening. These rooms could easily have been theirs, and the mirror set at the other end of the passage quickly prepared for the other guests.

Unless there was something he was not seeing. The secret was not in the furniture, so it had to be in the room itself. In the walls...

The sitting room walls were lined with wood paneling that made it quite difficult to make out the bedchamber doors in poor light. Louis went to the outside walls and peered closely, raising his candle to check every inch he could reach.

The tiny hole was almost invisible, like a dark spot in the grain of the wood, but it was enough clue for Louis, who began to push at the wood paneling around it until with a sudden click, a door opened inward.

Beyond was a dark, narrow passage that had to run between the walls. Louis entered. As he pulled the secret door closed behind him, he found a lever that obviously opened it from the passage side. He found the tiny hole which had first drawn his attention to the panel and put his eye to it. It gave him a fine view of the sitting room.

Turning, he followed the passage along to some roughly cut stairs leading downward, along another short passage and up a shorter set of stairs that came to a dead end.

But no, another wooden lever, similar to the one at the other end of the passage, only smaller, stuck out above his head. When he pulled it, a trap door unlocked, and Louis, suddenly, could smell horses.

Warily pushing up the trap door, he climbed out. He was in a stall of the hotel stables.

This was the reason those particular rooms were being reserved, presumably, at the hotel owner's discretion. The occupants would have a secret way out, if necessary. A way to avoid unwelcome visitors or even to spy on those one had invited.

Louis blew out his candle and left the stables. Dawn was breaking, and the stable boys would soon be out and about. It was time to walk up to Braithwaite woods and meet Anna.

The passage was an interesting discovery, but one he decided not to share with her yet. At least, not until he had discovered who she truly was. Not until she was won. Excitement stirred in the pit of his stomach. Oh yes, it was time.

ANNA WOKE THE following morning, full of both excitement and certainty. The way Louis had looked at her last night, the way he had just stood silently by her side as she gazed out of the window... He was ready to eat out of her hand. A kind word, a kiss, and she would win. She felt in her bones how close she was. The victory, as well as the prospect of the kiss, made her heart drum.

When she opened the curtains, the bright beauty of the land under snow added to her anticipation. Like a child, she wanted to go out and play in it, be the first to make her footprint in the pristine whiteness.

She dressed in the dark riding habit as usual, though as a concession to the cold, she donned a dark red military-style spencer under her cloak. She used only the hood of the cloak to cover her hair and sallied forth.

She could hear the sounds of servants moving around various parts of the castle, cleaning and setting fires, carrying water and preparing breakfast. She left by one of the quiet side doors and walked through the crisp snow, leaving a trail that would be easy for anyone who cared to follow. It didn't matter. By the time she returned, she expected her business to be completed. She would travel back to London with him...in separate vehicles, of course, but she could rely on him, surely, to go there just to meet her. If she promised enough.

The snow seemed to muffle all the usual sounds of early morning. All she could hear was the crunch of snow under her boots. Her breath streamed out in front of her.

As she entered the woods, a bird flapped above her, dislodging some snow from a tree branch that scattered over her head and shoulders. The woods looked different, the paths hidden, the trees white and silvery like some magical land in a fairytale.

Coming upon the fallen tree, she brushed a patch of snow off it with her gloves and sat there to wait for him.

What if he doesn't come, and I'm wrong about everything?

I'm not wrong. I'm not.

She could hear him, the faint crunch of snow, the rustle of brushed branches. At least she hoped it was him. Her fingers strayed to the stiletto, not in her gloves today but in a different pocket in the folds of her habit.

But it was Louis who wandered through the trees, moving easily and without hurry, as if he, too, was enjoying the first snow of the winter. He wore his gentleman's morning clothes, buff pantaloons and a blue coat beneath his open greatcoat. He carried his hat, and his dark blond hair had fallen forward over his forehead. He looked boyishly handsome, almost angelic—which he was not.

"Anna."

She stood, meaning to go to meet him as she had planned, but he increased his pace, catching her before she had taken more than a step, and taking both her hands. As she looked up at him, smiling, her hood fell back, barely covering her head at all. She thought it would make a charming image, and he appeared to agree.

"How beautiful you look in the snow," he said softly. He stood so close that his breath mingled with hers in the cold air. "My enemy, my ally."

Her heart thudded. *Now* was to be her moment. Not later in the hour, when she would have grown more used to his nearness. "I don't want to be your enemy, Louis," she whispered.

His fingers slid up to her wrists, gently caressing. "Then don't be. Trust me."

"I do trust you. I'm meeting you here, alone, am I not?" She shivered as his hands moved up to her shoulders, warm and heavy. But she felt no panic, only a thrill of anticipation.

"Why?" he asked. "Because you care for my wellbeing? Because you are drawn to me as I am to you?"

"Yes," she admitted. The truth was no longer so hard to say.

His arm went around her, pulling her against him, his palm flat against her back. His other hand caressed her arm, brushed against her waist. Everything about him was hard, strong, and yet it was his gentleness that beguiled her.

"What shall we do, Anna?" he murmured, inhaling the scent of her hair. "Is there a way forward for you and me? Together?"

"Yes," she whispered. "There has to be. Louis—"

Too late, she felt the soft play of his fingers dip suddenly into the folds of her gown, not in a bold caress, but to withdraw the stiletto from its hiding place. She made one instinctive move to snatch it from him, and then was still, for his expression had not changed. Neither his face nor his voice threatened her. And yet for the first time, he did not veil the fierce intelligence in his eyes. Her stomach dived with sudden fear.

"Did you come to kill me, Anna?" he asked evenly.

She shook her head, blindly. He'd always known about the weapon, watched the movement of her hands whenever she felt unsure or threatened.

"I needed to protect myself," she whispered, raising her face closer to his. She didn't know if she was fighting now for his trust or for her own life. "You must understand that. I need to protect *us*. Louis, tell me everything. We have to go now to safety, to save you and to end the war. Nothing else matters."

"Do you believe you and I can do such things?" he asked.

"If we save *you*, it is a start. I feel it." Her heart pounded. Their lips were so close she could taste his breath—coffee and a faint, fresh tang of herbs. "We can be together, Louis. Kiss me and you will know. Kiss me and come with me. It is the only way for us."

His hand slid into her hair, pushing the hood aside to cup the back of her head. "There is another way. I will not argue the kiss, but trust must begin with you. *You* must tell the truth."

His eyes were warm, his breath unsteady. Whatever was happening to her, she was still winning. She could agree to anything. One kiss would reel him in completely.

"I have always told you the truth," she whispered. "You will see."

His lips quirked and he angled his head, closing the last hairsbreadth between them. His mouth covered hers and parted her lips. Wonder, not panic, filled her, for this was gentle, too, his lips moving on hers in a soft, sensual caress. And then his mouth clung and sank into hers, and she gasped in shock as waves of emotion flooded her, battering her like a stormy sea.

There was no escaping it, for his hand behind her head held her steady. His other arm crushed her to his body as the stiletto fell into the snow, and the kiss went on and on, a tender tangle of lips and tongues, blinding, terrifying in its sweetness, utterly overpowering her.

For a long, long, moment, she didn't even know she had lost, so overcome was she by this new pleasure. And then she knew. She understood the feeling at last.

She cared. And she could not hurt someone she cared for. Worse, she knew she had betrayed the fact with her devastated lips, as surely as if they had spoken the words.

A tear squeezed out the corner of her eye and trickled down her cheek.

One kiss and everything changed. It bound her, defeated her, and now only the truth would do.

His fingers caressed her throat and cupped her cheek as slowly, gradually, he detached his mouth from hers. "Who are you, Anna?" he said huskily.

"I'm Anna Gaunt," she whispered. "And my brother-in-law, Henry Harcourt, sent me to help you escape the fort. You did that without me…"

"And what exactly is Henry Harcourt?"

"He has a position at the foreign office, is building himself a unique career in finding information no one else can. I help him."

"Does he pay you?"

"When he can. I do it for fun, mostly."

"I hope I am the most fun."

A laugh that was more like a sob broke from her. "You are the most of everything. I've failed and I don't even care."

To her surprise, his head dipped and he kissed her again, when there was no need, when she was already won. Daringly, because she would never have another chance, her hand crept up to touch his cheek.

"It's gone beyond success and failure, winning and losing," he said against her lips. "Who is Banion?"

She drew back, frowning. "*Banion?* What has he to do with anything?"

He smiled, and she knew she had said something that pleased him. "Something more important than our little game is happening here, something I suspect threatens both our countries. Banion is Gosselin, my enemy and yours." The smile faded as he touched her cheek. "Why so stricken, Anna? Do you care for him, after all?"

She blinked. "Banion? I barely noticed him. You suspected me, used me all along." *I thought you liked me. I thought you were different.*

"I have been doing this a long time," he said. "Too long."

"Doing what?" she asked. Stupidly, she felt like weeping. She, who never wept.

"Asking questions, listening, learning, playing so many roles that there is no longer any difference between them and me. They are all part of me. I cannot even wish to be different any more, and I certainly don't wish you to be." He bent, brushing his cool lips against hers. "You are magnificent, Anna Gaunt, and I wish you were mine."

She pushed him away. "Who is pretending compassion now?" she snapped. "I do not need it. And I can still have you arrested."

"But you won't," he said with so much certainty that her fist clenched. "Because, like me, you have to know how this ends."

Her brow twitched. "This? Do you mean Banion? Or you and I?"

"All of it."

She drew in a shuddering breath. She felt as if the earth she stood on was sinking, that all the foundations she had so carefully built for her life, had crumbled. Because of him. And yet, he had not hurt her, had not taken her information and run, safe in the knowledge that she would not betray him. He had not even taken advantage, beyond the kiss she had offered, and those she had allowed for reasons she couldn't fathom save for the fact that they were sweet and thrilling. And she had always craved thrills. She had just never found them in a man before.

"You're cold," he said, pulling her cloak more closely around her. He bent and retrieved the fallen stiletto and unerringly returned it to the pocket in her habit. A smile twisted his lips. "*Madam, will you walk? Madam, will you talk with me?*"

Chapter Eleven

A BEAM OF pale sunshine filtered through the trees. The whiteness seemed to fold them into their own isolated world.

"Did you know?" she asked. "Did you know all you had to do was kiss me?"

"All? I would like to do a great deal more. But if you had not invited me, I doubt I would have gone even that far."

"You said we could be friends," she recalled. "But...you do not like me in *that* way?"

He looked startled. "Oh, I like you in every conceivable way there is. It was not *my* preference that concerned me but yours."

"I thought you knew I liked you." Somewhere, she couldn't quite believe she was having this conversation.

He shrugged. "I knew you were not indifferent. I am observant... And I confess I felt your pulse to see if your reaction was genuine. For at other times, you avoid me and flinch."

Warm blood seeped into her cold face. "I do not like to be touched."

"Which made it hard to seduce you."

"I am still not seduced," she said hastily.

His eyes laughed though his voice was grave. "Quite right," he said outrageously. "It gives me something to aim for."

"And allows me another chance to win," she suggested, and this time he laughed out loud, and lifted her fingers to his lips.

"I look forward to that... You do not flinch anymore."

"I am used to you," she said at once.

The smile in his eyes began to fade and she looked away.

"Did something happen to you, Anna?"

"To me...to all of us, through me." She turned suddenly, hitting him in the chest with her clenched fist. "Stop it!"

He caught her hand and held it there. "Stop what?"

She could not look at him. "Stop...*working* on me. I will not tell you this."

Beneath her hand, his heart beat strongly, steadily. "You need tell me nothing. But there is no *working* with you, Anna."

Slowly, she raised her eyes to his face. "Why not?"

"Because we are not objects, machines to be switched off and on. And I care for you."

Almost unable to help it, she let her cheek fall against his chest. His arms came around her and held her.

"You have not lost, Anna," he whispered into her hair. "God help me, I have not won unless—" He broke off on a hiss of laughter. "But there, there are some things a man like me cannot win from a marquis's daughter."

She understood what he meant. She had been around men enough, flirted with them enough, to know. But the disgust that normally came with such recognition seemed to be absent. It did not *fit* him.

Her arms lifted, tentatively embracing him. "A man like you is not the problem," she said into his coat. "A woman like me, is. And I do not mean my family's rank." Her fingers curled in the hair at the back of his neck. "I cannot give you what you want."

Instead of stepping away, his arms tightened. She should have felt threatened, but she didn't. She felt...safe.

"And yet," she said with something like awe, "And yet, I confess I am...curious."

She felt the stretch of his lips against her hair as he smiled. "Let us settle for curious," he said. "For now."

In a little, they walked on again. Anna did not feel at all as if she was with a dangerous French spy who had just extracted from her the admission of her work for Henry and the Foreign Office, to say nothing of the more personal. She felt as if she were walking in the snowy woods with her lover, her suitor. Which was ridiculous in so many ways it was laughable. And yet, it was undeniably blissful.

He said, "Someone is coming to Blackhaven. Someone important is coming secretly to the hotel. I got into the reserved rooms. The bedchambers are all made up, and the sitting room is set with a table and lots of blank paper and pens. More than that, it is my belief someone is also going to Roseley, where your friend, Mrs. Alban—"

"Mrs. Lamont," Anna corrected. "Alban is her husband's Christian name."

"Mrs. Lamont," he allowed, "seems to be preparing for an important visit, too. I think Gosselin is here for that meeting—to protect it, to disrupt it, I don't know which. I do know it's more important to him right now than I am."

"We could have him arrested," Anna suggested. "I'm sure it would be easy enough to convince Mr. Winslow."

"Or I could kill him," Louis said brutally. "Either way, it would stop him. Only..."

"Only what?"

"What if he is doing something *right*? What if stopping him is the wrong thing to do?"

Anna stared at him. "Are you and I likely to agree on the right and wrong?"

"No," he admitted. "But it would help both of us to know. Can you find out from your brother-in-law who is meeting in Blackhaven?"

This, of course, was what he needed to know. Perhaps she should have been hurt, but the boundaries between the personal and the professional had become so blurred that she simply accepted that they both needed the answer to his question.

"Henry doesn't know anything about it," she said impatiently. "Even if the meeting had been arranged after I left, he would have found a way to tell me if he knew it. But...Henry is only *building* his empire. He does not yet hold a senior post. And if this meeting is as important as you think, and as secret as you think, then it could easily happen without his knowledge."

"Damn."

"You saw the hotel book," Anna reminded him. "Was there no name for the rooms they're keeping?"

Louis grimaced. "Mr. Smith."

"How unimaginative." She glanced at him. "*Could* it be a real name?"

"Of course. But there are too many other coincidences. Every instinct tells me this is no mere Mr. Smith."

"We have to be discreet," Anna said. "If we draw attention to this, we risk ruining something...for Britain or for France. And yet we cannot do nothing if your evil Gosselin is involved." She regarded him thoughtfully. "Why do you hate Gosselin?"

"Like yours, that story must wait for another day. Someone is coming too close. I must flee before your brother calls me out."

"He is not so straight-laced. It's my belief he and Serena used to have assignations here, too."

"Perhaps. But he would not permit anyone to hurt you."

It was true, though she wasn't sure how Louis knew it.

"Au revoir," he said, tilting up her chin. He swooped and kissed her mouth. Desire unfurled deep inside her, novel and yet increasingly recognizable. Oh, yes, she was curious.

"But this is insane," she whispered against his mouth. "We are still enemies."

"No. Our countries might be. Not you and I."

And then he was gone, striding off through the snow, and she realized she was cold. And yet happier than she could ever remember. Because she cared. Because her enemy did.

LATER, OF COURSE, without the thrill of his oddly spellbinding presence, she castigated herself for a gullible fool. There had been no reason to tell him what she did for Henry, just because he had kissed her and she had found she was not so cold as she'd always thought.... Very well, that she cared. That his kiss shattered her. How could she have built a simple kiss into an event that meant she won or lost?

Her pride writhed inside her, while her brain tried to make sense of the information they had exchanged. And in truth, as she had admitted, she had very little information to give. Henry Harcourt was a small if clever fish in a pond of large, important ones. And that is what saved her pride in the end. If he still sought her out, knowing all that, then she was right to believe he cared for her. Was she not?

With her head spinning and her mood fluctuating between despair and wild elation, she almost didn't catch Tamar's words to her in the library that afternoon.

Eventually, she glanced around from the window to find him gazing at her with a tolerant kind of frustration.

"I beg your pardon," she said mechanically. "Did you speak to me?"

"I asked if you were not primping for tonight's ball."

She frowned. "But the assembly ball is on...oh. Tonight."

This was the regular assembly room subscription ball for the quality of Blackhaven and its environs, as distinct from the invitation-only masquerade which had been sponsored by Mrs. Winslow and Mrs. Grant.

"You don't sound happy about it," her brother observed. "You haven't quarreled with Lewis, have you?"

"Not exactly... I mean no, of course I have not."

"You do seem very preoccupied." Tamar threw himself into the chair beside her and sprawled, hooking one leg over the chair arm.

She said, "I do not like...not being in control."

"I know."

She swallowed. "I want him gone from my life."

"And if he goes?" Tamar asked.

"I will die." A laugh that was almost a sob forced its way out. "Does that make me insane, finally?"

Tamar gave a twisted smile. "No. It makes you normal. Or as normal as a person can be in love."

"Love?" she repeated with revulsion.

Tamar laughed, and unwound himself from the chair. "Exactly." And sauntered out looking far more amused then concerned.

GOSSELIN HAD NOT left Blackhaven. Instead, he had taken a small and insalubrious room at the local tavern. Such accommodation suited neither his dignity nor his personal tastes, but he could no longer stay in the pleasant house on Cliff View. Louis Delon would find it too easily. At the tavern, at least, he could blend with the scum who frequented it, and who turned out to be beneficial since he was able to hire a slippery villain to find out who the devil Delon was pretending to be.

Gosselin had to admire Delon's gall. To have escaped his prison and not only survived his injury but placed himself in the Blackhaven Hotel, right in the heart of the town's society, was impressive. Not only that, but he'd clearly made friends with the most important family in the neighborhood, for he had been standing on the hotel step, waving off Lord and Lady Tamar. And the beautiful Lady Anna, who stirred Gosselin's blood.

Not that Gosselin would do anything about the latter, of course. His pursuit of Lady Anna was largely to provide himself with an innocuous reason to stay so long in Blackhaven, but her beauty, nevertheless, disturbed his sleep. Whenever they were in the same room, she drew him like a magnet. And if he was truthful, part of his irritation at discovering Colonel Delon was that he had clearly been in her company, a more favored suitor than he.

But, of course, the more important question was, what the devil was Delon doing here? Was he just hiding where no one would expect him to be, until he could slip away? He could not return to France without being arrested. Gosselin and Fouché had seen to that...

Or did he guess why Gosselin was in Blackhaven? That possibility troubled Gosselin most, although he could not see how Delon could have learned anything like this from prison.

The other possibility was that Delon had recognized him earlier and stayed to kill him when opportunity rose. Gosselin had no intention of giving him that chance but all the same, his flesh crawled at the idea of Delon of all people observing and following him for days.

He would have to kill Delon first. Unfortunately, he could not just walk up and shoot the cur, or he would be locked up and unable to carry out his important task. Even provoking a duel would land him in trouble he could not afford. Nor did he rate highly his chances of breaking in to Delon's hotel rooms and strangling him in his sleep. The rumor may have been that the escaping prisoner had been shot, but he didn't look seriously weakened to Gosselin.

No, the best solution to the problem would be if Delon were simply put back in prison.

Gosselin, washed and shaved, pulled his trunk from under the rickety tavern bed, and drew out his black satin knee breaches and black evening coat. Once dressed with his usual care, he donned the disreputable hat and muffler and the dirty old greatcoat before leaving the tavern. In his tatty satchel, he carried a better overcoat. He had learned a lot from Delon over the years.

The night was bitter, freezing a harder crust over the snow that lay on the ground. Having slouched around the harbor for a little, looking for any ships anchored close by, Gosselin ambled down to the beach, and walked along to Blackhaven Cove, where, with relief, he tore off the smelly coat and hat, swapping them for the coat in his bag, where he stuffed his disreputable clothes instead, and hid them in the mouth of a cave. The soldiers were still watching further up the coast, so as far as Gosselin could tell, he was unobserved.

He walked quickly up the path, past his old house in Cliff View and on to High Street and the assembly rooms, where he would plead for a dance with the fascinating Lady Anna. At the masquerade ball, she had strung her admirers along by refusing to dance with any of them—

including himself—but he had later seen her waltzing in the arms of a man in black. Gosselin hoped to be the favored partner this evening.

He also hoped to find Colonel Delon in attendance.

Almost as soon as he walked into the ballroom, he saw Anna holding court, drawing more attention than the dancers.

Not for the first time, he wondered what it was that drew men to her. It was certainly not her fortune, because apparently, she had none. Which probably explained why she was still unmarried in her twenties. And why she appeared to be wearing the same silver-grey gown she'd worn at the masquerade. She did not make play with her fan, or flirt in other ways. And yet she talked and laughed with utter confidence...and supreme indifference. It was as if she tolerated her admirers only for amusing conversation, while retaining her own air of mystery. Even being laughed at or ignored only seemed to inspire her admirers to try harder.

Well, he would not join the throng and become one of the many. The apparently favored "Sir Lytton" was not in attendance either, so perhaps he was employing the same strategy. Gosselin would be happy to steal a woman from under his enemy's nose if opportunity arose. Not that the cold-hearted cur would care.

There was no sign of the cur in the ballroom or the card room. Gosselin was disappointed, for Winslow the magistrate was present, as were several army officers. It would have been a good time to have him arrested, while Gosselin himself could play the hero. He would have every opportunity to monopolize Lady Anna then.

While he waited for Anna to grow bored with her current crop of admirers, Gosselin made himself agreeable to other pretty women instead. It was no hardship. For a small town on the edge of England, in the middle of nowhere, Blackhaven seemed to boast a high number of beautiful and charming females, married and otherwise. When he had first come here, he had expected most of the women to be ageing and sickly, visiting Blackhaven only for their health. That this was not so, had been a pleasant surprise.

When Anna finally stood and walked away, shedding her admirers like a puppy casting its coat, Gosselin was ready for her. Snatching up two glasses of champagne from a passing waiter, he tracked her across the room, halting when she paused to speak a few words to people on her way. Her eyes strayed to the entrance more than once. So did Gosselin's. He wondered if they were looking for the same man.

When she moved on again, Gosselin stepped out from behind his pillar and presented her with one of his glasses. She halted, her eyes widening with just a hint of startlement.

"Lady Anna," he greeted her with a slight bow. "I took the liberty of bringing you this—before you sent me away to fetch it."

"Mr. Banion."

He couldn't help being gratified that she remembered his name. Or at least his alias.

After an instant's hesitation, she accepted the glass. "How very observant of you."

"It is something I cannot help, when in the same room as you."

She regarded him without either gratification or timidity and took a sip of her champagne. "Then you will know how much flattery bores me."

"Not flattery," he insisted. "Simple honesty. And the desire to secure the waltz with you."

"Thank you, sir, but I do not dance."

"Yes, you do. I saw you at the masquerade."

She waved that aside with one elegantly gloved hand. "A single occasion—with an impudent fellow. Tonight, I do not dance."

"Not even with another impudent fellow?"

"Especially not."

He hid his disappointment, though he did not give up. "Then you will take a turn about the ballroom with me?"

She met his gaze, speculation in her own, "Very well," she agreed, beginning to walk. "Are you a native of Blackhaven, Mr. Banion?"

Piqued that she had not even troubled to discover that much about him, he replied, "No, alas. I arrived only a few weeks ago, hoping to benefit from the waters."

"Then you have not been well?"

He wrinkled his nose with what he hoped was charming self-deprecation. "A nasty bout of the measles, my lady. Which I know full well is neither manly nor romantic."

She laughed. "I don't believe any illness is! And have you not found the waters beneficial?"

"I believe I have. But there is more than water to keep me."

She changed the subject, as most modestly brought up young women would have, but she did not abandon him. On the contrary, he found himself telling her about his life in Blackhaven and interspersing that with anecdotes from his real life. To all of this, she listened with flattering attention, laughing where appropriate and asking questions to encourage him.

Once she stopped to speak to a gratified young couple who were just returning from the dance floor and introduced them to him as Mr. and Mrs. Bradley. "Although you may know each other already," she added, "since you must both stay at the hotel."

"No, we have never met," Mr. Bradley assured her. "Which room do you have, sir?"

"Oh, I don't put up at the hotel," Gosselin said easily. "I took a house on Cliff View."

"Quite right," Anna said. "I believe the hotel is horrendously expensive for a long stay. I suppose the tavern is cheaper."

So much so that it almost reconciles one to the odor of stale beer and fishy humanity. Even to the prospect of having one's pocket picked on the way out the door. Lulled by Anna's interest, and eager to impress her with his wit and knowledge, he almost blurted the words aloud, all in the hope of winning a smile from her.

"But hardly recommended," he managed, before he saw that Anna was no longer listening. Following her gaze to the entrance, he saw Colonel Delon.

"Sir Lytton Lewis," the major domo announced.

Gosselin's chest tightened. He excelled in intrigue not in physical danger, and despite his intention of confronting his enemy in public, his courage almost failed at the sight of him. After all, Delon had every reason to want Gosselin dead, too, and had considerably more personal skill and experience in such matters.

Gosselin tried to prepare himself for the imminent meeting, but to his surprise, Anna turned and walked the other way with a mere, "Excuse me," to the Bradleys. Since she didn't forbid his presence, he hastily caught up with her.

"And you, my lady," he said pleasantly. "How long do you stay in Blackhaven?"

"I cannot tell. Serena has invited me to stay for Christmas, and I probably shall, now that the weather has turned. I should not care to travel post haste into a snow drift!"

"Indeed not." Just ahead, Mr. and Mrs. Winslow were delivering up their daughter to a young man for the next dance.

It did not take much to steer Anna in their direction. In fact, he did not even need to draw attention to them by greeting them, for Anna was already saying. "Good evening, Mrs. Winslow. Mr. Winslow."

Now, he had the perfect witness for his accusation. There was even an army officer in a smart red uniform close-by. Annoyingly, however, Delon seemed in no hurry to pursue Anna. Nor did she summon him with so much as a look. It began to dawn on Gosselin that Delon was no longer the favored suitor, and in spite of the difficulties it created now for his own plan, he couldn't help being maliciously glad. Perhaps he could even seduce Anna and make sure Delon knew before he died in that English prison…

However, this pleasant daydream was interrupted by the reforming of Anna's court around her now that she stood still once more. Gosselin had to use his elbows to avoid losing his place at her side.

Then, to his annoyance, Delon finally approached, and the young men around Anna seemed to part for him, allowing him immediate access. It was little consolation that Anna clearly saw and ignored the movement. She certainly did not greet the newcomer.

Emboldened, Gosselin raised his voice and addressed the army officer who, with his friends, appeared to have joined the outer fringes of Anna's court.

"Sir, does not this fellow look familiar to you?"

The officer, nudged into awareness, glanced at Gosselin in surprise. "What fellow?"

Gosselin pointed dramatically at Delon. "*That* fellow!"

"Well, yes, he's Sir Lytton Lewis," the officer said easily.

"He's not Sir Anything," Gosselin said scornfully. "Look beneath the speech and the smart clothes! Is he not your escaped prisoner?"

The group around them quieted at last with a hint of unease. Until Delon laughed. "Banion," he said affectionately. "You will have me hanged one of these days."

"Oh, I hope so! Well sir?" Gosselin snapped at the officer, who looked at him as though he were mad. "Is he not the Frenchman?"

"How would I know?" the officer demanded, uncertain whether or not to be amused. "I was never in the fort."

It was a blow. Gosselin had assumed all the soldiers around Blackhaven were part of the same regiment and shared the same duties.

"Neither was I," Delon lied easily. "Let us go together Banion and be done."

But if he thought to threaten Gosselin, he landed wide off the mark.

Gosselin did not smile. He looked from the officer to the bewildered Mr. Winslow and back. "Believe me, if you do not arrest this man now, and return him to the fort, you are going to look very foolish indeed."

Chapter Twelve

IN THAT INSTANT, Louis saw that Gosselin had his listeners. He doubted anyone would arrest him on the spot, but awkward questions would now, surely, be asked.

Under the suddenly tense observation of the Winslows and Anna's sea of admirers, Louis met his enemy's gaze with a tolerant amusement he did not feel, while he tried to decide on the best way to deal with the situation.

And then Anna's laughter broke across them. "Mr. Banion," she scolded. "What a tease, you are! You almost had me believing you. Had not the Braithwaites' governess—who you must know has been more than once in Sir Lytton's company!—already identified a quite different man!"

In the general, somewhat bewildered laughter, she actually took Gosselin's arm and began to walk with him. "I suppose you must be very old friends with Sir Lytton," she confided, "to play such a joke on him."

"Very, very old," Louis murmured as his enemy all but brushed against him. Gosselin seemed as bewildered by his companion as by the sudden vanishing of his dangerous accusation. But Gosselin and his little trick no longer concerned Louis. What worried him was that Anna had not so much as glanced at him since he had entered the ballroom.

Even now, even through the fraught moment of Gosselin's accusation, Louis's body still hummed from the excitement of holding her in his arms this morning. Her surrender had elated him, her untutored, instinctive response to his kisses had thrilled him. Her wonder and confusion were so at odds with her usual bold confidence that she only fascinated him all the more.

Nor could he doubt that she had found that first kiss as shattering as he had. She would not otherwise have spilled out the truth. The naivety of that moved him. For the rest of the day, even as he'd continued tracking Gosselin, and making his own arrangements, she had been there in all his thoughts. And although he had followed Gosselin here, he would have come anyway, just on the off-chance of seeing Anna again.

And there she was, having turned a dangerous moment for him into a mere jest. And she was all the more convincing for wandering off with Gosselin. Even though it made Louis's blood boil with fury and fear for her.

Keeping her discreetly in view, he stayed with the Winslows for a little longer, discussing the Bradleys' run-in with the highwayman which, Winslow said, was so like Sir Lytton's own experience that it had to be the same man.

Louis nodded sagely. "But there has been no further sign of him?"

"Nothing around here or over the border. Someone did try to hold up the Edinburgh mail but the coach never stopped and the driver said the assailant appeared to be drunk. I doubt it was the same man."

"Well, providing he has stopped, I find I bear him no ill will," Louis confided. "Since I would not otherwise have come to Blackhaven."

Anna quickly abandoned "Banion" and was seen next with two young army officers. She did not dance but flitted like some restless butterfly from place to place, never gravitating closer to Louis.

Louis gave her time, by dancing with the Winslows' daughter. After that, he hunted her down, for he would not lose her.

The thought sparked a deep twinge of unease. He would not lose her? He could not keep her, even if he won her. Neither his choice nor hers mattered when they were enemies, when the French and the British both wanted him dead. And despite all the plans he formulated, he wasn't sure he could ever abandon France to its fate. Even for her.

At this moment, though, he needed to convince Anna that this morning's encounter had come from genuine feeling. Dear God, how could it not?

She saw him coming, of course, and retreated further away. But in this part of the ballroom, closest to the door, it seemed she had no acquaintances to protect her. So, refusing to be cornered, she simply walked out.

He was in time to see the train of her gown vanish into the ladies' cloakroom. Although he could think of no reason why she would go outside, just to be sure, he lounged near the ballroom entrance, from where he could see the cloakroom door.

She emerged a couple of minutes later and walked back toward the ballroom. She entered briskly, heading directly for Serena and the vicar's wife who sat together enjoying what looked like a comfortable gossip.

Louis fell into casual step with her. "You are avoiding me," he said pleasantly.

"Can you blame me?" she said at once. "Who wants to be seen with the French spy?"

"Thank you for that. I foresee a great future for your bother-in-law with you behind him."

"So do I," she said cordially. "Did you want something before I continue to avoid you?"

"Many things," he replied at once. "But I would settle for five minutes of your time." He let his fingers brush against hers and she snatched her hand back as though using it to adjust her other glove. He let it go for now. Other matters were more urgent. "You defended me," he pointed out, low-voiced. "You must be on your guard against him, now."

"I am always on my guard."

"I know."

At last, she looked at him, a quick, darting glance. "Then what did you really wish to say?"

"What I just did," he said firmly. "And also, to entice you into the alcove to our left."

This time, she met his gaze properly, challenging him. "Why?"

"I want to kiss you," he said softly.

Color seeped into her face. "Why?" she repeated.

"I liked it the last time and I want more."

"Don't be silly. We both had parts to play."

It was her means of self-defense. He understood but could not let it stand. He could not allow her believe that he used her, that such was all she would ever know. With a low growl of irritation, he cast a quick look around and, grasping her fingers, whisked her into the alcove and let the curtain fall behind them.

Giving her no time, he snatched her into his arms and crushed her mouth under his. There was an instant's resistance and then she just let him kiss her. It was delicious, heady, but not enough. He needed her response, that instinctive, fiery passion he'd tasted this morning. And so, he coaxed her, caressing and opening her lips wider, exploring her mouth while he stroked her smooth, elegant neck and the pulse that beat at its base.

With a gasp, she seized the hair at the back of his head, but not to pull him off her, to drag him nearer while she kissed him back at last. His soft groan was more relief than triumph.

"There are no *roles* here, Anna," he whispered. "I want you and I won't pretend otherwise."

Her fingers fluttered against his cheek, his lips. "I can't give you that, Louis."

"And perhaps I wouldn't take it if you did," he said at once. "That doesn't mean we can't enjoy the persuasion."

Laughter caught in her throat, and he released her, though only to take her hand and peel back her glove to press a kiss on the inside of her wrist and another on her bare arm.

"You had better go before we are discovered," he said. "If we are careful, we can steal many such interludes."

The risk appealed to her, as he had known it would. Her eyes gleamed with it. And there was definite desire in her quickened breath, the faint, sensual tremble of her lips. She made his heart ache.

Then she simply smiled and walked away from him into the noise of the ballroom.

HER LIPS STILL tingling from his kiss, her heart curiously light, Anna stepped back into the blazing light of the ballroom and moved immediately away from the alcove. The only gaze she encountered was Banion's. Gosselin's. She didn't care. He must already suspect some collusion between them and romantic intrigue would make it seem less dangerous to his plans. Whatever they were.

"You are playing with fire," Serena murmured at her side.

"And I thought I was being so discreet."

"In Blackhaven, there is no such thing as discretion. Everyone else knows your business before you do."

"I would be surprised," Anna muttered. "I hope you are not meaning to turn into a *strict* chaperone."

"I doubt that would achieve anything."

"It wouldn't."

"But you will take care?" Serena said anxiously.

Anna looked at her with as much surprise as curiosity. "You are worried about *me*."

"Who else would I worry about? *Him?*" She twitched her head in the direction of the alcove.

"Probably," Anna said ruefully. But secretly, she was touched by her sister-in-law's concern. She had imagined at first that it was only about the reputation of her family, but for some reason, Serena seemed actually to care about her. The thought came to her that Serena was her friend, which was yet another novelty. Anna had never had a friend before. Except Christianne, who was like part of herself. Or Rupert, when they remembered each other's existence.

The rest of the evening flew by for her, and she discovered that Louis was right. Their intrigue was fun. He sat beside her at supper, and while he spoke to Serena, he held Anna's hand beneath the table cloth. She did not jump when his fingers brushed and curled around hers, although she worried someone might notice the heightened color in her cheeks. Her skin tingled beneath the caress of his thumb.

She allowed it only for a few moments before withdrawing her hand to eat. On other occasions, his leg brushed against hers, and she knew that was deliberate, too. It did not appall her. It excited her.

"I think our friend has left," she murmured once, in an attempt to make things more normal, at least normal by her own and Louis's standards.

"He has," Louis agreed.

"Should you not have followed him to find out where he stays?"

"He's at the tavern. I searched his room before I arrived. There is nothing new."

"You leave no stone unturned, do you?"

"Not if I can help it."

For Anna, the departure of their quarry made the passages with Louis much more intimate. She was more than his tool, or his means of watching his enemy.

When, during the after-supper dance, Tamar decided he had had enough and wished to go home, Anna almost refused. But they were no longer children running wild around the countryside. Staying at the ball alone would not be tolerated by society, and that did not at the moment suit her.

Clandestine meetings would not be tolerated either, of course, which was at least part of their thrill. She did not at once accompany Serena to the cloakroom, since she was in the midst of a group of men who had all asked her to dance and been refused. While finishing her laughing conversation with them, she was searching the ballroom for Louis.

Failing to find him, she abandoned her admirers and left the ball-room with a faint sense of pique. Two women were entering the cloakroom as she crossed the foyer which was, otherwise, quite empty. Or at least, she thought it was until the door to one of the rooms on the left, opened and Louis stood there.

Her heart soared. A swift glance told her she was unseen, and then she simply ran to him in a rustle of skirts and laughing breath. He seized her, even as he closed the door behind her. In the darkness, his lips found hers.

She flung her arms around his neck, sliding her fingers into his hair. When the kiss broke, she pressed her cheek to his.

"You did not dance with me," she said, low.

"You do not dance with anyone else. People would talk."

Laughter erupted. "Really, Louis? Are you saving my reputation?"

"It's a fine line." He pressed little kisses down her ear to her neck and shoulder, where his lips clung to the line of her clavicle and paused. She felt the heave of his breath and then he straightened. "Tomorrow."

He released her. She heard the click of the door re-opening and light from the foyer drifted in. In the dimness and shadows, he was a stranger, her enemy. In was still true, though she had never felt it to be so wrong.

"It's clear," he murmured.

Because she couldn't help it, she reached up to touch his rough cheek, trailing her fingertips over his parted lips as she slipped past him and out into the foyer.

"WERE YOU ORDERED to kill me?" Louis asked casually.

It was early morning in the white-covered woodland by Braithwaite Castle. As they walked, Louis had again withdrawn the stiletto from its sheath in her habit and was examining the blade's point.

"Not unless I had to," Anna replied. "By preference, I was to persuade you to change sides and tell me—or Henry—everything you knew. If I couldn't, if you wouldn't..."

"Then you were to kill me to prevent me returning to the French ith what I'd discovered about Britain?"

"It was mentioned," Anna acknowledged. "I agreed I would use my judgement. I wasn't convinced you could have learned anything very useful rotting in a prison in the back of beyond."

He regarded her curiously over the top of the stiletto. "The prospect of such a task did not daunt you?"

"If your enemy is not human, he is easy to kill."

A frown tugged down his brow, though his eyes remained steady, un-accusing. "How can you have learned such a thing? How many enemies have you killed?"

"None, so far as I know. Though I certainly wounded a couple of thieves who attacked me in London." She lifted her chin. "Do you find me unnatural, unwomanly?"

"I find you disturbing and magnificent. You have a brave heart."

Her smile was twisted. "I have no heart at all."

He stopped and pushed his hand inside her cloak, placing his palm flat between her breasts. "Then what is it that beats for me?"

She stared at him, for the first time genuinely afraid. "Don't make me *weak*," she whispered.

Something in his face changed. For a moment, she thought he reflected her own fear. But then, it might have been pity or simple longing.

He said, "If we don't feel, it isn't *for* anything. I feel for you. I care for you."

She swallowed. Her heart seemed to slam against her ribs, against his hand. "And I for you," she whispered.

His hand moved lightly, caressingly over her breast as he bent his head and kissed her mouth.

PARTING FROM ANNA that morning was a wrench. This was more than caring. It was closer to obsession. And that was dangerous for both of them. To Louis, no problem was ever insurmountable in the long run, and he could hatch a hundred future plots to bring Anna and himself together. The trouble was, that in the immediate, even if he discovered Gosselin's plot, and killed him, he was still a discarded French spy with too much knowledge in his head, trapped in England with no friends or means of support. Or even protection beyond his own wits and his weakened physical strength.

Only his long-honed instincts made him aware of someone approaching through the woods. One man. He was prepared to meet Gosselin or any bravo hired by him. In fact, on the whole he wanted that, to learn what he could, even if he would not yet kill him. And so, he kept walking as if he had every right to be there, alert and poised for whatever action was necessary.

But the man who met him at the fork in the track was none other than Lord Tamar.

"I thought it was you," the marquis said, amiably enough. "Assignation with my sister?"

"Would you knock me down if I said yes?"

"I didn't knock you down for manhandling her at the masquerade, so possibly not. Though I reserve the right." He reached up, breaking a bare twig off the tree beside him. "I'm not used to this," he said disarmingly. "But I suppose I should ask you what your intentions are."

Louis's lips twisted. "I wish I knew."

It was probably not the answer Tamar expected. He threw the twig on the ground. "I won't let you hurt her. And if I can't stop that, I promise I'll beat you to a pulp."

"Because she has been hurt already?"

Tamar gave him a clear look. "Is that what holds you back? You fear she is not...pure?"

"Jesus Christ, no." Louis dragged his hand through his hair. "Such things do not weigh..." He dropped his hand and met Tamar's gaze. "What happened to her?"

Tamar searched his eyes, then said shortly, "She was assaulted when she was fourteen years old."

Louis had guessed, yet it still hurt to hear. His fists clenched and unclenched. "By the man in your picture?"

"By his brother, but there is an association for her. They were bailiffs, dunning us for money my uncle owed since they could not touch me or my late father. He caught my sisters alone." Tamar swung away from him, tight-lipped. "Anna bore the brunt of it."

"What happened to him?" Louis ground out. *Where can I find him?*

"I killed him," Tamar said simply.

Louis nodded once, forcing himself to breathe.

"But the damage was done," Tamar said. "The twins clung all the closer to each other. Christianne grew dependent, and Anna grew protective. And hard. For years, she could not bear to be touched. She still has to force herself to shake hands, even with women. But she made herself strong, as you may have noticed. She is not afraid of men. She merely learned how to despise them and how to use them. For amusement, I can only suppose."

Tamar turned back to Louis. "She is different with you. More natural. Which is why I didn't knock your teeth down your throat when we first met. I never thought she would kiss anyone. I don't object to more kisses, Lewis, if you're discreet, but I won't have you toy with her, or dishonor her."

Louis nodded once. His suspicions had been one thing. To hear the story, even without details as Tamar told it, was quite another.

Tamar took a deep breath, straightening his shoulders as though banishing the past. "Very few people know any of this, for obvious reasons. If I did not think you a decent man who cares for her, I would not have told you."

The blood seemed to drain from Louis's face, rushing to his feet so fast he felt dizzy. *"Decent?"* The word escaped him with something very like revulsion. "And if I am not? If I am not what you think me?"

Tamar's eyes narrowed. "Are you already married?"

The guess was so wildly wide of the mark that Louis laughed. "No. No I am not married. I *am* a decent man, by my own lights, at least. But the rules I live by are not yours." His lips twisted. "Though, ironically, they may be hers. Goodbye, Tamar."

Abruptly, he walked on, all the pleasure of his morning lost in a flood of guilt and impossibility. Tamar did not for a moment believe "Lewis" was not a gentleman. Louis doubted he would be quite so understanding of a Paris street urchin turned spymaster courting his sister. But that was not really the issue. Anna would go her own way, regardless of family or social conventions. She would not care for the loss of ton society because she had never known it. The issue was, Louis was the only man she had ever trusted enough to let near her. If he had helped her to heal, to be ready for the life most women of her rank longed for, that should be enough. He should walk away before her heart was fully engaged. Before he truly hurt her.

He suspected it was already too late for him.

Chapter Thirteen

ANNA, HOWEVER, WAS having too much fun in the present to be thinking of the future. The thrill of all the new feelings aroused by Louis combined with the mystery of Gosselin and the secret meeting in Blackhaven to make life irresistibly exciting. It did cross her mind that she was not carrying out the precise duties Henry had assigned to her—a fact brought home when she returned to the castle that morning for breakfast and found a letter from Christianne awaiting her.

Apart from her sister's usual everyday doings which included a large dinner party, a trip to the theatre, and the ordering of a new evening gown, there was a promise of wonderous news when Anna came home again.

Anna paused at that. Home. Frightening as the prospect had once been, she and Christianne were no longer part of the same whole. Her home was no longer with Christianne. Nor was it here with Rupert, for it wasn't really Rupert's home either. Braithwaite Castle was Serena's brother's, and as soon as Tamar Abbey was fit to receive them, the marquis and marchioness would make their home there. This comfort, this happiness Anna had found here, was only temporary.

She returned to her letter. Apparently, Henry was put out because of Sir Anthony Watters's resignation from the Foreign Office. Christianne couldn't work out why, but he seemed to think Anna would understand. *I did not even know*, Christianne wrote, *that you were acquainted with Sir Anthony or Lady Watters.*

Neither did Anna. But there was a reason he was telling her. There was always a reason for his innocuous little messages.

Between ourselves, Christianne continued, *he departed under something of a cloud, which has upset Henry and his colleagues.*

Now that *was* interesting. Sir Anthony was a fairly senior figure. She would have expected his departure to have initiated a major jostling for position among his underlings. But to have left under a cloud…

Could Sir Anthony Watters be the man awaited by the hotel? Was he meeting Gosselin?

That was one aspect. The other was, why Henry, who knew nothing of this expected event, particularly wanted Anna to know about Watters's resignation.

Watters. It was just a name to her, but she was sure she had heard it more recently than she had left London…

She became aware that she was frowning directly at the nervous Mrs. Elphinstone the governess. Who had been employed by Lady Watters for many years.

Anna laughed, and Mrs. Elphinstone's expression grew positively alarmed. "Forgive me," Anna said easily. "Was I staring? In truth, my mind was miles away and my eyes fixed on you without purpose. I did not mean to be rude."

Mrs. Elphinstone claimed to have been accosted by a Frenchman during her day off when she had been in Whalen. She had described the escaped prisoner accurately, causing the patrols here to be sent to join those at Whalen. And so, Captain Alban had been free to land his wife at Blackhaven Cove, unobserved by any but Louis.

But surely that innocuous event had not been Mrs. Elphinstone's reason. Not if she was still connected to her disgraced one-time employer. Someone else was coming here by ship, just as Louis suspected. Someone no one else was meant to see.

Anna finished her breakfast unhurriedly, waiting until the girls had trailed reluctantly after Mrs. Elphinstone to the schoolroom. The poor lady did not have a great deal of time for spying, Anna reflected as she rose and made her own way to the library. Here, she penned a brief note and folded it before going out to the stables, seizing her cloak on the way.

It was simple to find her favorite stable boy and give him the note with one of her shrinking supply of coins. "Deliver it only to Sir Lytton," she warned. "Not to any of the hotel servants. Bring any reply straight back to *me*."

The lad tugged his forelock, grinned, and ran off, no doubt glad to escape his duties for an hour.

Although she wanted to keep her time free to discuss her new discovery with Louis, she had promised to accompany Serena to help the vicar's wife in some charitable work. When she received no immediate reply to her note, she went grudgingly with her sister-in-law, more concerned with the possibility of running into Louis in Blackhaven than with the plight of the poor souls to whom she found herself ladling soup and distributing gloves, coats, boots, and blankets.

It was only gradually that their tragedy began to move her. She recalled her early life at Tamar Abbey, when they'd given old clothes and food to the villagers who had needed them. And later, when her father had died, how they had had less and less to give. She and Christianne were reduced to words and taking the odd turn watching the sick and the dying. It had been one of the few things to pierce her protective armor, and so, she was glad to have left that duty behind when she went to live with Christianne.

Now, distributing things provided by other people to injured old soldiers and sailors, and to the poorest and least appealing of the town, the memory pushed through again. How was it that now she had more, she gave less? Because she didn't like being reminded that there were people worse off? People who had suffered more than her and continued to do so.

She didn't care much for this idea. She could pretend the work she did for Henry was great work for her country, but much of it, surely, was for Henry himself. And to combat her own boredom. As always, the shame and guilt made her smile more brightly, talking and laughing with the stream of broken humanity with whom she worked those two hours.

And they seemed fascinated by her, brightening when she did, grinning at her from across the room while they ate.

"They like you," Mr. Grant said warmly. "It's an art—being kind without *appearing* to be. Thank you."

"It is easy," Anna said. "I am not kind."

It was only a couple of hours, but they shook her out of her comfort, and she did not even have the satisfaction of encountering, or even seeing Louis. Nor was there any message waiting for her back at the castle.

As she wandered restlessly, trying to think of the best thing to do, she came upon her brother in a room at the top of the old part of the castle. He and Serena had apartments lower down, but they seemed to have taken over several other disused rooms, too. Rupert had set up his easel and was painting the sea. He did that a lot, in different light and weather and time of day. Like Christianne, he always found the pleasure, the beauty in his surroundings.

"I hear Grant wants to employ you permanently," Rupert said cheerfully.

Anna wrinkled her nose. "He wouldn't if he had me there permanently." She walked past him, poking among his brushes and paints until she found a long eye glass of the kind sailors used. "What is this for?" she asked, picking it up.

"It brings everything closer. Helps me to see the movement of the waves and the ships."

Ships. She put it to her eye and looked out to sea. Rupert leaned over and adjusted it for her. He was right. Everything was much closer and sharper, which did not interest her much when there was only the sea to gaze at. But passing vessels, anchored vessels, were another matter. From various places in the castle you could see right around the headland, the town, the harbor and, beach, Blackhaven Cove and, of course, the beach below the castle.

"Fascinating," she murmured. "Rupert, may I borrow this?"

"Whenever you like. Just put it back here when you're finished so I always know where it is." He gave a quick, slightly sheepish grin. "It was a gift from Serena."

"I always thought you would end up married by accident to some tavern wench or a harridan you were too polite to refuse."

He cast her a sardonic glance. "Did you?"

"You didn't even marry her for her money."

"No," Rupert agreed. "Although I almost *didn't* marry her because of her money."

Anna hesitated. She was growing soft, but she wanted him to know she was glad for him. "Christianne will like her," she said abruptly, then left him.

WITH RUPERT'S EYEGLASS, she kept a look-out for distant ships, especially anchored ones that might disgorge boats to come ashore at night. But in truth, the weather was so bad that she barely saw any vessels at all. No one would choose to sail at such a time who didn't absolutely have to. If they came at all, the visitors Louis expected would surely arrive by land.

Not that she had the chance to give him her opinion, for he did not contact her that day. Nor did he meet her in the woods the following day. They had made no definite assignation, but still, it had become such a regular meeting that Anna was somewhat piqued by his absence. And then worried.

"I think I shall go out this afternoon," she said at lunchtime. "A long ride is just what I need."

"Not too long, I hope," Serena said. "We are expecting guests for dinner this evening."

Anna hid her impatience. "Who is coming?"

"Oh, just the Benedicts, the Grants and the Winslows," Serena replied. She cast Anna a quick, teasing smile. "And Major Doverton and Sir Lytton to make up the numbers."

"Is Sir Lytton still in Blackhaven?" she asked, deliberately careless.

"Well, he was this morning," Tamar said. "I met him in the coffee house. He didn't mention leaving."

And that was almost worse. While relieved nothing had befallen him, she could not understand why he was ignoring both her letter and her person.

Because he has always been using you and no longer needs you. His care, his tenderness, were all a sham.

Or for some reason he had come to believe hers were.

I have grown soft, but I will not be reliant. And she certainly would not rely on his assurances that he was watching Roseley. It was time she rode up there and saw for herself.

But even there, she was foiled. She had not been riding half an hour when Chessy went lame. Examination showed her the mare's shoe was loose and she had to dismount and lead her mount back to the castle. By then, there was no time to ride to Roseley and back before Serena's wretched dinner. She toyed with the idea of missing it and going to Roseley anyway, but for some reason it was not easy to be rude to Serena.

She stayed. Perhaps night was a better time to go anyhow. And at least she would see Louis at dinner.

Louis, however, was the last to arrive, full of apologies to Serena. If he had ever been the "street brat" he called himself, that child had vanished long ago into the charming, polished gentleman who greeted her with a smile, but no more warmth than he accorded Serena or Catherine Winslow.

"How do you do, Lady Anna?"

"Very well," she replied gravely. "How do *you* do, Sir Lytton?"

But there was no secret smile in his eyes. He merely moved on to Mrs. Winslow.

At dinner, Serena had placed her between "Sir Lytton" and Major Doverton. Catherine Winslow was on Louis's other side, and he seemed more inclined to speak to her. Anna laughed and flirted with the appreciative Major Doverton, until, finally, Louis turned to her as they finished the fish course.

"And what have you been doing since I last saw you?" he inquired.

She searched in vain for the warmth, the veiled teasing in his eyes, and again found nothing. "Writing letters, mainly," she replied, and lowered her voice. "Did you not receive them?"

"Of course," he replied.

"Then you have been busy?" *Too busy to reply* remained unspoken.

"Oh, terribly," he assured her. "Taking the waters, strolling about the town. When did you say were returning to London?"

The pain was so unexpected, so sharp that she could not breathe. With cool eyes and bored, careless tongue, he was annihilating her. Only now did she realize how far she had fallen, how much she had given and expected in return. She, who had never been fooled or taken advantage of since she was fourteen years old, had been used up and discarded. As she had meant to do with him, before...

Before what? Before he had beguiled and enchanted her? Before she had turned into this needy, *weak* woman she despised.

"I don't believe I did say." Somehow, she managed to turn away from him as the servants cleared away the plates and brought in the next course. By then, she was going through the motions, talking and smiling with Major Doverton while ice reformed around her heart like a life-saving dressing.

Never, ever would she admit to this pain. She could not bear to think just yet of what to do with him, now that he had so clearly decided he did not need her. But she could and would carry on with the task Henry would have given her had he known anything about it. Then, she would deal with Louis.

When the ladies finally left the gentlemen to their port and brandy, she excused herself and went to purloin Rupert's eyeglass once more. It gave her something to do while she planned her next move, which would be to ride in secret to Roseley and discover if Mrs. Lamont had visitors.

She didn't really expect to see anything of interest, so when the glass revealed the dark ship anchored beyond the town, she had to look twice to be sure. Partially hidden by the headland, it appeared to be in darkness save for the odd light that came and went.

It could have been just a ship anchoring to wait out a coming storm. But if anything, the weather seemed calmer, the winds lighter, the air warming enough to begin a thaw. The sea was a little wild, perhaps, but not dangerously so. She wondered if it was Captain Alban, returned with a guest for the vacant hotel rooms...or with whoever Lady Arabella was cleaning the house at Roseley for.

And where the devil was Banion?

Excitement surged within her. Tonight, surely, the mystery would be solved. But first, she had to get through the remains of the evening. Joining the ladies in the drawing room, she allowed herself to be pulled into conversation which was, fortunately, entertaining for the most part. Catherine Winslow was quieter than most, although she appeared to regard Serena and Kate Grant as her friends. The senior Winslows clearly had a soft spot for Mrs. Grant but were somewhat aloof with Mrs. Benedict, who, as the governess, had married out of her station.

More for contrariness than compassion, Anna chose to sit by Mrs. Benedict, whom she found to be both wittier and more intelligent than most and was actually in the midst of genuine laughter when the gentleman entered the room.

Just for an instant, she caught Louis's gaze on her. She might have imagined the sudden spark in his eyes, or the way they lingered, but it was enough to jolt her, to make her question everything all over again. Though not to change her plans.

When Serena poured the tea and she took Louis his cup, she murmured, "You should check the hotel tonight." He inclined his head, accepting the cup.

Only later, as everyone moved and changed places, did she find him beside her. "Why tonight?" he murmured, as if there had been no interruption to their conversation.

"There is ship anchored beyond the headland. In darkness."

"Show me?"

She did not answer him, but went to speak to Major Doverton, who had just asked her to sing.

Only as the guests were leaving, and she joined Tamar and Serena in waving them off from the front steps, did she linger beside Louis, who had ridden up to the castle.

"Follow me," she invited, waving the carriages on their way, before she flitted around the side of the castle toward the cliffs. There, she looked again through Rupert's purloined glass, and then passed it wordlessly to Louis.

"I think it's the same ship," he said. "Alban's." He spoke calmly, but his body suddenly seemed full of controlled energy.

"They could have come ashore by now. You should hurry back to the hotel."

He cast her a quick, amused glance. "Thank you. I'm not convinced they will go to the hotel. Alban's connection is with Roseley."

"I will go there," she said, turning away.

"No," he said flatly.

She ignored that, holding out her hand for the glass. "We might meet in the morning to exchange discoveries. If you can spare the time from your hectic schedule."

Mechanically, he dropped the glass into her waiting hand. "Anna—"

"Goodnight," she said, walking away.

"Anna, don't go up there," he warned, leaping in front of her. "You don't know who you'll be walking into. And Alban's men are not...gentle! Promise me you will stay in the castle and I will tell you everything I discover in the morning."

She laughed. "I promise you nothing and I owe you nothing. Certainly not obedience, *Colonel Delon*."

Perhaps it was foolish to reveal that she knew his identity, but she wanted to stamp on his arrogance for many reasons, at least some of which had nothing to do with her task. But she wouldn't think of those, only watch his reaction.

His gaze fixed on her face. His own gave little away, and yet she knew, perhaps from his very stillness, that she had taken him by surprise. And then he smiled. Strangely, it wasn't an unpleasant smile at all. It was almost...proud.

"Why, Anna," he said softly. "You knew all along. Who has been playing with whom?"

She laughed as though she didn't care, had never cared, and walked past him back to the front door. He didn't follow. She thought she might have won back her pride, but it didn't make her feel better.

BY THE TIME she had returned the glass to Rupert and changed into her boy's clothing—pantaloons, shirt, coat, and overcoat, with thick leather gloves and sturdy boots—she had done all she could to suppress and banish her own intolerable feelings. Her only thought was to find out who was visiting Roseley. Perhaps then, she would know why and what, if anything, she should do about it. It wouldn't necessarily be the same as Louis—Delon—might want to do, but that was neither here nor there.

Some of the stable boys lived in the rooms above the stables. But everything was dark and quiet all over the building as Anna crept in with her lantern. Chessy, her shoe repaired, snorted gently when Anna opened her stall door. She slipped on a bridle and saddle, then led the mare from the stable as quietly as she could.

The ground outside was soft from the melting snow, muffling the sound of hooves. When they were some distance from the stable, Anna mounted astride and pointed Chessy toward Roseley.

Chapter Fourteen

ALMOST TWO HOURS later, the drumming horses' hooves, approaching from behind, drove her off the road. Abandoning Chessy so that the mare would look, hopefully, like a runaway, she darted ahead on foot, until she found a rocky outcrop to hide behind. Hastily, she doused the lantern, and lay waiting, her heart thundering.

The galloping hooves had halted. Peering over the rock, Anna saw the light from several lanterns and a group of men in a huddle some distance down the road.

Devil take them, they've stopped for Chessy... The mare's distinctive whinny preceded a sudden canter as the mare apparently eluded them. Hopefully before they discovered the saddle was still warm. She just hoped Chessy wouldn't bolt seriously and stray too far, for she still had to get back to Braithwaite Castle.

Low, male voices drifted to her on the breeze. One, more distinct than the others, said, "It looks like she's just thrown her rider and is enjoying her freedom."

"Perhaps," said another, more short and abrupt. "Keep your eyes open and your pistols cocked."

Wriggling further up the rock, Anna took Rupert's glass from her pocket and pointed it toward the group of men. Some of them had dismounted. A couple were searching around the rocks and scrubby bushes.

"If you would, sir," the short voice said impatiently. "We need to keep moving. My men will find anyone lurking in the vicinity."

No sooner had he spoken than a gloved hand clamped over Anna's mouth and she was dragged flat onto the ground behind the rock while the weight of a man's body held her helpless.

Old fears surged into the new ones, and just for an instant, panic screamed in her head, for she could not move, not to turn on her attacker, not even to bite the hand over her mouth.

And then she realized those were words being breathed into her ear, in French. "*C'est moi. C'est moi. Louis.*"

And although her whole body wanted to sob with mingled fury and relief, she forced herself to relax. His weight shifted, his hand released her mouth. And she finally saw why he had dragged her down.

Someone was approaching on foot from the opposite direction to the horsemen and would easily have seen her in another moment.

"All clear ahead," the newcomer called softly, and the men returned to their horses. One of them had a distinct, yet oddly graceful limp. He swung himself into the saddle without aid, although a smaller man hovered close by him as though anxious to help. The horses moved forward, once more at a rapid pace.

Anna flattened herself at the foot of the rock, but she could not resist casting her gaze upward as the riders galloped past. Their lantern light flickered over the face of the lame man, who was not young but possessed a haughty, curiously refined face.

Louis's arm remained heavy across her shoulders, both a warning and a secret comfort.

When the riders were far enough ahead, she threw him off and sat up. "Who are they?"

"The one giving the orders is Captain Alban," Louis murmured.

"And the lame man? Do you know him?"

"Yes." Even in the darkness, she saw the brief gleam of his smile.

"Then he is French… Who is he, Louis?"

"I can't tell you that until I know what you will do."

She reached for her lantern and the flint in her pocket. When the light flared up over his enigmatic face, she met his gaze. "What will *you* do?"

"I don't know yet. It depends on who he is here to meet and why."

"Did you know it was him?" she said suddenly. "Is that why you no longer have need of me?"

He looked away, and she wished she hadn't asked, hadn't acknowledged the change in him. But she would not give in to the pain, to the weakness. She would find out alone who the arriving Frenchman was, and why he was there.

But before she could move, his gaze suddenly returned to her, pinning her. "I didn't know until I saw him. And for the rest...perhaps I am learning to be the gentleman I pretend to be."

She stared, and then deliberately curled her lip. "What a pity. I liked you better before."

She rose to her feet, looking around for Chessy. Her lantern picked up a horse-shaped figure a hundred yards or so across the moor. The mare appeared to have found something to eat.

"Where are you going?" Louis asked as Anna began to walk in that direction.

"To Roseley."

"Don't be foolish. Alban's men will have the house and grounds totally secure."

Anna did not pause. "We shall see."

For the first time, he appeared to be genuinely flustered. "What will you do?" he demanded, catching up with her. "Claim acquaintance with Lady Arabella? In *this* guise?"

She laughed, spreading her hands. "I could be a stable boy, could I not?"

"No," he said flatly. "Anna, I am trying to keep you safe. It's all to keep you safe."

"I don't need you for my own safety," she said with contempt, and was even angrier when he actually fell back. She refused to look behind her until a cry of distress made her spin around in time to see Louis dragging someone upright from the long grass.

Instantly, she strode toward them, holding her lantern high. The discovered man swung wildly at Louis, who seemed to catch him with ease, twisting his arm up his back while holding him still. The light played across the features of Mr. Banion.

"Gosselin," Louis observed. "What a surprise. Now I may cut your throat and my day will be complete."

"In front of her ladyship?" Banion mocked. "How very vulgar."

"Oh, I doubt her ladyship falls to pieces at the sight of a little violence," Louis said indifferently.

"And what of *him*?" Banion asked with a hint of desperation, gesturing wildly with his eyes toward the road. "Are you ready to cut *his* throat, too, now you have gone over to the enemy?"

Louis's arm tightened at his enemy's throat. "Just yours. Never equate personal enmity with the patriotic variety."

"Does *she*?" Banion demanded, staring pleadingly at Anna. "Does she even know you are French?"

Anna laughed. "I even know *you* are." But unease slid up her spine, a warning of... Something rustled in the grass. "Louis," she said urgently, but he was already looking around.

Men rose up out of the darkness, blades glinting in the lantern light.

"Go," Louis commanded. "Run." He swung around to face the oncoming men, holding Banion—Gosselin—like a shield in front of him.

Anna held her breath, but the piratical newcomers, surely more of Alban's men, advanced without hesitation. Gosselin meant nothing to them.

Before she could tell Louis so, he released his enemy, pushing him so hard he stumbled to the ground. "You were followed, you imbecile!" Louis snarled, then sprang toward the pirates with a last yell of, "Anna, run!"

Anna ran, though only to circle around and approach the attacking men from the other side. Without conscious thought, she had drawn her favorite stiletto from her pocket.

Louis swung back to avoid the vicious swing of a knife, taking advantage of the wielder's subsequent imbalance to punch him hard in the jaw. As he fell, someone tried to seize Louis from behind, and was hurled backward by Louis's elbow and a backward kick. Someone else fell under his fist, but despite the dagger that appeared suddenly in his hand, he was far too badly outnumbered not to be beaten.

Anna's ears sang with fear and fury as she threw herself toward the fray. Or perhaps it was her own screaming. Louis could not die. He must not die, whoever he was, whatever he had done, whatever he had made her feel. Her heart pounded. Or at least, she thought it was her heart, but then, suddenly, it was horses' hooves. Chessy neighed loudly in her ear and then, before she could do more than haul someone back by his coat tails, hands seized her, yanking her up and onto Chessy's back.

Stupidly, she thought for an instant it had to be Louis, but when she peered over her shoulder, he had paused on the ground to stare after her. And then Alban's men hurled themselves at him and she didn't see how he could survive.

It was Banion who had somehow caught and mounted Chessy, and then seized her.

"Stop!" she yelled into Banion's face. "Help him!"

"Trust me, he will help himself," Banion said grimly. "He always does."

"But he is wounded! He cannot fight all of them. At the very best, his wound will open again…"

But Banion was not listening. Taking matters into her own hands, Anna threw herself forward and seized the reins, hauling on them to slow Chessy and turn her back.

Banion swore in French, seizing back the reins. "Don't be stupid! He will follow you!"

It made her pause, partly because he clearly wanted Louis to follow her. Why was that, when Louis was his sworn enemy? And how the devil could he when at least six pirates were beating him, killing him…

Banion's arm tightened around her waist, holding her in place while he tried to turn the horse once more. Revulsion swept over

Anna. From sheer instinct, as Chessy slowed, she wrenched herself out of Banion's grasp and threw herself to the ground. Chessy pulled up at last, and Banion shifted the horse, trying to block Anna's way back. At the same time, he reached down with one hand to help her back up.

"I won't hurt you," he promised. "But you must come with me." He grasped her shoulder. "It's the only way."

"No, it isn't," Anna said, lashing out with her stiletto.

His surprised yell of pain rent the darkness, but Anna didn't wait to see the result of her action. All but sobbing, she ran back to the fight.

But she could no longer see anyone.

WHEN LOUIS HAD told Anna to run, he immediately hurled himself at Alban's men to give her time. But he was under no illusions. Fit and well, he might have given a reasonable account of himself but the outcome would have been no different, not against six fighting sailors trained by Alban. On the other hand, it had not been part of his plan for Anna to escape in Gosselin's company. That terrified him more than anything.

His wound screamed in agony as a blow landed on it, and his left arm suddenly wouldn't obey him. He staggered back, knocking someone aside as he went. But his worst fear now was that he would be left unconscious or too weak to save Anna.

He straightened, circling as they all closed in on him. "Very well," he said amiably. "You've had your fun. Now take me to the captain before I feel obliged to explain your excessive enthusiasm."

"That's exactly where you're going," someone said aggressively. "You were *following* the captain."

"That wasn't me, you imbecile! The man who followed him has just ridden off! I was merely on my way to see Captain Alban when I found that fellow skulking in the grass."

"Then why did you attack us?" one of the men demanded, picking up a fallen lantern.

The light shone clearly on the sailor's face, and with relief Louis recognized him. Rummaging in his mind for the man's name, he replied, "Because I'd no idea who the devil you were. It never entered my head Captain Alban would have more men following so far behind. I apologize for hurting you, Cobb."

The name rushed back to him as well as several others connected to those men. They'd travelled on the same ship to England. These men had locked him up, fed him each day, and Louis had listened by habit to every interaction he could.

Cobb frowned at the use of his name.

Louis laughed and waved one arm toward the road. "You don't remember me, do you? Come, let's get to Roseley as quickly as possible so that I can discharge my business with the captain. Lead on, Brandy!"

The use of their names, which he could not have known without some dealing with their captain, seemed to convince them as he expected it to.

"You still don't remember me?" he asked, allowing amusement to seep into his voice as he walked confidently toward the road. "I'm sure it will come to you," he added, devoutly hoping it wouldn't.

Ahead, yet another man was walking to meet them, leading a horse by the reins. Louis's hired horse.

"Found him tied up on the moor," the man told Cobb.

"He's mine," Louis admitted. "I left him to discover who was following the captain. But I admit, I'm very glad to see him. You men hit too hard and I need to get to Roseley as quickly as possible."

He reached for the reins, and the man only cast a quick glance at Cobb before relinquishing them.

"Well, you shouldn't have fought so well yourself," Cobb said generously.

Louis managed a laugh as he hauled himself into the saddle. Every inch of his body seemed to protest, his shoulder most vociferously of all. He just hoped the wound hadn't opened again.

"Well, if you'll excuse me, gentlemen, I'll find the fellow you lost, before I ride on to Roseley. I'll see you there. Can you spare one of the lanterns?"

It was insolence, really, but it would be necessary in his search for Anna. Brandy delivered his lantern up without a quibble.

"I suggest you hurry," Louis said seriously. "You have wasted too much time here." He urged the horse to motion and then galloped off in the direction he had last seen Anna and Gosselin.

The difficult terrain forced him to slow before long. He could see no one riding ahead in any direction, though eventually he found the tracks left by Anna's horse in the slushy ground, and they eventually returned to the road, where they were indistinguishable. It looked as if Gosselin was taking her back to Blackhaven, but Louis did not believe that.

For one thing, Anna would not have been a comfortable companion. She would not sit submissively silent while he abducted her and tried to hide her in the middle of a town. He would take her somewhere quiet...either to lure Louis to her or simply to kill her.

Louis's blood froze. By choice, Gosselin would take the former course, if only to keep Louis busy during whatever business he had with the guest at Roseley. But Anna would not give him that choice. She would be too much of a handful. He could have killed her already. He could be in the act of killing her at this moment.

Ignoring the terror threatening to swamp him, he followed the road back to the point they had found Gosselin. If he had been forced to kill her so soon, he would do it where Louis would find her easily. Just for spite.

He left the road, swinging the lantern high over the grassy ground where they had found Gosselin. His heart thudded with fear. He could not endure to lose another friend. He could not bear to lose *her*. She had crept and clawed her way into his cold heart, far deeper than he had even realized until now when he faced losing her. More than that, he could not bear that she be alone and afraid, helpless once more in an evil man's power. That she should die in such horror when she begun to waken to the joys of life that had been so cruelly taken from her...

A figure rose up from behind a rock, faint and indistinguishable beyond that it wore male clothes. Except the rock, surely, was where he and Anna had hidden as Alban rode past. His throat constricted. He was afraid to even hope, and yet he rode forward to meet the figure at once. It began to run, and he saw with unspeakable relief that it was her.

He dragged the pistol from his pocket, aiming it at the rock in case Gosselin should show as much as a hand behind her.

He didn't. And the boyish figure, which truly looked nothing like a boy, flung itself at his leg, sobbing wildly. "I thought you were dead," she gasped. "I thought they had killed you!"

He bent from the saddle, grasping the back of her head in unutterable relief, pressing her cheek into his thigh. But it was not enough. He bent lower and swept her up by the waist, close into his body, burying his lips in her hair. But she tilted her head back at once, grasping his face between her hands, and he saw the tears streaking her pale, beautiful face and glistening still in her eyes.

"Oh, thank God," she said shakily and kissed him full on the mouth.

It seemed she could not stop kissing him, pressing her lips to his cheeks, his chin, his neck, until he held her head steady and sank his mouth into hers for the long, desperate kiss they both needed.

When the horse moved restlessly, he released her to pick up the reins once more. Shifting his weight behind the saddle, he settled her more comfortably in front of him.

"How did you escape Gosselin?" he asked, just a little shakily.

"I stabbed him in the hand," she replied impatiently, and in spite of everything, laughter shook him.

"Of course, you did. I should have known you would get away."

"I wanted to help you. He wouldn't go back. How did you get away from all these men?"

"I'd met some of them before," he confessed. "It was Alban's ship that brought me to England, to my prison. I thought I probably looked familiar enough to get away with it, so I pretended I was connected to Alban and on my way to see him." He dropped his cheek onto the top of her head once more, briefly squeezing his eyes shut. "Did he hurt you?"

"Banion? Of course not," she said scornfully. "No one hurts me now."

"You are wonderful," he said, smiling into her hair before straightening, and turning the horse's head back toward Blackhaven.

"Wait," she said, frowning. "We should go on to Roseley to find out about that man. Their guest."

"There is no point. We could talk our way past Alban's men, even speak to Alban, but they won't tell us why he their guest is there. To find that out, we need to know who he is meeting."

"Who is he?" Anna demanded.

And this time he told her. "Charles de Talleyrand-Périgord, Prince of Benevento. Napoleon's one-time minister of foreign affairs, and always a man to be reckoned with."

Chapter Fifteen

A NNA, DROWNING IN torrents of bliss because he was alive and because he *did* care for her after all, had to force her brain to think.

"Talleyrand," she repeated. "Why would Talleyrand come here? Is he betraying France to the British?"

"It is possible," Louis admitted. "It would explain Alban's involvement."

She twisted her neck to look at him. "What will you do if he is?"

"Try to stop him," Louis said evenly.

"How?"

"That would depend. What would *you* do in these circumstances?"

Anna's lips quirked unhappily. "I suppose I should try to prevent you from preventing him. I wish we were not enemies."

"We are not enemies. Look on us as potential friends...which makes me sound a little like Monsieur de Talleyrand!"

"Is he a likely traitor? Do you trust him?"

"Lord, no I don't trust him. He is too busy seeing the larger world that he ignores the human cost of what he does."

The pain in his voice was not obvious, but Anna knew it was there. "Did he betray you?" she asked.

He shook his head. "I don't think so. He has not been in favor for years. I believe Gosselin convinced Fouché our stream of informants would work without me, that I was tainted and should be removed. Along with those too close to me. Talleyrand would have considered such action foolish."

"Would he consider changing sides and betraying France to the British foolish?"

Louis shrugged. "Not if it would save France. He has already given certain information to Austria and Russia to hasten the Emperor's fall. I doubt he would find it harder to provide the British with something similar. It bothers me more that Gosselin is here. And he is not with Talleyrand's party. And yet, he knew Talleyrand was coming. Who could have told him?"

"Sir Thomas Watters?" Anna guessed. "He has recently been forced to resign for reasons no one seems to know. But these reasons upset Henry."

"Watters used to send us information in exchange for money," Louis admitted reluctantly. "But he was unreliable, too careless. I cut him off."

"Ah." Anna was disappointed. "Perhaps that was all that has been discovered against him."

"Perhaps," Louis said thoughtfully. "Or Gosselin cold have drawn him back in. He certainly knew about Watters."

"And the Watters' French governess is at the castle. What if she is passing messages, or connected in some other way with Gosselin, too?"

Louis inclined his head. "Perhaps you should talk to her. While I have another look at the vacant rooms in the hotel."

They fell silent, each, no doubt, thinking their own thoughts. Anna leaned back against him, more involved in the pleasure of his nearness than in the mystery she had been so determined to solve. Being with Louis brought mystery enough. She didn't quite understand why she loved his touch and yet still shrank with revulsion from everyone else.

Is Rupert right? Do I love Louis?

She had certainly gone to pieces at the prospect of his death.

He came back for me. The warmth of that knowledge folded around her, protecting her from the bitter cold of the night. She held the lantern, while Louis's arms enclosed her, handling the reins.

"We are on different sides," she said, almost dreamily. "And yet I find I don't care."

"I tried to push you away," he confessed. "So that it would hurt less for both of us when we part. I lasted only a day. It seems what is done is done. We cannot go back."

Anna closed her eyes. Even in the darkness, some things seemed easier to say like this. "I want to go forward."

His lips whispered against her ear. "With me?"

"With you. But I don't know how." She opened her eyes, sure once more that he wanted her.

"In a year, perhaps less, we will no longer be enemies," he said. "But you will still be a marquis's daughter and I a nameless brat from the slums of Paris."

She frowned. "Why do you imagine I care for such things? Can you see me as a matron of the ton?"

He smiled. "Yes. You would twist everyone around your finger, whatever their social standing."

"The ton would bore me in a week. Less. There are too many rules."

"Perhaps. But if you came with me, would Lord Tamar cut you off? Would your sister? Would Henry Harcourt?"

She thought about it. "No. No one expected me to make a splendid match. No one expected me to marry at all."

The horse moved on, its pace even and rhythmic.

Louis said, "Would you marry me?"

Her heart beat in rhythm with the hooves, hard and sure.

"You spoke to Rupert," she said. "That's why you were cold. Did he not tell you what...happened to me?"

"A little," he replied steadily.

She closed her eyes once more, swallowing the lump in her throat. "I am not...pure," she whispered.

And both his arms held her tightly. He kissed her temple, her cheek, and when she lifted her face, gasping, he kissed her mouth, long and thoroughly.

"Never think that," he said against her lips. "It's a silly concept thought up by men. The man who assaulted you is the only one to blame. If Tamar had not already killed him, I would. But you—your courage has lifted you up, allowed you to do things few men would dare. You are magnificent."

She held his arms around her, trying to come to terms with his words, his ideas. "I have never met anyone remotely like you before."

"Does that mean you will marry me? When we can?"

She could not breathe. The weight of the promise she was about to make pressed down on her but could not break the happiness. She dragged his hand up to her lips and tasted the salt of her own spilled tears. "I will marry you."

AT ABOUT THE same time as Louis and Anna were beginning their homeward journey, Serena was wakened by an all mighty pounding on the front door of the castle. She had no idea how long it had been going on, but she suspected some little time if it had finally managed to penetrate her sleep in a distant part of the castle.

"It's the middle of the night!" Tamar exclaimed in annoyance. "Who the devil is that?"

Serena threw off the bedclothes and reached for the flint to light the bedside candle. "We had better go and find out. We can't expect the servants to attend to French prisoners and highway robbers or whatever other unsavory characters there are in the vicinity."

"Actually," Tamar said, climbing into his pantaloons as Serena walked across their bedchamber with the candle in her hand, "I had better go. *You*, my love, are not wearing anything."

Serena blushed, more at the memory of *why* she was wearing nothing, that with any residual modesty at being seen by her husband in such a state.

"Well, neither were you until an instant ago," she accused, setting down the candle and picking her night rail off the floor. Tamar strode to the door, still struggling into his shirt, while Serena threw a wrapper over her night rail, and seized a shawl against the cold. She ran after him downstairs and through the freezing cold rooms to the main entrance hall. Paton, in his nightcap and a rather natty dressing gown that she was sure had once been her father's, had already opened the door. Two footmen, half-dressed and each carrying a branch of candles, flanked him to provide light and moral support, while Mrs. Gaskell and several maids dangled over the staircase bannister with wide-eyed excitement.

"Lady Anna!" Paton exclaimed in horror.

Tamar whitened, rushing across the hall with Serena at his heels. She slid to a halt as Anna entered the house with a total stranger. They both looked pale and frozen. Anna, dressed for travelling, was shivering.

"We are so sorry to disturb the household as this time of night," Anna exclaimed, with far more apology in her voice than Serena was used. "But we had no idea how long the journey would be and the post boys would not wait…"

"Post boys?" Serena exclaimed, startled. "Anna, come right in for goodness' sake, you look utterly frozen. What on earth…?" *What on earth are you doing travelling in the middle of the night with a total stranger?* She knew Anna was wayward, and the dangers were unthinkable, but it was not her place to scold, and certainly not before the servants. So she bit her tongue.

"Lady Serena," Anna said apologetically.

"How formal," Serena observed, baffled by this new attitude.

"Not really," Tamar said beside her. "It ain't Anna. It's my other sister, Christianne."

Serena stared in disbelief, for the woman really *was* Anna—until she smiled, a singularly, sweet, warm smile, far more open than that of the sister Serena knew. And Tamar actually embraced her, which he had never done with Anna, and casually offered the strange man his hand.

"Doorstep introductions," Tamar said cheerfully. "Serena, my sister Christianne, and her husband, Mr. Henry Harcourt. Now, can we please go somewhere warmer so you can tell me what the deuce you're doing here?"

Mr. Harcourt bowed low over Serena's hand. "I hope the intrusion is not too great. It was an impulsive decision. My wife was missing her sister and anxious to meet your lady, Tamar, so when I was granted a couple of weeks' leave, we posted up here. We did not mean to arrive at this unconscionable hour, but—"

"Impulsive, Henry?" Tamar said skeptically as he led the way upstairs to the drawing room where the remains of last night's fire still kept the chill at bay. "You?"

Christianne laughed. "Rupert. You know he came to please me."

"Paton, I think perhaps some tea. And hot soup for our weary travelers," Serena said, recovering enough to remember her duties as hostess. She took the branch of candles from the nearest footman. "Um...I'll just go and see if Anna is awake." She couldn't imagine anyone would have slept through this racket. Her sisters and even Mrs. Elphinstone had joined the maids on the bannisters. "Bed," she ordered her sisters. "You may meet Mr. and Mrs. Harcourt in the morning!"

"Lady Serena!" Christianne caught up with her. "Would you mind if I came with you? I can't imagine Anna is asleep. She'll know I'm here, and I am so worried about her."

"Worried?" Serena repeated in surprise. "I assure you she is well. Or at least she was three hours or so ago when we went to bed."

"I know, but something upset her, just tonight. I felt it." She gave a small, deprecating laugh. "I know it is bizarre, but we feel each other's pain."

Serena frowned thoughtfully. "Well, I think she has quarreled with Sir Lytton...it might have upset her more than I realized."

Christianne fixed her gaze on Serena's face as they walked. "This Sir Lytton...is he a good man? A kind man?"

Serena blinked. "He seems so. Rupert believes he is good for Anna, though of course none of us have known him for very long. Did she tell you about him?"

"She mentioned someone," Christianne said vaguely, and Serena knew she would never break her sister's confidence.

Arriving at Anna's bedchamber, Serena knocked and went in first, bearing the candles. "Anna? Look who has arrived! Are you awake?" Although she half-expected Anna to be leaping through the bed curtains, they remained closed.

Serena opened the curtains to reveal the empty bed. It was neatly made and had quite clearly not been slept in at all.

"She is not here," Christianne said flatly, before she even looked. She sank on the bed, her fingers curling into the coverlet. "Oh, drat you, Anna, where are you this time?"

"In the library, perhaps," Serena said, with much more lightness than she felt. With Christianne trailing after her, she checked in all the likely places on her way back to the drawing room. Christianne said little, but it struck Serena that, considering the obvious tie between the sisters, she was taking the nighttime disappearance much more casually than one might have expected.

And in the drawing room, Tamar, apprised of the facts, only sighed and shrugged.

"Should we not organize a search for her?" Serena urged.

"And have your servants know she is abroad alone at night?" Mr. Harcourt interjected. He looked a little whiter, a little tighter around the mouth than he had on arrival, but he clearly was not anxious enough to do more than try to preserve his sister-in-law's reputation.

Serena turned in disbelief from him to Tamar, "Rupert, *anything* could happen to her!"

"It could," Tamar agreed. "But it's unlikely to. If Anna does not wish to be found, she won't be. Frankly, it's highly unlikely someone dragged her from her bed and abducted her. She has gone out of her own free will and no doubt will be back by first light." He met Serena's gaze. "It isn't the first time she's done such things. Even in London, when she used to give Harcourt palpitations with her starts."

"But what on earth can she be doing?" Serena demanded. She paused, staring at her husband. "Oh Rupert, you don't suppose she has eloped with Sir Lytton?"

FOR ANNA, THE night time journey home was unimaginably intimate. The darkness seemed to isolate them from the rest of the world, with just the glow of the lantern to unite them in their private bubble where even the cold of the December night could not penetrate. Held securely in his arms, she ached with the kind of happiness she had never known before, and she never wanted it to end.

Not that their conversations were always comfortable or light-hearted, For the first time he told her of the tragedies that had blossomed from Gosselin's betrayal, the arrests and deaths of the only people Louis had ever called friends, people like him who had lived in the shadows, with constant risk. Some did it for money, some for love, but all were utterly loyal. Until they were gone, he hadn't realized how much he had cared.

"They were like the children I knew I would never have. And I let them down. I failed to care for them, to keep them safe."

"How could you know your own people would turn on them? On you?"

"I *should* have known. I was arrogant. It never entered my head I was endangering them by going my own way. I would rather have died than let them."

She kissed the corner of his mouth. "I am selfish enough to be glad you didn't. You have more to do, Louis."

He kissed her fingers. "I have had enough. After this, after Gosselin, I want no more of it. I want to live on a farm with you."

"Can we have dogs and horses?"

"Lots."

She smiled and rested her cheek on his good shoulder. They talked a lot about such futures, although she was sure neither believed in them. They were fantasies that might come true one day. For now, while their countries were enemies, the present was all they truly had.

"Why do you trust me?" he asked once. "Knowing what you do about my life, my work, why do you trust me?"

She thought about it. "I don't know. I suppose it is the same reason I like you—only you—to touch me. I love you."

"Love is no protection from betrayal. It must enter your head that I could be lying to you."

"Does it enter yours that so could I?"

"Yes," he admitted. His smile was rueful as he pressed his lips to the top of her head. "But not often enough to stop me."

"I am the same," she said, curling her fingers around his wrist. "It's as if...I understand you."

"I recognized a fellow spirit the first night we met."

"How strange life is," she said, sleepy with contentment.

"We are nearly at the castle road," he observed. "You should be able to get back in before the servants are up."

"But you will tell me as soon as anyone takes up the hotel rooms?" she said anxiously.

"I might."

She frowned. "I will have to come myself. Take up residence in your dining room and entertain a constant stream of respectable ladies for coffee and luncheon and tea...The trouble is, we don't know who the enemy is—for either of us!"

"It is an interesting situation." Louis allowed. He turned the horse up the road to the castle gates, which stood open as usual, and rode through them.

Feeling his scrutiny, she twisted round to face him. "What is it?"

He smiled. "I was wondering about coming right into the castle with you and taking you to bed. Does that appall you, my love?"

"A little," she admitted. "But not like it used to. Mostly, it makes me glad." She reached up and pressed her mouth to his. Her heart thundered with anticipation and excitement and sheer need. There may have been fear in there, too, but she could not find it. "Come with me, then," she whispered. "Stay until dawn."

His breathing quickened. He sank his mouth on hers in a long, sensual kiss that melted her bones. Of its own volition, apparently, the horse moved a little faster, as if sensing its own rest and comfort was close at last.

They led the horse into the stables as quietly as they could. But they took no more time than to throw a blanket over it, and make sure it had hay and water. And then Anna took Louis's hand and led him into the castle via the side door. She lit the candle she had left on the table. He took it from her and she led the way through to the main staircase.

As they walked, his thumb gently stroked the sensitive skin of her trembling hand. Louis had become her all, her one desire.

As they climbed the staircase, Anna thought she heard a voice, muffled by distance. She cast a quick glance at Louis, to see if he had heard it, too. He raised one eyebrow but did not pause. On the landing, she hesitated, for there was light coming from the long gallery, from under the drawing room door.

Louis's breath was hot in her ear, thrilling her. "Come."

Smiling, she turned with him toward her bedchamber, just as the drawing room door flew open and someone she had never expected to see bolted out in a sudden blaze of light.

"'Tianne," Anna whispered.

Christianne stopped dead, staring from her to Louis. Behind her, inevitably, came Henry and Tamar and Serena. They all goggled at her, which seemed excessive until she remembered she was wearing boys' clothes. And now she wanted to laugh.

"Anna?" Serena said, tearing her gaze from this odd attire to Anna's face. She sounded faint with relief. "Please tell me it *is* you this time."

"What the devil is going on?" Anna demanded.

"That was my next question," Serena said breathlessly. "Are you well?"

"Come into the drawing room," Henry said hastily. "We don't want to rouse the servants."

"Again," Christianne added.

"Oh dear." Anna could not look at Louis. Part of her still wanted to laugh, because they had been caught in such a ridiculous way. But mostly, she wanted to scream, because she had so wanted this time with Louis.

Without releasing her hand, Louis strolled forward, tucking it into his arm in a more respectable manner. They might have been entering a ballroom in glittering evening dress.

Chapter Sixteen

H IS INSOUCIANCE MUST have rubbed off on Anna, for as the door closed behind them all, she said carelessly, "Sir, my sister Christianne and her husband, Mr. Harcourt. This is Sir Lytton Lewis."

"I believe we know exactly who he is," Henry said.

Of course, he would suspect. "Then you'll know I'm perfectly well and may all go to bed," Anna said impatiently. "Please don't tell me you were all waiting up for me?"

"Of course, we were," Serena exclaimed. "You weren't in your bed!"

"We went for a moonlight ride," Anna said brazenly, ignoring the almost total absence of moon that night. "What I don't understand is why Christianne and Henry are here. Did you arrive in the middle of the night?"

"I'm afraid we did," Christianne admitted. She seemed to have difficulty taking her eyes off Louis. "But Lady Serena has been most kind and understanding."

Anna glanced a little ruefully at Serena. "You must find us all very odd guests."

"I find very little odd since I met Tamar," Serena retorted. "But I do think, Sir Lytton, you have behaved badly."

"Nonsense," Anna said at once. "He merely brought me home."

"And felt unable to leave you at the door?" Henry said, scowling. But he was playing a part. His gaze was speculative rather than truly angry. If anything annoyed him, it was Anna allowing herself to be caught.

Serena had come right up to Anna, searching her face. "Are you truly well?"

"I am truly well," Anna said. She couldn't help the smile that flickered across her lips. "In fact, I have never been better."

A moment longer, Serena gazed into her eyes, then she nodded and turned away. "Then I think we should say goodnight to Sir Lytton and go to bed."

Louis inclined his head but looked at Anna.

Reluctantly, she slid her hand free of his arm. "It is probably best. Good night."

His smile was warm, feeding her longing. "Good night."

He bowed civilly to the others. No one would have guessed from his manner that he had just been caught by her family sneaking with her into the house at dead of night. Tamar and Serena conducted him to the door, waiting to see him off the premises.

Anna wanted to laugh, especially when he cast a wicked glance over his shoulder, sharing his humor.

Serena led the way, Tamar following Louis. Although, a moment later, Tamar stuck his head back in the door, frowning at Henry. "Don't you go reading her the riot act. It won't wash. She don't *know* what's proper." His lips twisted. "And if she did, she wouldn't care," he admitted, and closed the door before hurrying after his wife and Louis.

"Is that *him?*" Christianne asked, low, slipping her hand into Anna's.

Anna squeezed her fingers. "Yes."

"His manners," Henry said with distaste, "seem quite *French.*"

"There's no need to insult him, Henry," Christianne admonished, floating back to the sofa by the fireplace. "If Anna likes him, he is a gentleman."

Henry stood beside Anna, watching his wife. "Your sister has some very strange ideas about you," he murmured.

"No. You just don't understand our definitions."

"And this Lytton Lewis? Is he Delon?"

"You know he is."

Henry's lips twisted. "Of course. If he weren't, you would not be with him. Have you won him over?"

"Up to a point," Anna said carefully. "There are some things he will help us with. Did you really come all this way to satisfy yourself as to my progress?"

"Of course not," Henry said contemptuously.

"I needed to see you," Christianne said sleepily, stretching out on the sofa.

Anna waited for a few moments before she said low, "You, however, had no need to see me."

"On the contrary, I had to know what you were doing with your spy, because I have just pursued Lord Castlereagh to Blackhaven."

Anna's lips fell open. "Castlereagh? The foreign secretary? My God, he is here to see Talleyrand."

Henry's eyes widened. "Talleyrand? I thought he was falling into Delon's trap, wanted to be sure you knew, and could find a way to prevent it. He is meeting *Talleyrand*? Why? How do you know."

"I've seen him."

"But you cannot know that unless…Delon identified him. Anna—"

"Let her sleep, Henry," Christianne said faintly from the sofa. "We all need to sleep."

"Didn't Serena give you a bedchamber? They seem always to be prepared for guests."

"Yes," Henry affirmed. "But it seems to be too late for Christianne. I shall stay with her."

It was, probably, the only reason Anna tolerated him—his devotion to Christianne. Well, that and the "work" which had given Anna's life purpose and had led her in the end to Louis. She nodded and walked toward the door.

"You and I shall talk in the morning," Henry said significantly.

Anna was fairly sure she would avoid that, but at this moment, she was too tired to think. She stumbled upstairs to her bedchamber and fell fully clothed into bed.

AFTER A MERE couple of hours sleep, Gosselin took up his post in the coffee house once more. It was only just light, and he was the only customer. Even the waiter was yawning.

Although news from London had dried up—Delon, damn him, had always claimed Watters was useless—Gosselin had every reason to hope that Lord Castlereagh was now close. With Talleyrand in the country, he surely had to be, and Gosselin's finest moment was at hand.

At least, he hoped it was. Right now, he felt anything but fine. He raised his coffee cup in his bandaged hand, thinking bitter thoughts about unladylike, violent English noblewomen like Lady Anna Gaunt. She had stabbed him quite brutally in the hand before he even knew she had a weapon, and then ran off to join Delon in a fight with some very vicious seamen. Her stupidity annoyed him, for he had never thought her remotely stupid before.

It was another weakness to add to Delon's and give him back some sense of wellbeing. The little coup d'état Gosselin and Fouché had enacted against the over-powerful Delon might not have succeeded in killing the cur. But it had, finally, betrayed the first weakness he had ever found in his commander. He cared for the fools who did his bidding. Which made eliminating them all the sweeter, and almost made up for Delon fooling him and giving himself up to the British.

Gosselin had begun to suspect that Anna, clearly Delon's tool in Blackhaven, was another weakness. Now, it seemed Delon was also hers. Which irritated Gosselin, who rather wanted her for himself. Besides which, he would far rather have tied her up or even killed her on the other side of Blackhaven and sent Delon searching all over the country for her while Gosselin completed his task in peace. And hopefully escaped back to France before Colonel Delon came hunting for *him*.

It was, surely, only a matter of time before the British arrested Delon once more. Gosselin would prefer to tie up this loose end if he could, but since Delon knew he was here, he doubted his chances.

Unfortunately, Delon also knew about Talleyrand. Gosselin only hoped it would not enter Delon's head that the Prince of Benevento would wander into the Blackhaven Hotel in the full view of the populace. But at least now that Talleyrand had arrived, Lord Castlereagh could not be far away. After all, neither man could hope to remain inconspicuous for very long.

Gosselin sipped his coffee and while he watched the front door of the hotel, he allowed himself to dwell with some bitterness on the events of last night. It had begun well, witnessing the night time landing of Talleyrand in Blackhaven Cove, and following undetected, as he had imagined. Seeing both Delon and Anna waiting ahead had been a blow. As if they had known where Talleyrand was going.

Being discovered by Delon had been another blow, and from there it had all gone to pieces. He had salvaged nothing from that, except knowledge of Delon's latest weakness. But he still had his task to perform and with luck, Delon would sleep his way through that.

This happy thought must have calmed him so much that he nodded off in his chair, for he came to with a jolt to see an unmarked coach stopped in front of the hotel across the street. Even as Gosselin sat up, the coach drove off again, and four men entered the hotel: three well-dressed gentlemen and a valet. Of the three gentlemen, one was particularly well muffled—against the cold, one would have thought, if one did not suspect him of merely hiding his identity. It was impossible to see his face. Gosselin quelled the urge to run across the road and peer at him in the foyer. No one could arrest him for looking.

Fortunately, he stayed with the plan and waited, keeping his eyes now on the first-floor windows of the all-important room... And, yes! The curtains twitched. A man's face—one he did not recognize— appeared briefly, parting the curtains only slightly to allow in some light.

The rooms were occupied. Now they just awaited Talleyrand...

But Castlereagh must have been travelling through the night. He would be exhausted. No one but an imbecile would face Talleyrand in such a state. Castlereagh would sleep, which meant so could Gosselin.

Before he could even take the coin from his pocket to pay for his coffee, someone slid into the chair opposite him.

"Good morning," said Colonel Delon.

Gosselin's stomach rebelled, threatening to eject the recently consumed coffee.

Delon smiled. "Who are you protecting now?"

"I was enjoying a cup of coffee before I go home," Gosselin retorted.

"To Cliff View? You might as well, you know, for I can find you just as easily at the tavern."

Gosselin couldn't stop his eyes widening, and Delon laughed. "Poor, poor France."

"I have never pretended to be as experienced as you in matters of low spying," Gosselin said, trying for dignity.

"Then you have no business taking on such a position. But we both know that. What happened to your hand?"

Thrown by the sudden change of subject, Gosselin blinked at his bandage for a moment before he said resentfully. "That she-cat you have made such a pet of, stabbed me. If you ask me, she is no more a marquis's daughter than I am!"

"But then, I would never ask you for information."

A dangerous glitter had formed in Delon's impenetrable, unblinking eyes, urging Gosselin to poke further.

"I would not turn your back on that one," he sneered. "I certainly wouldn't *sleep* at her side."

"No," Delon agreed, standing abruptly and looming over the table so that Gosselin feared he had gone too far. "You wouldn't. Your tongue is also too loose for your position. Good-bye, Gosselin."

He swept out of the door, looking, Gosselin thought resentfully, rather magnificent. Rather as Gosselin himself wished to appear. What he could not understand was why Delon had come in in the first place. He had asked him no probing questions, nor threatened him. It was almost as if he had just come to *look* at him.

Gosselin's stomach jolted unpleasantly. There had used to be all sorts of nonsense talked about Delon. They said he could tell the tiniest lie from the tone of your voice. That he could tell exactly what you were thinking from simply looking into your eyes. For several seconds, Gosselin felt frozen with terror that Delon had learned his whole plan from that hard stare.

But, of course, that was rubbish. And just in case Delon was still watching him, he threw a coin on the table, and went deliberately back to Cliff View to sleep. Even Delon himself would have to sleep some time.

LOUIS HAD BEEN sitting on one of the hotel foyer sofas, apparently lost in his newspaper, when the four men had bundled through the front door. Without appearing to look up from the paper, he picked out the chief of them immediately. Tall, thin, unexpectedly youthful and aristocratically handsome, he allowed the others to surround him, to conduct business at the desk before he was whisked upstairs, followed by two porters with their baggage.

Standing up, Louis saw that they were met on the landing by the lofty and rarely glimpsed figure of the hotel owner himself.

Satisfied, Louis strolled out of the hotel. As usual, Gosselin was fixed in his seat at the coffee house window. Which was annoying. Louis had hoped the arrival might pass him by unnoticed. Nor could he discern the direction of Gosselin's gaze. So, he walked across the road to the coffee house. Gosselin's head did not turn to follow him.

When he entered the coffee house, he saw at once that Gosselin's attention was fully on the hotel, and he was gazing upward. To be sure, Louis walked right over to him, and as he sat, followed his enemy's gaze up to the first-floor window. Gosselin knew.

Of course he did. It was why he had never risked attacking Louis there and bringing such attention to the hotel that the meeting was moved...

But he would do nothing until Talleyrand arrived. Why else would he have been following him last night if the prince was not central to his plans?

Like Gosselin, Louis retired to bed. Unlike Gosselin, however, he needed only a couple of hours of sleep to thrive, and he had a well-trained ability to wake at more or less exactly the time he wished to.

He rose and dressed before midday and sent for some breakfast. When the knock sounded at his door, he opened it to take the tray from the maid and forestall any of the flirtatious behavior that had become tedious to him.

But it was not the maid who stood there. It was not even his breakfast. It was a veiled lady in black crepe like a widow.

The disguise did not fool him for a moment, though he hoped devoutly it had misled everyone else. Grasping her wrist, he jerked her into the room and closed the door.

He kissed her through the veil, and when that was not enough, he drew it up over her head and kissed her naked lips.

"What the devil are you doing here?" he all but groaned into her mouth.

"It's Castlereagh," she breathed, drawing back.

"I know."

She frowned. "Damn you, *how* did you know?"

"I saw him arrive. How did *you* know?"

"Henry. It was the real reason he posted up here. It scared the wits out of him to think of a French spy in the vicinity of the foreign secretary. Which is quite funny when one thinks of Sir Thomas Watters who must have been in his vicinity for years."

Louis shrugged. "But he never gave us anything useful. He just took the money. Until now. He must have known his colleagues had discovered his past treachery and given Gosselin this meeting as a parting gift. He must have been *extremely* well paid for that." He took her face between his hands. "What are you doing here?"

"Escaping Henry, who will only ask me awkward questions about you. Don't you like the disguise? I made it from an old mourning dress of my mother's."

"I like it very well. I like you in all your guises, but you are taking a risk. And not, I suspect, to come to my bed."

She flushed, as he had hoped she would, though she answered openly. "I doubt it would be sensible if Lord Castlereagh is already here. Why do you suppose he is meeting Talleyrand? And which of us should be concerned, you or I?"

Louis sighed and released her, walking to the window. "Concerned by their secret meeting? Neither of us, probably. I imagine it is some ploy of Talleyrand's to secure favorable terms for France in the peace that is sure to come by the spring. What worries me is Gosselin's part in this."

"Would even Gosselin not want favorable terms for his country?"

"His country is of purely secondary interest to Gosselin," Delon said dryly. "Neither he nor Fouché, his master, would thrive in peace time. His aim must be to prolong the war."

"So, he must disrupt the meeting," Anna said slowly. "Or prevent it altogether." She met Louis's gaze and the smile he loved flickered across her face. "In this, if in nothing else, we must be on the same side."

"I like that."

"So do I," she whispered.

He walked back to her, his pace deliberately slow and predatory. "Then what should we do?"

"Stop Gosselin," she said breathlessly.

He took her hands. Folding them behind her back, he drew her against his body. In winter, her skin smelled of summer flowers. Her softness melted into him. He felt the rapid beat of her heart, the faint tremble of her response.

"How?" he asked.

"I thought you could knock him down. What would you advise?"

"I thought you could threaten him with your dainty stiletto. Though when I hold you like this, in my power, I find I don't care very much about anyone else."

She tilted her head, her breath warm on his lips. "What a wicked spy."

"A poor spy," he corrected, pushing his hips harder against her. He might have been trying to distract her with a little bodily lust, but he suspected it was he who was losing. She pushed back, even swayed, gently, caressing him with the soft curves of her breasts and stroking the hardness in his pantaloons.

Her eyes, hot and clouded, begged him. Her parted lips, luscious and trembling, seduced him without even touching.

He caught his uneven breath. *To hell with it.*

At the moment of his decision, a knock sounded at the door. His breakfast. He stared down into Anna's beautiful face. She made no effort to free herself. He could ignore his breakfast and take Anna to bed at last. He could think of nothing against that plan at all. It would distract her and enable his mind to focus, eventually, on something other than her person and sheer, unutterable lust.

Another, louder knock irritated him. For a second longer, it hung in the balance. And then, because this wasn't the right way with Anna, he released her hands.

"Enter," he said quickly, before he changed his mind. At the same time, he strode to the door and took the tray from the girl—his usual, flirtatious maid—and closed the door. "Join me for breakfast," he invited.

She gazed at him, so clearly wondering what had changed his mind that he blurted, "Don't tempt me. If I take you to bed, I won't leave you alone, and Gosselin will do his worst."

She sat down at the table and poured a cup of coffee, taking a sip before she pushed the cup and saucer across the table to him. "So how should we set about stopping him?"

"*I* shall stop him," Louis said firmly. "He owes me his life many times over. You must keep Henry away from the hotel or he will ruin everything from ignorance."

Anna didn't speak, merely searched his face. He suspected she saw through his instructions to his main aim—to keep her safely out of the way.

"And then?" she said at last.

"And then I shall call at the castle, as a good suitor should, and tell you how it ended."

"That seems very tame. From my point of view."

"I shall endeavor to make it...er...not tame."

A smile flickered in her eyes. The reality of "afterward" was already upon them. "And will that be the last we see of Sir Lytton?"

"Perhaps," he admitted. "It depends how quietly everything can be done." He reached across the table and took her hand. "Anna. Until the war is over, there can be no certainty between us. Only promises."

"I keep my promises," she said.

He smiled. "So do I."

She drew in a shaky breath and rose to her feet. "Then I shall leave you for now. *Au revoir.*"

He rose with her. "*Au revoir,*" he said softly.

ANNA LEFT HIM with her emotions in turmoil. But her mind was clear and full of plans. Since she knew he would be watching, she left the hotel and walked up the high street in the direction of the harbor. After a little, she turned left and returned from the side street, walking close in to the wall as she approached the front door so that he would not be able to see her from his window. It was less noticeable than a lady blundering about at the kitchen entrance.

Again, veiled, she sailed through the foyer to the stairs. By then, she must have been a familiar sight. This time, she did not go on up to the second floor but walked along the first-floor passage. None of the doors were guarded. But by walking the length of the passages repeatedly, and skulking a little, she began to narrow down the rooms likeliest to house Lord Castlereagh.

And when she encountered a friendly maid stripping down the bed in one of the other rooms, she stopped the maid in the passage with a trivial question while her arms were full of clean bedding. Anna helped her carry it into the bedchamber and struck up a conversation with her.

As she left, Anna paused at the door, and thoughtfully lifted her veil. "I wonder if you would consider helping me?"

"Of course, ma'am," the girl said at once. "Anything."

Anna stepped back inside the bedchamber and closed the door.

Chapter Seventeen

A T ABOUT HALF past three in the afternoon, Talleyrand arrived at the hotel. He wore an elderly fur-lined cloak, which effectively covered his habitual elegance of dress, and he was accompanied not by Captain Alban but by a man Louis recognized as Alban's surgeon.

Louis gave him time to cross the foyer and walk up to Castlereagh's rooms on the first floor. Then he rose and donned his coat, still somewhat gingerly, for although his wound had not reopened, it was somewhat tender again after his exertions of the previous night. He tucked a sheathed dagger into the top of his pantaloons, and into the other side, he placed the bulky, stolen pistol. He hoped fervently he would not have to use the latter, since he suspected it fired wide and was as likely to blow his own head off as anyone else's. Like Talleyrand, he threw a winter cloak around his shoulders to hide the state of his dress.

As he left his room and walked downstairs, he noticed a difference in the hotel. Large men lounged in slightly ill-fitting gentlemen's clothes on the first-floor landings and near the front door of the hotel. They were Captain Alban's men. And Alban himself lounged on one of the foyer sofas with the lady he had landed in Blackhaven more than a week ago.

This could have proved difficult, for it was possible Alban would have a better memory for prisoners than his men did. However, Louis was fortunate enough to spy Mrs. Winslow entering the hotel and hurried to greet her. She seemed delighted to see him, but then spotted Alban's wife—the duke's daughter—and abandoned him with unflattering haste. Louis, with the seal of her acquaintanceship passed out of the hotel, if not unnoticed, then at least not recognized.

Another of Alban's men stood chatting to the doorman outside the hotel. Louis strolled past them and round to the back of the hotel where the stable and coach house stood. Alban's men were also guarding the kitchen entrance, but no one paid Louis much attention as he entered the stable. They might, of course, notice if he didn't come out again, but he doubted they would waste time trying to discover him and leave the back door unguarded.

As he had expected, the trap door in the empty stall was unfastened. Louis lifted it as quietly as he could, climbed down the steps far enough to replace the trap door, and then listened in the darkness.

There was no one in the immediate vicinity. The stairs and the passage were black and he had to feel his way along them, which made it difficult to move as silently as he would have wished. But at least no light meant he was alone, that Gosselin had not yet entered the passage. If, indeed, he knew of the secret entrance and meant to come this way. If he didn't—which Louis thought unlikely—then Louis could still observe what occurred inside the room and act accordingly.

However, when he reached the top of the second lot of stone steps and turned into the final length of the passage, the faintest glow reached him from the far end. A few warier steps confirmed it. A moving flame, a hand-held candle. Gosselin was already there.

Louis flexed his fingers. He thought of Marguerite and her child, of Dupré and Sanchez and all the others wiped out solely for this man's ambitions…but anger was not the path to a clear head. His first duty was to preserve the men in the room beyond. At least until he knew the purpose of their meeting.

And yes, Gosselin had come to kill. As Louis crept closer, he could make out the two pistols in his enemy's belt. He was dressed like a rough seaman and was peering through the peephole. The candle was set now on the flat stone table beside the secret door, a spare one lying beside it. Gosselin had, apparently, thought of everything.

Except that Louis would find him.

Gosselin was so intent upon his spying that Louis actually began to believe he could reach Gosselin and strangle him, before he even knew Louis was there. But inevitably, Louis's luck ran out. His foot crunched on loose gravel, only very slightly and he paused at once, but it was enough.

Gosselin jerked around, staring. The candle flame flickered at his movement, its faint light quivering across his white, wide-eyed face.

"You," he uttered in hoarse astonishment. "My God, are you *everywhere*? Do you know *everything*?"

Louis smiled unpleasantly. "Yes." And he leapt forward before Gosselin could recover his wits.

Gosselin panicked. Perhaps he knew he could not win any fight with Louis. Perhaps he was simply running away by the only route possible or meant to finish his task before Louis had the chance to stop him. Whatever his reason, he lunged at the door lever and all but fell into the dazzling light of the room beyond. The door crashed back on its hinges, presumably startling everyone.

When Louis ran in, the occupants of the room were leaping to their feet. Four men stood around the table in the middle of the room, which was already full of papers, pens, and ink bottles. There was also wine and a tea tray, still gripped by a hotel maid who, terrifyingly, bore an uncanny resemblance to Anna Gaunt. But he couldn't think of that.

Gosselin had his pistol pointed directly at Talleyrand's haughty head, and at the range of barely two yards, was unlikely to miss. It did not comfort Louis to understand Gosselin's plot at last. He meant to kill Talleyrand and blame British treachery, thus both disgracing the one-time foreign minister whom Napoleon wanted back and encouraging enough ill-feeling to continue the war.

And the knowledge of death flickered in Talleyrand's clever eyes as Louis flew at Gosselin, bringing him down in a flying tackle.

The pistol exploded as it fell to the floor. Talleyrand still stood, but the instant Louis took to check gave Gosselin his opportunity. Elbowing Louis in the face, he rolled free, and from the floor, aimed at

Lord Castlereagh who was already lunging toward him.

This would be the alternative plan. It worked just as well if Castlereagh died instead of Talleyrand. The prince was still disgraced and the British, incensed by Castlereagh's assassination, would almost certainly refuse to make peace.

Even in that moment, it disgusted Louis. Did the fools really imagine that Napoleon could recover enough to save them any power?

Dagger in hand, he was about to throw himself at Gosselin once more, when Anna leapt in front of Castlereagh, spreading her arms in instinctive protection. Terror closed Louis's throat. Everything, everyone in the room seemed to slow down. Men burst into the room from the passage, but Louis paid them no attention. He found himself praying that Gosselin would turn his pistol back on Talleyrand.

He didn't. He recognized Anna, and actually smiled as he began to squeeze the trigger.

He was still smiling when Louis's dagger took him in the throat. Thrown with the deadly accuracy of long practice, without thought or planning, it killed him instantly.

The gun did not go off.

"My dear girl," Castlereagh said, appalled, staring at Anna as he moved her aside. She didn't seem to notice. Her gaze was locked with Louis's.

Stumbling to his feet, he strode to her and pulled her roughly into his arms. If she hadn't protected Castlereagh and given Gosselin that instant's pause to imagine his own petty revenge, no doubt Castlereagh would have been dead.

Questions were being hurled around the room. "Who in God's name was that?"

"How did he get in here?"

"Sir, are you hurt?"

"What in hell happened here?"

"Are you well?"

"Is this man one of yours?"

Louis heard the words in a cacophony of pointless sound. In that instant, the only thing he cared about was the vital, brave woman he all but crushed in his arms. And she did not shrink. She melted.

"As I live and breathe," said a soft voice in French, "I believe I look upon Colonel Delon. So, this is where you have been hiding."

Talleyrand.

Releasing Anna, Louis turned slowly to face him, and bowed. "Sir."

"I heard that you were a prisoner of the British. Who did not know what they had."

"I escaped."

"*You* are the escaped prisoner?" That was Captain Alban, a pistol in his hand, staring at him hard. "By God, you are. I brought you in *The Albatross*. Then who the devil is *this*?"

Castlereagh stepped forward to look. "The man who attempted to kill both Monsieur de Talleyrand and myself."

"His name is Gosselin," Louis said. "A rogue French spy, representing neither the Emperor nor Monsieur de Talleyrand."

"And who, exactly," Alban asked, "do *you* represent?"

Louis smiled cynically. *No one.*

But before he could speak aloud, Talleyrand said, "Me. He represents me and my aim of peace in Europe."

Louis met his gaze. He could not deny that his heart beat faster at this first claim that his country needed him. He understood at once that Talleyrand was giving him his escape from Britain, from being returned to prison. As Talleyrand's man, he would be allowed to leave with him.

"I believe we all have cause to be grateful to this gentleman," Castlereagh said. "Colonel…Delon is it? And to this girl who would have died preserving my worthless life."

"Hardly worthless, sir!" Anna objected, causing Castlereagh's eyes to widen at her cultured speech.

He frowned. "Do I know you, madam?"

An interruption came from the passage door where one of Alban's men had dragged another inside before slamming the door firmly. "My lord, this gentleman claims to be one of yours."

"Harcourt, my lord," Henry said, shaking off his escort. "I came to warn you then I heard the gun shot…" His gaze fell on Anna, and then on Louis, and he swallowed convulsively.

Castlereagh's frown deepened. "You *knew* of this plot?"

"I only suspected," Henry said hurriedly, "but when I tried to see you in London, I heard you had posted up here. I followed you." He looked directly at Anna.

ANNA WAS AFRAID suddenly that he was about to pretend she was Christianne. Which, considering her recent open embracing of Louis, would be somewhat humiliating for both Christianne and Henry. She remembered that she had meant to prosper through Henry's success and had no objection to helping this along.

"I was here already, to reconnoiter, as it were," Anna said smoothly. "I am Mr. Harcourt's sister-in-law. Though I confess my impulse to swap clothes with the hotel maid would not have met with his approval. I could think of no other way to get in here and be sure everyone was safe."

"The passage was meant to ensure our safety," Castlereagh said ruefully. "We never thought of being attacked through it. My apologies, Monsieur."

Talleyrand poked the fallen man with his toe. "None necessary, milord, or I shall feel compelled to apologize on behalf of my country for this filth. Perhaps he could be removed and then we might continue our conversation. I know we are both pressed for time."

"Use the passage," Louis murmured as Alban gestured his men to remove the body. "It comes out in the stables."

"Harcourt," Castlereagh said, "you had better stay. I don't want you believing there is anything remotely treasonous about this secret meeting."

Henry tried not to preen, but he clearly knew, as Anna did, that this could only be good for him.

Castlereagh said urgently, "I believe we may thank everyone else later, in a more appropriate fashion. For now, please, clear the room. Alban, will the gun shot not have brought the Watch and who knows else?"

"Probably not," Alban said calmly, as everyone began to leave via the secret door and the passage door. "It wouldn't be the first shot they've heard in the hotel. Lord Daxton has stayed here. And *him?*" Alban indicated Louis.

"I would like him to stay," Talleyrand said.

Castlereagh inclined his head. He glanced at Alban. "I believe your escaped prisoner may never be recaptured."

Alban gave a sardonic twist of the lips and held the door open for Anna. At the last moment, she glanced back over her shoulder and met Louis's gaze. Her heart ached with gladness and pain. He had Talleyrand's protection now. He could go home, vindicated, welcomed, useful. And she...

"You are Tamar's sister," Alban said, falling into step beside her. "He is downstairs in the foyer with my wife."

"Then if you allow me to exchange clothes once more with my accomplice, I shall be happy to renew my acquaintance with her."

Anna paused outside the room where she had left the maid. "I need to see him again," she said with difficulty.

Alban's hard eyes searched hers, his expression inscrutable though hardly encouraging. "Wait with Bella," he said shortly and walked away.

The little maid, who looked rather good in Anna's clothes, trembled with anxiety. "Did someone shoot at you, Miss?" she demanded. "Did you shoot them? Oh, Miss, am I in trouble?"

"Of course not," Anna soothed, letting the maid loosen her fastenings. "No one was shot. A pistol was fired by accident. Sort of. And no one knows anything about you. If you have been missed below, just tell them you were held up by all the important people along the hall."

Five minutes later, back in her widow's weeds and discreetly veiled, she descended to the foyer, where all appeared to be as calm as Alban had foreseen. Tamar sat on one of the sofas, beside Lady Arabella, with whom he seemed very taken. In fact, while he talked he scribbled with a pencil on a piece of folded paper in his lap. As she drew nearer, Anna saw that it was Arabella's profile. She had an interesting as well as pretty face, Anna allowed. She could see why her brother liked it.

Tamar glanced up and saw her. He almost looked straight through her before he frowned, peering closer. "Anna? What the...?"

"Do be quiet," Anna said, nodding civilly to Arabella. "My lady. Your husband has asked me to wait with you. So Tamar might go home."

"Might I?" Tamar said. "What has been going on? Where's Henry?"

"In an important meeting," Anna said. "You might want to ask him about Mrs. Elphinstone and decide whether or not to keep her with you."

Tamar regarded her with fascination. "Might I?"

"Well, Serena and Lady Braithwaite might."

He let that go. "And the shot we heard?"

"Nothing. No one is hurt." Apart from the man who lay dead, who was responsible for this mess and so much more cruelty.

"And you?" he asked quietly.

"I am perfectly fine," she replied with impatience.

"Serena, and even Christianne, were convinced you'd run off with Lewis."

"I didn't."

"So I see. But he does *live* here. Anna, are you in a pickle?"

Without warning, the concern of the brother who had always looked after her, who had killed for her, brought a lump to her throat that she could not swallow.

"A little," she whispered. "But I shall come about."

He didn't take her hand. She couldn't have borne that much sympathy. Her time with Louis was almost ended and she felt she would die.

"Shall we go back to the castle?" he said. "Lady Bella can come with us."

Anna pulled herself together. "No. Lady Bella and I shall wait here. You should go, though. Set Christianne's mind at rest." She smiled with difficulty. "And Serena's. You are lucky to have her, Rupert."

"I know." He stood, presenting his drawing to Arabella with no more than a grin. "Then I'll leave Henry to bring you back."

As he was about to go, something propelled Anna to her feet. For the first time since she was a child, she threw her arms around her brother's neck, and kissed his cheek through the veil.

"Thank you, Rupert," she whispered. She meant for everything. She had never said it before, and suddenly it was vitally important that he knew.

Although he must have been stunned, he hugged her back briefly. Since he didn't know what troubled her, he didn't speak, for which she was grateful. He merely grinned to lift her spirits and sauntered out of the hotel.

Darkness had closed in since Anna had arrived here. It seemed a lifetime ago.

She became aware of Lady Arabella's regard. "I saw your husband upstairs," she offered. "He is well. So is your…guest."

"You know who he is," Arabella guessed.

"And I know your husband brought him."

"And will take him away again. It is in our country's interests. And Europe's."

Anna raised one eyebrow. "Does Captain Alban think so?"

"*I* think so," Arabella said vaguely. "Women do…don't they?"

"Think?" Anna said in some surprise. "Of course."

"And act, if necessary," Bella added.

"Are you accusing me of something?" Anna asked, faintly amused.

Bella looked surprised. "Only of acting as necessary, for good. Alban would not otherwise have sent you to me."

Anna regarded her with interest. It seemed the time would pass bearably after all, until she could see Louis again. Then, she would need all her strength.

IT WAS NOT Captain Alban but a gentleman Bella addressed as "Doctor", who escorted them from the hotel to the harbor, where a boat, manned by several rowers, awaited them.

When Anna hesitated, the doctor said, "The others will come in another boat. On *The Albatross*, one may speak with greater privacy. You will be brought safely back to shore and escorted home with every propriety."

"Propriety," Anna repeated and laughed. With a sailor's aid, she stepped into the bobbing boat, and sat on the bench beside Lady Bella.

There was something soothing about the rhythmic splash of the oars. Even in the bitter cold, the glow of the lanterns seemed to hold them in a bubble of safety, in a place between joy and grief. She could pretend happiness was still possible. And who knew? Perhaps it was. Whatever happened, she was happy for Louis.

The journey to the ship was quicker than she expected. Before long, she was climbing aboard the famous *Albatross*.

"Is the captain aboard?" Bella asked.

"Yes, ma'am," came the immediate response. "And he's asked that I take Lady Anna to the second cabin."

Bella accompanied her, leading the way below decks, out of the biting wind. Anna swayed, holding on to the walls as the ship rolled. Bella knocked and opened a door on a decent-sized cabin that boasted a decent sized bunk with velvet curtains, and a desk which was spotlessly clear apart from several pens and a neat pile of blank paper. In front of it, stood Captain Alban, whose harsh face softened almost imperceptibly when his wife walked in.

Anna followed her in time to see Louis striding from the sloping window. His eyes looked restless, almost turbulent, although the gleam of longing in them thrilled her. Without hesitation, she went to him, giving him both her hands, which he kissed, one after the other.

Alban said, "I promised them a few minutes." Taking Bella's hand, he strode toward the door. "Be warned," he added over his shoulder. "Himself will be back at any moment."

"Himself?" Anna asked bewildered, as the door closed behind the couple.

"His name for Talleyrand," Louis said, taking her face between his hands. His eyes seemed to devour her. "God, Anna, I don't know if I am more proud or terrified by what you did."

"Or I by what you did," she retorted.

A hiss of laughter escaped him as he pressed his cheek to hers.

"Were we right to save them?" she blurted. "What did they talk about?"

"The future. What to do after the war is ended. How to keep a balance in Europe to prevent future wars. Which means not annihilating France in her defeat. There were no specifics, only principles and an agreement to negotiate in the future—whatever that future holds. I believe we were right."

She tangled her fingers in his hair. "Then you can go home? Is Talleyrand enough protection for you?"

"Perhaps. The Emperor wants him back in his government, but I'm not sure he will go. I think he sees the writing on the wall."

"As you do."

"In the short term, he wants me to go to Basel where Prince Metternich and other allied rulers and ministers are meeting, to see what I can learn."

She clung to him. "I am glad," she whispered.

"As soon as there is peace, as soon as I can come to you, I will."

"I know." She closed her eyes, lifting her face for his kiss. She wasn't sure how she could bear the parting, but she would. Because one day, in six months or a year, or maybe two, they would be together.

"Will you wait for me?" he asked fiercely against her lips.

"You know I will."

He kissed her again.

The door opened quietly, causing them to move reluctantly apart.

Talleyrand spoke in cynical English. "Bless you, my children."

As though struck, Louis stared at him.

But Talleyrand addressed Anna. "Colonel Delon has told me of your part in all of this. You are an exceptional young lady and I thank you from the bottom of my heart."

"There is no need. I would have taken the colonel's secrets if I could."

Talleyrand did not look remotely offended. He smiled faintly and limped across the room to sit by the desk. "You will excuse an old man his lack of courtesy."

"You are not old by any definition," she said frankly.

"I still have a few things to do. While you...are most unusual for an English noblewoman. I mean that as a compliment, without intending any insult to other English ladies. You are well suited to Delon. I only wish you were French."

Anna blinked.

Louis let out a breath of laughter. "When there is peace, that will not matter," he pointed out. "Sir...you were ordained a priest. Will you marry us now?"

Deprived of breath, Anna stared at him.

So did Talleyrand. The prince's lips curled. "My dear Delon, supposing I even remembered how, I doubt my officiation would be considered legal in this country."

Louis met Anna's gaze. Her breath rushed back with a surge of yearning so powerful she swayed. Or perhaps it was the rolling of the ship. She grabbed Louis's arm for support.

"It would be legal to us," she said clearly. "Binding to us. If we are to part for months or years, give us this."

The tender, joyous smile that broke across Louis's face was all the reward she wanted. Almost.

Talleyrand laughed and shrugged. "I'll do it. Fetch in Captain Alban and his lady, and I'll perform the ceremony before God if not the law."

Chapter Eighteen

A ND SO, ANNA and Louis were married by the Prince of Benevento, the Bishop of Autun, duly witnessed by Captain Alban and
Lady Arabella, who signed the document Talleyrand made in their real
names of Alban and Arabella Lamont. For Anna, although she was
desperate to remember the whole ceremony as a comfort in the
coming months, it passed in something of a blur. She saw only Louis's
face, heard only his voice.

And nothing in her life had ever seemed so right.

When it was done, Talleyrand blessed them with a mere hint of
sardonic humor and Bella led them to a nearby empty cabin.

"You can be private in here to say your farewells," she said practi-
cally, lighting the lamp by the bunk. The cabin was barer than
Talleyrand's, but there were sheets and blankets on the bunk, and
water and towels by the night stand to refresh themselves. There was
even a light supper spread on the table. Anna realized she hadn't eaten
all day.

"I won't sail until high tide," Alban said. "I'll have someone take
you ashore in a couple of hours. Feel free to use the ship as your own
until then."

As the door closed on them, Anna turned slowly to face her husband. "Am I really Madame Delon?"

"I don't know," Louis said, incurably honest with her. He
shrugged off his coat and threw it on the chair, standing before her in
his shirt sleeves. As though he were too hot on this wintry night. "In
any way that matters to me, you are my wife."

"I feel the same," she whispered. "I will miss you, Louis."

"Hush." He took her in his arms, smiling into her hair. "We have ages before we need to miss each other."

"Two hours," she said in despair.

"Then let us make the most of them," he said hoarsely, and dragged his open mouth across her jaw to her lips.

This time, there was a strange urgency to the melting of her bones. She didn't just want the thrill, the pleasure to go on forever. She wanted more, she wanted to be as close to him as she could get, and she wanted it at once.

Gasping into his mouth, she kissed him back with fervor, instinctively pressing her breasts and hips against him. And that felt so good, she pushed harder, dragging him closer yet, writhing against his exciting hardness.

He swept her off her feet, striding the two paces to the bunk before falling with her. His weight landed on her, the most thrilling sensation she had ever known, and yet she was helpless under him. He caressed her with his whole body, making her moan with delight and need, before he lifted her from the waist, unfastening her gown and stays and drawing all that black crepe from her body. And then her chemise vanished, too, and she was naked in his arms, bathed in the warm glow of the lamp.

"Oh, let me look at you," he breathed, his eyes wondrously hot as they devoured her from head to toe, and then he lowered his lips to her breasts, and his hand stroked everywhere, learning her every curve. Only when she plucked with increasing annoyance at his shirt, did he remove his own clothes, revealing all his own distinctive beauty. She smoothed her palms against his chest and back as she had so wanted to do since she had first seen his wounds. He wore only a light bandage around his shoulder now, so there was a lot of hot, velvet skin to caress and kiss.

"I want this, I want all of you," she whispered desperately. "Take me as your wife."

"Oh, I will," he got out before claiming her mouth once more. He wrapped her hand around his hard shaft, and she felt only awe as she stroked it.

She loved his hands, the way they played her body like some delicate musical instrument. And it seemed he would give her no time to be afraid, for his fingers slid up the inside of her thigh and played there, too, so softly and sweetly that she moaned and arched and gasped and let the sudden ecstasy engulf her.

"That is what I'll give you," he whispered through the pleasure. "Only more. More intense, more urgent, more…everything."

And then it was no longer his fingers which pushed and caressed, and he was inside her, not hurting beyond the one jolt of discomfort. In new wonder, she held on to him, her eyes locked to his as their bodies moved in the age-old push and pull of love. His eyes were clouded, lost in lust, and yet they worshipped her with the rest of his body.

"Anna, my sweet Anna," he whispered shakily as he kissed her mouth and the pleasure built and built and the ecstasy swept over her once more, just as before only different, deeper, harder. He fell on her, groaning and she clutched him to her, knowing she was his at last, as he was hers.

SHE DID NOT weep as she stood with him on the deck of *The Albatross* while the sailors lowered the boat into the water. Hand in hand with him in the cold night, she gazed at the moon and the stars, knowing they would always be above both of them, however far apart they were. It was a comfort.

"My men will land you at Braithwaite Cove," Captain Alban said, "and see you safely back to the castle."

"Thank you," she answered. She cast a smile over her shoulder at Lady Bella. "I hope we can be friends one day."

"We already are," Bella said. "Good luck to you, Lady Anna."

"And to you, Lady Bella." She turned to Louis and lifted her face for his last, brief kiss. Their true farewells had been made in private, with her tears well hidden behind genuine joy and laughter. "*Au revoir*," she breathed. "Be safe, my love."

"*Au revoir*," he said hoarsely. "Stay out of trouble if you can."

She managed a smile. "Of course I can't."

And then she climbed down into the boat and the sailors' respectful hands helped her to her seat. She didn't even know she was crying until she could no longer see the ship in front of her. She wiped at her eyes.

"Long parting, Miss?" the coxswain asked with simple sympathy.

"I fear so," she answered as lightly as she could.

"Rough." He was silent for a long moment while the oars pulled and splashed, and Anna shivered, drawing her cloak closer around her. Then the coxswain said, "I thought the foreign gent married you."

Anna nodded, and he nodded sagely back.

"Not always easy to stay together at sea," he acknowledged. "Even married."

She gazed at him, frowning slightly. She was going home to inflict herself on Rupert and Serena, who would be just as happy without her. Or to go to London with Christianne and Henry. Christianne missed her, but increasingly less as Henry took over her life. And there would be children. She was sure that was Christianne's news, saved up for when they were alone.

But I have a life of my own now. I have a husband, a lover. I don't need Henry's tasks to give my life meaning. Louis is my meaning...

She stared at the coxswain as they drew closer to the beach beneath the castle. Two of the men jumped out into the shallows to haul it ashore.

"What am I doing?" she said aloud. And then she laughed, breathless at her own stupidity and how close she had come to wasting even more of her life. She threw herself forward. "Wait! Come back. I've changed my mind. Would you please be so good as to row me back to *The Albatross*?"

LOUIS WATCHED THE boat grow smaller and smaller as it neared Braithwaite Cove. Letting her go had been the hardest thing he had ever done. But it was a selfless, honorable decision to keep her safe at home with her family until he could come to her.

And what if I have just given her a child?

They had already discussed that possibility. She was to announce her secret marriage to Sir Lytton Lewis, immediately, just in case.

"It might get confusing later," she had joked, "when we have to merge Madame Delon with Lady Lewis."

He was leaving her alone to try and rebuild his life, betting on Talleyrand's success, which was not entirely assured, whatever happened to France.

Walking blindly toward his cabin, he encountered Captain Alban striding toward his. Frowning, Louis said abruptly, "Alban, you married above you, did you not?"

"Undoubtedly. I suspect you have done the same."

"Even more undoubtedly. But Lady Bella sails with you."

He shrugged. "Most of the time. We spend time at home, too, of course. But for reasons the rest of us cannot fathom, she prefers my company to the lack of it."

Louis frowned. He said slowly, "Leaving Anna to make my fortune, as it were, seemed perfectly sensible until she stepped into that boat."

Alban regarded him. "It seems to me, in your line of work, your lady would be quite an asset."

Louis smiled crookedly. "Even on different sides."

"It did you no harm in saving the late conference."

"True," Louis allowed. "But she has family in England who care for her..." And didn't he have an identity in England already, one that could be built on? Sir Lytton Lewis, husband to Lady Anna, the Marquis of Tamar's sister. No one would doubt him. There were things he could do for Talleyrand here, surely, that would compromise no one's honor, and even if not, he could find other employment.

He became aware he was staring at Alban. "Launch another boat. I'm going back with her."

Alban stared back. "And Himself?"

"Tell him I'll write." And he pushed open the hatch and bolted back on deck.

Behind him, he was grateful to hear Alban shouting orders. It took only a few minutes to get the smaller boat in the water and organize a crew.

"I must be going soft," Alban commented. "Either that or I've lost my mind. I'm putting everyone out just to help a French enemy abduct an English noblewoman."

"No, you're not," Lady Bella said behind him. "You're helping a man be with his wife."

Louis gave her a quick, grateful grin over his shoulder, and began to lower himself down into the waiting boat.

"I can't wait long," Alban called after him. "My men will return in an hour, with or without you."

"Understood," Louis said, getting comfortable. It was cold and spray from the sea pattered against his face. He barely noticed. Nor did he feel his wound. His whole being strained toward the shore with boundless energy. He wanted to snatch up the oars and row himself, just to get there faster.

But Alban's men had their own strict way of doing things. So all he could do was sit and watch, staring into the darkness in the hope of seeing her boat ahead, or her figure climbing the path from Braithwaite Cove to the castle. He should have known when his whole being cried out against it, that leaving her was wrong. But she had had to physically go before he let himself even think that what seemed the honorable thing wasn't necessarily a *good* thing. For Anna or for him.

They had rowed about half way from the ship to Braithwaite Cove when he saw the bobbing shape on the water approaching them.

"It's the first boat," one of the sailors said. "On its way back."

Louis scowled. To be returning so quickly, they must have left her to walk up to the castle alone. Of course, she had probably insisted and his Anna generally got her own way by one means or another. So did he.

As the boats drew nearer, the sailors from each crew began to call to one another. Louis opened his mouth to shout his own questions, when he saw the small figure huddled among them.

"Anna," he whispered. He stood abruptly, rocking the small boat, and suddenly Anna was on her feet, too, waving madly.

"Louis! I'm here, I'm coming with you!" she shouted.

The crew of her boat tried to make her sit, but she was speaking to them urgently and refused. Louis shook off the man trying to yank him back on his own seat.

"You'll tip us all in the sea!" one of them yelled. "Oh, God's teeth, what's she doing, now?"

Louis's attention snapped back to the other boat, for as they came alongside, the men had to draw in their oars, and Anna was holding on to the side and climbing. Louis felt the blood drain from his face in fear. He threw himself to the side of his own boat, opening his mouth to tell her not to be an idiot. But one of her crew was already throwing a rope to him and he caught it and hauled. And Anna leapt.

She won't reach! Dropping the rope, he made a grab for her, just as her foot slipped and she began to fall. But he'd grasped her wrist, and her other hand clung to his and he pulled with all his strength until they both fell backward into the boat.

The sailors swore as the boat rocked dangerously. But Louis knew they were safe. They had to be now. Somehow, he dragged her with him onto the seat.

"You fool," he uttered, crushing her to him, his hand tangled in her hair. The veil had vanished, no doubt into the sea. "What were you thinking? You could have drowned!"

"I had to tell you," she gasped, clinging to his wrist. "I'm coming with you, wherever you go."

He frowned, tilting her head back to stare down into her face. In the silver glow of the moon and the weaving lamp on the boat, she was bedraggled and smiling, and more beautiful than he had ever seen her. He said, "I was coming to tell *you* that *I'm* staying in England."

She laughed, her cold fingertips caressing his face, his lips with something very like wonder. "Well, we're about half way between the ship and shore. Which will be more fun?"

He searched her face, seeking his way. "England will be safer."

"For me. Not for you. Besides, safety isn't fun."

He didn't mean to smile, but his lips were curving of their own volition. "You're just a little mad, you know."

"I know," she whispered, and kissed him.

Louis lifted one hand and pointed back toward *The Albatross*.

TALLEYRAND REGARDED THEM with a frown, but Anna thought he was more amused than annoyed. However, his gaze was speculative as it lingered on her.

"As a couple, certainly, there may be more opportunities," he said. "Opportunities that might not be open to a single man in Basel."

"I do not, however, work for you," Anna pointed out.

"I am sure you will find a way to pass information to your brother-in-law," Talleyrand said dryly. "And do you know, I believe Lord Castlereagh himself may turn up in Basel before too long. At this stage, your country and ours has increasingly little difference in aims. Can we agree on the peace of Europe as our goal?"

Anna nodded.

"Then we may all look after our own countries as best we can within that greater goal. Do I have to bless you a third time before you go away and let me sleep?"

"No," Louis said. "Good night."

They made their way back to what was now their own cabin. They had nothing but the clothes they stood up in, but Anna had never been happier.

"What of your family?" he asked.

"I'll write to them. They'll understand," Anna said optimistically. "They're used to my mad starts. Even Serena. She loves my brother, after all." The word *love* rolled off her tongue more easily now.

She sighed with contentment, melting as he took her into his arms. "What changed your mind?" she asked at last. "Why did you come after me?"

"For the same reason you came back. We are meant to be together. I would have come back for you as soon as I could, you know I would, but...it came to me, finally, that abandoning you here for however long might not make you happy."

She pressed her cheek to his. "It didn't. It wouldn't. That's why I came back. I know you need me. You're the only one who *truly* needs me as I need you."

His arms tightened. "You will drive me to distraction. I'll worry and fret and probably shout, trying desperately to keep you out of danger. But we *will* have fun."

She laughed, already eager to face her new life in all its aspects. "I know. And I will go my own way and interfere in yours. But I trust you, Louis, and I'll always love you." Her smile lingering, she turned up her face and he kissed her mouth long and hungrily.

"I know we'll be happy," he whispered against her lips. "Happier even than this."

And they were.

Mary Lancaster's Newsletter

If you enjoyed *The Wicked Spy*, and would like to keep up with Mary's new releases and other book news, please sign up to Mary's mailing list to receive her occasional Newsletter.

http://eepurl.com/b4Xoif

Other Books by Mary Lancaster

VIENNA WALTZ (The Imperial Season, Book 1)

VIENNA WOODS (The Imperial Season, Book 2)

VIENNA DAWN (The Imperial Season, Book 3)

THE WICKED BARON (Blackhaven Brides, Book 1)

THE WICKED LADY (Blackhaven Brides, Book 2)

THE WICKED REBEL (Blackhaven Brides, Book 3)

THE WICKED HUSBAND (Blackhaven Brides, Book 4)

THE WICKED MARQUIS (Blackhaven Brides, Book 5)

THE WICKED GOVERNESS (Blackhaven Brides, Book 6)

REBEL OF ROSS

A PRINCE TO BE FEARED: the love story of Vlad Dracula

AN ENDLESS EXILE

A WORLD TO WIN

About Mary Lancaster

Mary Lancaster's first love was historical fiction. Her other passions include coffee, chocolate, red wine and black and white films – simultaneously where possible. She hates housework.

As a direct consequence of the first love, she studied history at St. Andrews University. She now writes full time at her seaside home in Scotland, which she shares with her husband, three children and a small, crazy dog.

Connect with Mary on-line:

Email Mary:
Mary@MaryLancaster.com

Website:
www.MaryLancaster.com

Newsletter sign-up:
http://eepurl.com/b4Xoif

Facebook Author Page:
facebook.com/MaryLancasterNovelist

Facebook Timeline:
facebook.com/mary.lancaster.1656

Made in the USA
Middletown, DE
13 October 2018